To Hervé and Mimi
Many Fêtes

PARIS TRANCE

'The usual plan is to take two couples and develop
their relationship. Most of George Eliot's are on that plan.
Anyhow, I don't want a plot, I should be bored with it.
I shall try two couples for a start.'

D.H. Lawrence

'Even the loveliest dream bears like a blemish its difference
from reality, the awareness that what it grants is mere
illusion. This is why precisely the loveliest dreams are as if
blighted.'

Theodor Adorno

When Luke came to Paris with the intention of writing a book based on his experiences of living – as he grandly and naïvely conceived it – 'in exile', he was twenty-six years old ('a fine age for a man,' according to Scott Fitzgerald). As far as I know, he made absolutely no progress with this book, abandoning it – except in moments of sudden, drunken enthusiasm – in the instant that he began leading the life intended to serve as its research, its first draft. By the time we met, at the Garnier Warehouse, this book had assumed the status of a passport or travel visa: something which, by enabling him to leave one country and pass into another, had served its purpose and could be, if not discarded, then stored away and ignored. So it's fallen to me to tell his story, or at least the part of it with which I am familiar. *Our* story, in fact, for by recounting this part of my friend's life I am trying to account for my own, for my need to believe that while something in Luke tugged him away from all that he most loved, from all that made him happiest, it is his life – and not mine – which is exemplary, admirable, even enviable.

The events recorded here concerned only a handful of

people and, quite probably, are of interest only to those people. Especially since 'story' is almost certainly the wrong word. Whatever makes events into a story is entirely missing from what follows. It may well be that what urges me to preserve these events in the way I have – the only way I could – is exactly what stops them becoming a story.

Luke arrived in Paris at one of the worst possible times, in mid-July, when the city was preparing to close down for August. Parisians claim this is the best part of the year – it's easy to park, they say (after a certain amount of time in a city the parking is all you care about) – but for someone who had just arrived it was the worst. The only people around were tourists and those forced to cater for them. Many shops and restaurants were shut and the few that *were* open closed far earlier than usual. Luke had rented a horrible apartment in the First arrondissement. On paper it had sounded perfect: right in the middle of the city, a few minutes' walk from the Louvre, the Arcades, and other famous tourist sights. Unfortunately that's all there was: museums and tourist sights. The temporal heart of the city, the part that makes it what it is today – as opposed to preserving what had been magnificent in the eighteenth century, or mythically bohemian in the 1920s – had moved east into the Eleventh, close to what had once been the edge of town.

The apartment itself was a stained place with a sad curtain separating the sleeping area from the living area and nothing to separate the living area from the smells of the cooking area (the cooker itself comprised two hot plates, electric, one of which warmed up only reluctantly). It was the kind of apartment where, if possible, you avoided touching anything. The surfaces of the cooking area – you couldn't call it a kitchenette, let alone a kitchen – were all sticky. Even the worn linoleum floor was sticky. The fridge had never been defrosted and so the ice-box was just that: a box of furry ice in the depths of which, preserved like a thousand-year-old body in a glacier, could just be glimpsed the greenish packaging of a bag of frozen peas. Years of unventilated steam had made the paint in the bathroom bubble and peel. There was mould on the walls. Clothes hung up to dry on the cord above the bath never did. The shower curtain was grimy, the toilet seat warped, possibly dangerous. There were yellow-brown cigarette burns on the flush. To stop the taps dripping Luke had to twist them so hard he expected the pipes to snap. The window in the living area – the only window in the place – had not been washed for a long time. In a few years it would be indistinguishable from the wall. Already it was so grimed with pollution that it seemed to suck light out of the apartment like an extractor. An extent of patterned material had been stretched over the lumpy sofa but as soon as anyone sat down (Luke himself essentially), it became untucked so that the cigarette-scarred arms and blotched back were again revealed. The only stylish touch was provided by a black floor lamp with a halogen bulb and foot-adjustable dimmer switch. By keeping the light turned as low as possible Luke sought to keep at bay the simple truth that it was an ugly sofa in an ugly, sticky apartment in the middle of a neighbourhood that was really a mausoleum. At intervals he was filled with rage – immigrant's rage – that Madame Carachos had had the nerve to rent this dump to him. On arriving in the city he had turned up at her lavish apartment and handed over a wad of bills to cover the rent for the two months they had agreed upon. They had taken a coffee together and then Madame

Carachos, like everyone else, had left the city to the tourists, to those who could not afford to leave, to Luke.

He spent as little time as possible in the apartment. Mainly he walked, and everywhere he walked he glimpsed apartments where he wanted to live, restaurants where he wanted (one day) to eat, bars where he wanted to drink with friends he did not yet have. When he grew tired of walking he went to the cinema. (Ah, cinema, solace of the lonely young men and women of all great cities.) He saw a film a day, some-times two. He became a connoisseur of the non-time that preceded the films themselves, especially in small cinemas where there were no advertisements or previews, where the audience was made up of four or five people, all of them alone. It was easy to see why, in films, fugitives and wanted men went to the cinema: not just to hide in the dark but because these intervals between performances were out of time. To all intents and purposes you might as well not have existed – and yet, simultaneously, you were acutely conscious of your existence. When the lights faded – always that same sequence of perception: the lights are fading, no they're not, yes they are, yes – and the curtains cranked back slightly to extend the tiny screen, there was always a moment, after the studio logos had been displayed, when the blaze of projected colour lit up the screen like Eden on the first day of creation. Disappoint-ment and boredom often set in very soon afterwards but, for a few minutes at least, Luke's head filled with verdant images of city and sky, landscape and trees, and he believed utterly in the cinema's loneliness-obliterating promise of brightness and colour. If this faded he tried to stay there anyway, tried to become absorbed in the simple clarity, the to-no-avail lucidity of the projected image. As he began to lose interest in the film so the idea of the city began to lure him out of the darkness of the cinema. The sun hovering over buildings, light striking walls and shutters, people moving, cars massing at bridges, the river winding through the centre of the city: all the things he had hoped for from the film he had come to see were actually to be found outside. The cinema was a dungeon from which he could escape into a world of colour and light. He sat for a while longer and then got up and pushed open the exit bar, stunned when the brightness of the street crashed into him again.

On one occasion he went to the cinema and found that he was the only person there. He was the audience. It was a Kieslowski movie, *A Short Film About Love*; to Luke it seemed An Interminable Film About Fuck-All and after forty minutes he left. Out in the street he wondered if the screening had been abandoned after his departure; or had the film continued even though no one was there to see it? He walked home, stopping, as he often did, in the Tuileries, which was only a few minutes from his faucet-dripping apartment. In his first month in the city he passed through there almost every afternoon. It was filled with sculptures from a time when, relatively speaking, it was easy to manufacture statues of exceptional power. One was of a naked man, walking, one hand clutching his face in despair. Another was of a man staring at the sun, his hands chained behind his back. Luke's favourite, though, was of a centaur bearing off a woman. He did not know which biblical or mythical characters were depicted but the statues' power was scarcely diminished by his ignorance. The theme in these sculptures was always the same: rapture, punishment, suffering. Passion.

He walked by the centaur, looked at the veins pulsing in

his belly. The fingers of one hand dug into the woman's waist, the other tugged her stone hair. His front hoofs had been broken off and she had lost a hand; her other hand grasped his arm but it was impossible to tell if this was a gesture of resistance or abandonment, if he was rescuing or abducting her, if what was being demonstrated was violation or rapture. If it was a violation then it was a rapturous one. Her missing hand – the way her fingers grasped the sky – would have provided a clue but, as things stood, only a pun remained: she was being carried away. Luke stared at the statue, the centaur rearing up on legs that bore the entire weight of stone, head tilted up to the sun, framed by blue.

Most of the other statues were also damaged in some way. Many lacked arms or legs, an unfortunate few were headless, all were being rotted by pollution. Rain soaked their naked skin, the sun scorched their backs. Pigeon shit fell on them. In the extremes of passion depicted, however, such indignities barely registered – so there was an implicit consolation in their fate. Essentially, they endured. The figure clutching his head in despair – had he been blinded? – was walking, putting one foot in front of the other. In spite of the immensity of his affliction, he kept going. Mere survival turned punishment into triumph. Condemned by the gods the statues became gods themselves. They protested their sentence even while accepting it. Always, in some way they were resisting or trying to rise above the fate to which they were condemned. The character in chains struggled against gravity, towards the tormenting sky. And yet, at the same time, the fact that they were made of stone, would never free themselves, meant that at some level they were resigned. Yearning and endurance were indistinguishable. They accepted their

sentence even while protesting it. They accepted the sun that
dazzled them, accepted the darkness to which blindness had
condemned them.

'O light! This is the cry of all the characters who, in classical
tragedy, come face to face with their fate.'

After a week of rain the sky became solid blue. The heat
was tremendous and though Luke was consoled by the statues
the park itself was a source of torment. Arranged at discreet
intervals, young men and women sunbathed, read, dozed.
Many of the women wore swimming costumes. The park was
like a beach and, as on a beach, Luke was aghast at how beautiful they were, these women. Several came for their lunch
hour, stripped down to their swimming costumes, ate their
sandwiches, dressed and left. Back at their desks they may
have been plain, ordinary, but for that interlude of near-
nakedness they were beautiful. Luke walked around the park
and then, like a respectful pervert, chose a spot where he
could watch a particular woman, could watch her arms, her
legs, her breasts, her hair, hoping that she would catch his eye,
return his gaze. The park seethed with a potent mix of sex and
celibacy. No one could read for more than two pages without
looking round at the other readers. Everyone was reading as
displacement activity or disguise but this disguise was so effec-
tive that to violate it was inconceivable.

What hell it was, this park! It was so different from the
parts of the Seine frequented by cruising gays. Walking along
the river on his way to the park Luke always felt uncomfort-
able, obscurely offended by their stares, by the flagrant desire
conveyed by their looks. They made him feel prudish,
affronted. Then, when he reached the park and began looking
at women with exactly the attention that, a few minutes

earlier, had been focused on him, that gay world seemed nothing short of idyllic. He envied the men their common currency of glances and desire. How perfect it would have been to have caught the eye of a woman who was hoping to catch his eye, to have exchanged a few words, to have walked back to his dismal room and ripped each other's clothes off. His thoughts were as crude as a prisoner's but as strong as these desires – far stronger in fact – was his acceptance of the idea that it was not on to disturb a woman when she was pretending to read, that she had a perfect right to sit on her own in a park reading a sexually explicit book and not be pestered by men. A couple of times he had seen men make approaches but the women on whom they had imposed themselves had never seemed flattered or pleased by these attentions. Or almost never. On one occasion he had watched a tanned American sit next to a woman with short blonde hair and a lovely shy laugh. Luke heard that laugh a lot in the next half hour and then he saw them gather up their things and leave together.

It never happened like that for Luke. Even on days when the park was ablaze with women he left as he'd arrived, on his own. On the way out of the gates he always passed an old woman who sat patiently in a chair, holding a card on which was written 'DITES MOI' in thick black ink. She seemed happy enough, sitting there, announcing her wish to talk without any hint of pleading or supplication. So matter-of-fact was the announcement that it seemed as if she were not requesting conversation but providing a service: 'If you need to speak to someone, here I am.' Perhaps that was why no one ever took her up on her offer. Luke had never seen anyone speak to her: people were embarrassed by her loneliness because it so frankly mirrored their own. And the sign itself was strangely off-putting. Having externalised her desire for speech in this way she was left in the most complete silence imaginable. The card rendered her mute, dumb; all the language of which she was capable had been set down, framed and preserved in those two words: DITES MOI. Luke was fascinated by her, by the way that she had decided what she wanted, did what she could to obtain it, and then sat and waited, apparently without desire or hope. He wanted to know her story but, oddly, he never considered asking her, speaking to her. Instead he walked back to his stained apartment, lay down on the unerotic bed and masturbated – an act that left him feeling sadder than ever. If an orgasm was a petite mort then this was petite suicide.

Instead of spending his afternoons prowling the parks and jerking off like this he should have been working on his French which was so poor that even the simplest tasks – deciphering menus, buying bleach to clean out the toilet, ordering sandwiches – became major exercises in pantomime diplomacy. Rarely understanding how much shopkeepers and waiters were charging him, he paid for everything with fifty- or hundred-franc notes and came home with sagging pockets of change. The most efficient way to have used this money would have been to enrol in one of the many courses in French conversation and grammar but Luke persuaded himself he could absorb the language passively, by osmosis, without effort, by reading the French subtitles of American films.

Even more than learning French he should have been making progress with the book he had come to write but what in London had seemed a romantic, attractive option immediately took on the character of an arduous, pointless task that

he had no idea how to go about. Which made it all the more
important that he found a job – but during the summer there
was no work to be had and since he was unable to find a job,
incapable of learning French or getting on with his book and
was, in addition, lonely, bored and consumed by sexual frus-
tration, he seemed better off going back to England.

England: as featured from the ferry on the day he left. A
rare bright day in the Channel. Breezy (to put it mildly). He
had stood at the stern and looked back at the Dover cliffs, yellow in the sunlight. Then he had turned to the man next to
him – a stranger – and said,

'There you are: the teeth of England.'

'Excuse me?'

'I said "The Bowmen of Agincourt",' said Luke, and
headed back inside the chip-smelling lounge . . .

Yes, he could go back to England – and it was that phrase
that made him stay. Going back to England: it was difficult to
think of four words more redolent of defeat because what they
actually meant was going back to living so deeply within his
limitations he would not even be aware that they *were* limitations: they would pass themselves off as contentment. Not
that he had ever felt content in England, more like a perpetual rumbling of discontent . . . And yet, at the same time, he
thought constantly about going back to England. Returning
was a tormenting possibility, simultaneously to be resisted and
to draw strength from. How comforting to have been forced
into total exile, forbidden to return on pain of death. To know
that there was no choice but to begin a new life, to learn a
new language, to start over definitively and construct a
mythic, idealised vision of the homeland that could never be
challenged or undermined by experience.

The weeks passed and Luke stayed in Paris. More exactly, for the experience expressed itself negatively, he kept not going back to England. He stayed by increments, in exactly the same way that, until a few months previously, he had kept up a programme of boring weight training. He'd hated it, hated turning up at the gym and going through the funless routine of warming up, reps, and warming down. He'd known that at some time in the future he would give up but had forced himself to keep going in order to postpone the day when he *would* give up. He remained in Paris – where he made no attempt to join a gym – in the same way: putting off his return on a weekly, sometimes daily basis. In this way, although he was not happy, he was able to hold out for happiness, for the happiness promised by the city.

His knowledge of which expanded daily. Crucially, he discovered the 29 bus which ran from the Gare Saint Lazare to Montempoivre. Though impressive, the route itself – past the Opéra and the Pompidou Centre, through the Marais and round the Bastille – was less important than the design of the bus: a small balcony meant that a handful of passengers could stand at the back and watch the life of the city unfurl like a film. Luke often rode the 29 from terminus to terminus, glimpsing hundreds of little incidents whose origins (he could only see what lay behind) or consequences (the bus, in this traffic-free month, moved swiftly on) were revealed only rarely. Under the influence of Alain Tanner's *In the White City* (which he had seen a few weeks earlier) Luke formed the idea of making a film comprising super-8 footage shot from the back of the 29. He would call it *Route 29*. All he needed was a camera and a Carte Orange.

In the meantime he received an unexpected, very

welcome phone call. Andrew, the one person he (vaguely) knew who was in the city for the summer, invited him to a party. A party! This, he was sure, would prove a turning-point.

He spent a long time in the shower, shaved carefully, chose his clothes carefully, checked to see that he had a pen and paper – for phone numbers – and set off early to catch the Métro and arrive at the party in good time. He had walked down the stairs from his apartment and was out in the street when he realized he had forgotten the condoms that he had bought weeks earlier, in London. He walked back up, unlocked the door, put the packet in his pocket and set off again.

The party was in the courtyard of a house in the south of the city. Andrew welcomed him and was immediately called away to the phone. Luke scanned the women and felt immediately deflated: no one caught his eye. Nothing about his life was more depressing than the way variants of that phrase – catching his eye, catching her eye – had come to occupy a position of such prominence in it. He stood drinking. After half an hour he spotted a woman he had not seen before. She looked Brazilian, was wearing a brightly patterned dress, orange mainly. He looked for Andrew, hoping he could introduce them, but the host was nowhere to be seen. Luke manoeuvred so that he was close to her but she was cordoned off by the two men she was talking with. He was unsure what to do next: talk to someone in the vicinity and have his freedom of movement restricted, or stand on his own, feeling conspicuous, awkward and alone, but ready to move when the chance arose to introduce himself to her. He compromised in the worst possible way, by talking to another English guy who was also standing on his own: a young banker who was just beginning a six-month stint in the city. Together they gave off a double helping of solitude. One of the men talking to the Brazilian woman went to get a drink. The other was briefly distracted by an Italian in an improbable cravat. Luke abandoned his new friend and stepped in front of the Brazilian without having any idea of what he was going to say. Opting for boldness he offered her his hand and introduced himself. Somewhat startled she shook his hand and said her name, which Luke did not catch.

'Are you Brazilian?' he said in English.

'I'm Italian.'

'Ah, Italian.'

'What about you? Are you Brazilian?'

'Me, no . . . Though I am a great fan of that Brazilian drink: caipirinha.'

'Excuse me?' she said, exactly like the man on the ferry. On this occasion Luke prolonged their non-exchange for a couple more minutes until, the instant a pause afforded her the opportunity, she excused herself and moved away.

After that encounter he felt that he was treated suspiciously by the other guests, as if they regarded him as the most pitiful of individuals: a loser on the make. Already slightly drunk he made his way to the kitchen to get another beer. Going to a party to pick up women demanded a single-mindedness of purpose that he didn't have. He relaxed, drank, talked to anyone who came his way, indiscriminately. It was easier like that, and far more enjoyable. On his way to the toilet he saw the Italian-Brazilian woman again, chatting in Spanish or Portuguese to a man with chubby fair hair and a baggy suit.

In the toilet Luke reminded himself that this party was his one chance of the summer, there would not be another

like it, and admonished himself to pursue his original intention. Within minutes of coming out of the toilet his resolve
had collapsed. It was futile, this self-inflicted ruthlessness. He
thought about leaving and then forced himself to stay, hoping
crazily that he would be able to get the phone number of the
woman he had talked to earlier. One look at her told him it
was impossible: she was laughing with the man in the baggy
suit, liking him, and he was leaning against the wall in a way
that suggested they were already on the outskirts of a kiss.

Luke left the party and walked to the Métro. The station
was closing, the last train had left moments before. He began
walking home. It had been his chance, the party, and he had
blown it. In spite of this he felt happy to be walking, relieved
to be free of the tension generated by impotent prowling. He
knew that in the morning he would wake up feeling abject but
now, as he walked past benches and parked cars, as he saw the
yellow lights of traffic coming towards him, as he passed couples walking home and old men walking their dogs, he did not
feel unhappy. There were lighted bars and late open shops on
each side of the street. He would stop and have a beer before
he went to bed but he wanted to get near home first. He
headed north, feeling neither tired nor depressed. His fingers
touched the packet of condoms in his pocket. They reminded
him of an evening when he had bought tickets for a concert
and then, due to a catalogue of mishaps, had failed to get
there. He was still miles away when the concert was due to
begin. When he realized he would not make it he had
thought, calmly, that it didn't really matter because in two
hours the concert would be over and everything would be the
same anyway, whether he had been there or not. Ultimately,
it was futile, self-defeating, this logic of negative consolation,

but it was difficult to be depressed while walking. He passed another Métro station and found, to his surprise, that this line was still running. Within seconds the last train arrived. As soon as it left the station the train pulled above ground. Suddenly the train was passing over the Seine and there was a perfect view of the Eiffel Tower, its reflection lying on the water like a pier. Everyone in the train was looking across at the Tower and Luke felt his relief turning to elation.

It had been years since he had felt as wretched as he had at the party, as he had on afternoons in the Tuileries. He could not remember a time when he had felt so lonely, lost, but that isolation had now been redeemed by a simple Métro journey. The two sensations, the two states, were linked, dependent. You could not experience one without the other. He looked at the lighted windows, hoping to see a woman undressing or combing her hair in front of a dresser. He saw nothing like this but he was happy. No day was uniformly terrible. Even the worst days had moments of relative happiness. And if there were not these moments of happiness then there was always something to look forward to in the coming day. There may not be anything to get up for but there was always this urge to wake up. Like this, life went on, tolerable and intolerable, bearable and unbearable, slipping between these extremes. It was not a question of hope, it was part of the rhythm of the day, of the body. And it was part of this rhythm that tomorrow he would wake up with desolation lying over him like a thin blanket, would try to remain asleep a little longer, wanting to put off the claims of the day, to prolong the comforting sense of not yet being quite alive. But there might be a letter in the mail box and that would be enough to get him out of bed . . .

As he got off the train and stepped up into the street he

was already looking forward to checking his mail, to buying a paper and ordering coffee, to sitting in the same chair he always sat in, the chair he was heading for now, where he would have one drink before going back to the sad apartment, where he would undress, splash water on his face, and climb in his bed to sleep.

The body has its own economy. Faced with extreme sexual recession Luke's lust gradually diminished until, by the time of his birthday on 20 August, it had all but vanished. By then he had become sufficiently accustomed to loneliness that an absolute lack of birthday cards did not seem particularly demoralising. He spent the morning checking his mail box; in the afternoon he walked over to Invalides where football matches – kick-arounds, really – allegedly took place on Saturdays. The Esplanade was occupied by the usual assortment of sitters, readers and sleepers and it seemed unlikely that any kind of game ever took place on these traffic-surrounded squares of grass. He returned home, checked his mail and took a nap.

In the evening he went to see *Brief Encounter*. It was a tradition: on his birthday he always saw *Brief Encounter* in one form or another. Usually he had to settle for video; seeing it on the big screen – albeit a tiny big screen – was enough of a treat to compensate for the fact that he was spending his birthday alone. He loved everything about the film: Milford Junction, the boring hubby with his crossword in the *Times* and *The Oxford Book of English Verse*, the woman with 'the refined voice' who works at the station buffet, the irritating Dolly who gabbles away and blights Laura and Alec's final moments together. He loved it because it was a film in which people went to the cinema, and because it was a film about trains. Most of all he loved Celia Johnson, her hats, her face, her cracked porcelain voice: 'This can't last. This misery can't last. Nothing lasts really, neither happiness nor despair. Not even life lasts long . . . There'll come a time in the future when I shan't mind about this any more . . .' What Luke loved more than anything, though, was Trevor Howard's final 'Goodbye': the way he managed to strangle his whole life into that farewell ('no one could have guessed what he was really feeling'), to make that last syllable weep tears of blood.

After the film he walked across the Pont des Arts where four friends – two men, two women, French-speaking, younger than Luke – had prepared a lavish candle-lit dinner on one of the picnic tables. A lemon-segment moon hung in the blue-dark sky, glowed faintly in the river. The young people at the table were drinking wine from glasses, laughing, and when Luke had passed by he heard them singing: 'Bon anniversaire, bon anniversaire . . .'

Luke drank a beer over the zinc at a café. A sign behind the bar read 'Ernest Hemingway did *not* drink here'. Then he went to the Hollywood Canteen, a burger place where you could sit at the bar and not feel – as you did in restaurants – like you were eating conspicuously alone. The burgers were named after Hollywood stars. Luke ordered a Gary Cooper, fries and a beer. The burger, when it arrived, tasted weird, not like beef at all. He mentioned it to the guy serving.

'Mais c'est pas du boeuf, monsieur. C'est de la dinde.'

'Dinde? Qu'est-ce que c'est?' said Luke falteringly.

'Turkey,' said the grinning barman. 'Turkey.'

And in this way, Luke's first summer out of England – and his twenty-seventh birthday – passed.

*

It is impossible, obviously, to believe that anyone's life is pre-destined – but who knows what is programmed into an individual's chromosomes, into their DNA? Perhaps each of us, irrespective of class and other variables, is born with a propensity towards a certain kind of living. Each of us has a code which, in the right conditions, will be able to make itself utterly apparent; if an individual's circumstances are far removed or totally at odds with that initial biological pro-gramming, it may hardly be able to make itself felt circumstantially – but all life long that individual will feel the undertow, the tug of a destiny rooted in biology, urging him, only slightly perhaps, away from the life he has. The dis-satisfaction and pointlessness that a rich and successful man feels on contemplating all that he has achieved in life is per-haps the faint echo of an initial code that he has thwarted, evaded, but can never quite silence. But a certain way of life will enable you to get closer to that initial blurred blueprint. Perhaps this is what it means to live in truth, even a disap-pointed truth.

In September the city began coming back to life. Traffic and noise increased. Delivery trucks blocked the streets. Tanned women hurried to work. Restaurants opened. Office workers returned to their favourite bistros and Luke returned to Invalides where a couple of games of six- or seven-a-side were in progress. He sat behind one of the goals and watched, gaug-ing the standard of play, checking to see he wasn't going to be helplessly out of his depth. He asked the young Algerian who was keeping goal if he could join in. After some discussion among the older players Luke was granted permission to play on the opposing side. Many of the players were extremely skilful and apart from an ongoing skirmish between a couple of Senegalese the game was played in just the right spirit: competitive without being aggressive. The fact that the ball bounced into traffic every five minutes – and threatened, on each occasion, to cause a three- or four-car pile-up – was an added attraction. Luke concentrated on not making mistakes and learning the names of his team-mates. A few called out *his* name but most settled for 'Monsieur, monsieur!' or 'Monsieur l'anglais!' It didn't matter. Once he had made a couple of tackles, headed the ball and, crucially, hit the ball into the path of a passing BMW, Luke felt quite at home. After only half an hour, unfortunately, the police came and brought the game to an end.

'C'est chaque semaine la même merde,' Said, the little goalkeeper, explained. 'On joue ici et puis les keufs se pointent et nous embarquent, ces bâtards!'

Luke said goodbye to his team-mates, some of whom waved back or shook hands or smiled and called out 'À la prochaine.' He walked home happier than he had been at any moment since arriving in Paris: for the duration of the game and the brief interlude after it had ended, as they gathered up their belongings and pulled on jeans and changed shoes, he'd had *friends* – from Algeria, Africa, Poland and France.

Back home he got a call from an English friend, Miles, who had lived in Paris for ten years. He had been away all summer, he said, was glad to hear that Luke was in town. He invited Luke to dinner on Monday, the first such invitation he had received in almost two months.

Miles lived in the Eleventh, a part of the city Luke had never visited before. He turned up half an hour early so that he could explore a little – and decided immediately that this was where he wanted to live.

'You'll be lucky,' said Miles, opening another bottle of wine (he was finishing off the first as Luke stepped through the door). Ten years ago, when he and Renée, his wife, had moved here there had been nothing. They had bought this place because they needed space for their kids and this was the only part of central Paris they could afford. It was a neglected working-class area but in the last five years it had begun to change. Following the well-established trajectory of neighbourhood-enhancement the world over, artists had moved in, a few galleries had opened, then bars, clubs, restaurants, more expensive galleries, more bars, more clubs. Rents were going up. As befitted a man who had anticipated a trend Miles explained this dismissively, contemptuously, even though these developments – for which he was partly responsible – suited him nicely. He was fifty, the father of two children. He had lived in Afghanistan and claimed to have slept with his sister even though, as far as Luke recalled, he had no sister. He lived on red wine, cigarettes, coffee. He drank beer like water, to clean out his system. Food wasn't important to him. Mainly he ate omelettes. Luke had met him in London but had not seen him for two years. If he looked only slightly worse now that was because he had long ago achieved the look of definitive decrepitude that would last him a lifetime. Luke had assumed that Renée would be around, but there was no sign of her or the kids. Come to that, there was no sign of dinner.

'They're off at something at the school,' said Miles. 'Some loony play or other. Would you like another drink, Luke?' It was one of those houses, Luke realized, which relied on its own internally generated chaos to function happily.

'Are we thinking of eating something?' said Luke.

'How about an omelette? Would you like an omelette?'

'Perfect.'

And what an omelette it was: an egg base with every-thing in the fridge thrown on top, in no particular order (the onions went in last, as an afterthought) with the flame turned permanently to maximum. Miles was a messy chef. In the process of cracking the eggs he smashed the cup he was bang-ing them into. By the time they sat down to eat, the cooker, work surfaces and floor were awash with debris.

'You can't make an omelette without breaking the kitchen,' said Luke sagely. Very sagely, as it happened, for at the last moment Miles had emptied half a pot of it into the pan.

'Quite. How's the omelette?'

'Great,' said Luke. 'Almost completely inedible.'

'Marvellous. You know, I'm so happy you're here. Would you like some more wine?' Luke held out his glass. His vision was becoming somewhat slurred. Miles, meanwhile, contra-dicting his earlier claim, said that there would be no problem finding an apartment to rent in this neighbourhood.

'Really?'

'We'll find a place tomorrow. I'll put the word around. You can get a place easily. I've got two or three in mind already. People are going away the whole time on some loony expedition or other.'

'Really? That's great because I've got to move out of the dump I'm in at the moment in a couple of weeks.'

'We'll sort it out tomorrow.'

'And you mentioned earlier about maybe being able to get a job at some warehouse.'

'Oh yes we'll do that tomorrow as well.'

'Really?' said Luke, conscious that his side of the conversation was coming to consist entirely of 'reallys'.

'Yes. Really,' said Miles. In a moment of surging clarity Luke saw his future as fixed, settled.

In the morning it looked blurred, as unsettled as his stomach. After the omelette and more wine they had gone out to a bar and drunk a few beers. Luke had walked home, not caring about anything. Now he felt awful, hung over, certain that Miles would have forgotten about both the job and the apartment. For the first time his circumstances offered a flattering reflection of how he felt. His mouth was parched, his head ached. It was a Tuesday morning and there was nothing to get up for except to wash the smell of smoke from his hair. When he had done that he dressed, checked his mail box – empty except for a menu from a new pizza pit – and went out for breakfast.

It was drizzling or not drizzling, warm. Once he had drunk his coffee he could think of nothing else to do but go back to his apartment. On the way he bought an English newspaper, a third of the size and three times the price of the non-export version. From now on, Luke resolved (as he did most mornings), I will buy French papers.

The phone was ringing when he stepped through the door of his apartment.

'Hello?'

'Good morning, Luke.'

'Hi Miles.'

'I'm not waking you am I?'

'No. I'm kind of hung over though.'

'Have you ever said yes to a single joy? Then, Luke, you have said yes to *all* woe. Besides, we hardly drank anything.'

'I think it was the omelette.'

'Ha! Now, Luke, I'm afraid nothing has come up yet on the apartment front but I do have the number of that loony who runs the mad warehouse. His name is Lazare Garnier. You should give him a call. He lived in America. He speaks English, or American. That's to say, he *swears* in American. Have you got a pen?'

By a fluke Lazare himself answered the phone when Luke called. He was furious because Didier had once again failed to turn up on a day when there was a massive backlog of urgent orders.

'Ah bonjour. Miles Stephens m'a dit,' Luke began, not very impressively. 'Excusez-moi. Parlez-vous anglais?'

'Sure.'

'Ah, yes. My name is Luke Barnes and I've been told by Miles Stephens—'

'Who?'

'Miles Stephens.'

'Who the fuck is that?'

'He—'

'Oh that English guy. The guy who lived in Afghanistan?'

'Exactly.'

'And?'

'He said that it might – that at certain times you took on people to work, packing. I wondered if there were any—'

'Where are you phoning from?'

'Um, the First.'

'What time can you get here?'

'Today?'

'No, next year. When the hell do you think I mean?'

'In about an hour and a half.'

'Make it just the half,' said Lazare. 'And you've got the job.' With that he hung up.

We were all working flat out that day. Lazare was in a temper (that is, he was in a good mood), bawling out orders, yelling at people for not having done things he hadn't told them needed doing. When Luke knocked on the office door Lazare was shouting at a client on the phone. He covered the mouthpiece with his hand and yelled at Luke to come in. Luke didn't hear. He waited, knocked harder.

'Oui.' Luke opened the door. Stood there.

'Monsieur Garnier?'

'Vous attendez quoi là? Un visa? Entrez . . . Attendez. Non,' he said into the phone, 'Je parle avec une espèce de con qui vient d'entrer . . . Ne quittez pas.' He cupped his hand over the phone again. 'Asseyez-vous, asseyez-vous,' he gestured to Luke and then turned his anger back to the phone. 'Écoutez-moi. Si vous êtes con . . . Allo? Qu'est-ce que vous faites? Il a raccroché, ce con!' With that he crunched the phone down and glared at Luke who had not yet sat down. 'Et maintenant, pour nous monsieur c'est quoi?'

'My name is Luke Barnes. We spoke on the phone this morning about my coming in to work.' Luke advanced into the room and held out his hand. Lazare waved him away.

'So get out there and start working. Bernard will tell you what to do.' He swivelled round, picked up the phone and began jabbing numbers.

Bernard introduced Luke to everyone. He was tall, confidently nervous. He was wearing jeans – which he almost never wore – and the blue work shirt which, as it grew older and softer, would be reserved for evenings when no wear and tear could be expected. His sleeves were rolled up above his elbows. He had that brittle friendliness of the Englishman adapting to a life larger than the one he had so far encountered. He seemed too tall to carry off the manners that he had evolved to diminish his awkwardness. Perhaps I didn't notice these things at the time. It is hard to say, difficult to preserve those first impressions because they are being changed by second – and third and fourth – impressions even as they are registering *as* impressions. Even when we recall with photographic exactness the way in which someone first presented themselves to us, that likeness is touched by every trace of emotion we have felt up to – *and* including – the moment when we are recalling the scene. He was tall, thin. He looked English – something in the set of his mouth. His face was angular, the jawline pronounced. He was handsome, attractive; as yet his circumstances had played almost no part in determining his expression. You could not yet read his history in his face; his looks were a fact of biology. The eyes were blue, full of looking, but – how else to say it? – *behind* the blue (or am I amending that first meeting in the light of what came later?) there was a remoteness, almost a refusal.

We shook hands. He had the handshake of a thin person who has learned how to make a good impression by shaking hands firmly even though that strength always feels as if it is made up of bones and nerves. He knew there was a way of getting an intensity of feeling into shaking hands but he had not learned how to do it. He was one of those people who have to learn everything. I say 'one of those people' and I am not sure why. Perhaps because, as I got to know him better, he came to seem so emphatically himself, so individual. Perhaps it is from people like this that we come to an understanding of types. When I met him that day – or so it seems to me now – he was poised on the brink of becoming himself, as I came to know him.

'Vas-y,' said Bernard. 'Je vais te dire comment qu'on fait.' Which was to clamber up to the second tier of storage racks and catch the packages of books thrown to him by Daniel before throwing them down to Matthias who piled them on to the trolley which Ahmed trundled into the post room. There had been some debate as to whether chaining packages like this was the most efficient way of getting them from the storage racks into the post room. Possibly it was not, but for anyone who had seen footage of soldiers – of the Eighth Army ideally, wearing shorts in the blazing heat of north Africa – tossing supplies from one man to another, it had an inescapable attraction. Also, there was that slight – very slight – element of fun, of sport, of risk, which comes from throwing and catching anything, even dull packets of textbooks. On Luke's first day, though, there was no time to relish these finer aspects of the job. A sudden rush of orders had come in, all needing to be dispatched that day. Lazare was banging on the office window constantly, phone in one hand, cigarette in the other, gesturing to Bernard to hurry, demanding to know why the order for Auxerre had not been sent out.

'Parce que c'est pas à expédier avant jeudi.'

'Pas celle-là merde, je te cause de la commande pour l'autre boîte. Comment elle s'appelle déjà?'

'Ouais, celle-là elle est partie hier.'

At which Lazare would permit himself a smile before

ushering Bernard back into the warehouse and calling out, 'Et qu'est-ce que tu as fait avec celle pour Lyon?'

He was a good boss, Lazare. Once you realized that whipping himself into a froth of anger and irritation was essential to his contentment it was easy to work with him. He had two children and a sweet-tempered wife. She came by occasionally and told us how, if Lazare had expended enough angry energy in the day, he would sleep perfectly. She was able to gauge his days by his mood in the evenings. If he was cranky and short that meant it had been an easy day without problems. If he came home smiling, relaxed, a bottle of wine in hand, that meant there had been a series of deadlines, problems and escalating difficulties.

'Le stress est son truc,' she said.

We worked late that first day. By the time we left it was growing dark and Luke's arms were numb with effort. We went to the Café Roma for a beer, another beer and a bowl of pasta each. We were all tired and the beer made us light-headed. Although Luke had hardly spoken to anyone he already felt that he belonged, was part of the group: an unexpected side-effect of Lazare's abrasive 'managerial' style was that the staff quickly developed a group identity. Luke didn't mention the book he had come to write. He didn't mention anything much. He spent most of that first evening sitting quietly, smiling, laughing readily enough but not initiating conversation with anyone.

We paid for the meal, tossing a pile of notes into the middle of the table and getting up to leave before the waiter came to collect them.

Outside, the sky was turquoise, streaked black with cloud. People waved goodbye to each other, began heading home. Alex asked Luke where he lived.

'In the First, rue de la Sourdière. For the moment.'

'Are you taking the Métro?'

'Yes.'

'Okay, we'll walk together. I live near there, near the Métro.'

People talk about love at first sight, about the way that men and women fall for each other immediately, but there is also such a thing as friendship at first sight. Although Luke and Alex had said little to each other there was an immediate ease and sympathy between them. Alex was shorter than Luke, strongly built. His hair was cropped army short. He walked fast, exuding energy, as if the idea of a stroll had never entered his head. Appropriately enough, he had come to Paris in March – though not, like Luke, with the idea of pursuing any kind of literary project – and had been working at the warehouse since late June. He'd been in the south of France for most of August and had only been back at work for a couple of days when Luke started.

'What's it like living in rue de la Sourdière?'

'Awful. The street is OK but the neighbourhood's not so good. And my apartment – well, it's a sad place. It's seen better days.'

'How long have you been there?'

'Almost two months.'

'And it's the first place you lived in?'

'Yes.'

'Everybody starts out in a dump. It's a rite of passage. You do your time in a cesspit, you're about to kill yourself, and then, hopefully, something better comes up.'

'What if it doesn't?'

'Then you go ahead and kill yourself.'

'And no one notices.'

'Neighbours, generally, are alerted by the stench.'

'My place smells bad enough already. No one would notice.'

'That's probably the previous tenant. Where would you like to live?'

'Round here.'

'You should. It's great.'

They walked in silence for a few moments, Luke hoping that Alex would suddenly remember that a friend of his was leaving an apartment just a few blocks away. Instead he asked Luke if he wanted a drink at the Petit Centre, the bar on rue Moret that is not there any more.

The Centre was crowded: overspill from a gallery opening nearby. They stood at the bar until two stools became available. Then they found themselves in the best position in the place: sitting at the end of the bar, part of the crowd but not engulfed by its pushing and shoving. Alex ordered two beers.

'My arms are so tired I can hardly pick up my glass,' said Luke.

'I know what you mean. Christ, what a day!'

'Bridge on the River Kwai.'

'Don't worry. It's not often like that.'

'How long have you been there, at the warehouse, I mean?'

'Since April, but I was away for the summer. I like it.'

'Tell me about the guys who work there. I wasn't sure who was who.'

'OK, Bernard is the number two, the foreman. He's French and so is Daniel. He and Matthias—'

'The German?'

'Actually he's Swiss but you wouldn't know it. Anyway he and Daniel are great friends – that is they're both great dope smokers. They do a lot of acid as well.'

'At work?'

'It has been known. Daniel deals a bit too.'

'What? Grass?'

'Mainly. But he's pretty good for most things if you give him a couple of days' notice.'

'How convenient.'

'It is actually. Then there's Ahmed who's Algerian. He's the guy I see most, out of work. And that's it. There's a woman called Marie who comes in occasionally to do secretarial work but you never know when she's going to show up. Like Didier. The guy whose job you've got. He was becoming less and less reliable. Today was the straw that broke the camel's back, Lazare's back anyway. He's been pissed off with him for a while but his not showing today clinched it.'

'I thought Lazare was pissed off with everybody.'

'That's just front. It's not even that his bark is worse than his bite. He's all bark, no bite.'

'So you think I can stay?' said Luke.

'Sure. I don't see why not. Where are you from anyway?'

'I lived in London for five years.'

'Whereabouts?'

'Brixton.'

'Me too. On Shakespeare Road.'

'I was on Saint Matthews Road.'

'Where's that?'

'Just off Brixton Water Lane.'

'I had friends who lived near there. Josephine Avenue.'

'What number?'

'I forget. A big shared house. They gave a lot of parties. The people I knew were called Sam and Belinda.'

'Was it the house with the purple door?'

'Yes.'

'I went to a party there.'

'Were you at the one the police raided?'

'By mistake?'

'Yes, exactly. They got the address wrong.'

'Yes. So we were at the same party. I bet we knew other people too. Did you know, oh what was that guy called? The artist, he had that great name—'

'Steranko!'

'Exactly.'

They had known the same people, eaten in the same places, drunk in the same pubs, and now they were drinking in the same bar, in Paris. It felt like an achievement. Luke pointed at Alex's glass which would soon be empty. 'D'you want another drink?'

'Ah, I see. We're doing it English-style: ordering another drink before we've finished the first. Yes. Please.'

As Luke collected his change a guy came in and slapped Alex on the shoulder: an American, in his fifties, drunk. He was with a Spanish woman who was also drunk and a friend who was French. Alex introduced Luke and then began speaking French. Luke sipped his beer, understanding odd words but unable to join in. Then the American – Steve? – started talking at him in English, telling about the private view they'd just come from: paintings of people looking at paintings in a gallery, seen from the paintings' point of view. Over their shoulders, over the shoulders of the people in the paintings, you could sometimes see some other paintings.

'Not that you could get anywhere near the paintings,' said the American. 'It was far too crowded. Are you an artist?'

'No,' Luke smiled. People always assumed he was an artist. Perhaps that is one of the reasons why he felt so little need actually to create anything.

'You look like an artist.'

'Thank you. How's that?'

'The hair, the clothes . . . What about me? What do I look like?'

'He looks,' said another man who had just pushed into the corner, 'like an overweight homosexual trying to pick up boys half his age.'

'That is not fair. Do you think I'm overweight?' Before Luke could reply he said, 'Have you met Michael?' Luke smiled and shook hands. 'Doesn't he look like an artist, Michael?'

'He look very nice. Look at that shirt.'

'You like this shirt? It's my favourite shirt,' said Luke.

'His shirt is a work of art.'

'It matches his eyes.'

'*He* is a work of art.' There was such a hubbub in the bar now it was necessary to yell things like this to get heard. Michael bought Luke a drink and began talking to someone else before Luke even had a chance to thank him. Alex had given up his stool for the Spanish woman who was actually Peruvian and who spoke neither French, Spanish nor English.

'As far as I can make out she speaks no language whatsoever,' Alex said, turning to Luke. 'How's your French?'

'Terrible.'

'You have to learn.'

'I know. If only it didn't require any effort.' Someone else Alex knew, an English woman, Amanda, had just been to a film. Luke asked her about it and she began summarising the plot. It was as if something were at stake. She had to recount what happened, in exactly the right sequence, omitting nothing, incorporating each twist of the unfollowably complex plot. Once, realizing she had made an error in chronology, she even retraced a couple of minutes of exposition and started over from the point where the mistake had been made. After that hiccup she really got into her stride. There was no stopping her. Luke nodded. Alex was communicating, somehow, with the Peruvian woman and was apparently paying no attention to this scene-by-scene reconstruction of the film. Luke wondered if he could endure any more of it when Amanda's attention was deflected, briefly, by the guy she had been to the cinema with. Alex turned towards Luke again.

'Quite a summary,' he said.

'I hate it when people do that. What makes them want to summarise plots like that?'

Alex shook his head. 'I like submarine films.'

'*Above Us the Waves*, *Das Boot*?'

'Exactly.

'*The Hunt for Red October*?'

'No.'

'Essentially, you're a Second World War man?'

'Through and through.' They slapped hands: allies.

'The Wolf Pack,' said Luke.

'The convoy.'

'Torpedoes: tubes one and two.'

'Depth charges.'

'Periscope depth.'

'The sea ablaze with oil. Survivors leaping into the blazing sea.'

'Crash Dive!'

'Two hundred fathoms down. Depth charges exploding all around.'

'No one making a sound.'

'Sonar.'

'Or is it Asdic?'

'I'm not sure. Sweating, unshaven.'

'Bloodshot eyes. Worried glances at the depthometer.'

'Well past maximum safety depth.'

' "Take her deeper!" '

' "She won't stand it!" '

'Creaking. Rivets pinging out like bullets.'

'Every eye bloodshot and every bloodshot eye fixed on the depthometer.'

'The hull about to be crushed by the pressure . . .'

Quite suddenly they ran out of steam. The bar had thinned out. People were still arriving, Luke thought, but more people were leaving than were arriving. Alex's glass was empty. Amanda and Michael were saying goodbye to everyone, including each other. Alex asked Luke if he wanted another drink.

'Yes,' said Luke. 'Always yes.'

'Irrespective of the question?'

'Almost.'

Alex paid for two more beers and passed one to Luke. 'It's a great bar isn't it?' he said. 'In fact it's the best bar in the world, brackets: indoor category.'

'What about outdoors?'

'The San Calisto in Rome. Do you know it?'

'I've never been to Rome.'

'Me neither,' conceded Alex. 'But it's something we could discuss.'

'Places we haven't been?'

'No. What makes a great bar?'

'Ah, a *bar* conversation.'

'I have pretty strong views on the subject.'

'And?'

'All great bars are primarily neighbourhood bars.'

'Correct.'

'But they are not exclusively neighbourhood bars.'

'Also correct.'

'You don't want to add anything?'

'You said it all,' said Luke, raising his glass.

Luke was back at work again the next day, sore from the previous day's exertions, relieved to find that things would be far less frantic. This was another benefit of Lazare's unusual managerial style: by imposing urgent, sometimes non-existent deadlines we often found ourselves with relatively little to do, especially if he was away from the warehouse, meeting clients, pitching for business. Typically we had two maniacally busy days and the other three were easy – which meant we could spend our lunch hours playing football at passage Thiéré. We had been mooting the idea for a while, had even played occasionally, but it was only after Luke began working at the warehouse that football became an established part of our week. Up until then we had spent most of our lunch hours *talking* about playing.

We took our lunch late and the playground was never crowded. If other guys were around – the Algerians from the workshop on the corner always wanted to play but it was difficult for them to get away for any length of time – we played together, four- or five-a-side. If it was just the five of us from the warehouse we volleyed and headed the ball back and forth, making sure that the ball did not touch the ground, embroidering this basic task – whenever possible – with displays of individual skill: flicking the ball from foot to foot and on to a thigh before heading it to the next person; bringing the ball under control and restoring the flow of play following a mis-kick. We kept count of how many passes and headers we could string together without letting the ball touch the ground. Sometimes we settled into a rhythm that seemed likely to continue indefinitely until one of us fluffed a simple kick and we were back to square one and had to begin the count again. I enjoyed this but it bothered me slightly that the game did not have a satisfactory name. Keepy-uppy, Headers and Volleys: neither was adequate. Alternatively – another game without a name – one of us went in goal while the others crossed and headed or let fly with palm-stinging shots.

After playing, especially if the weather was fine, we were reluctant to return to the warehouse and sat against the graffiti-mottled wall, the sun dazzling our eyes, gulping down water and chewing mouthfuls of bread and tomato, the minutes ticking by until, begrudgingly, like troops returning to the front, we tramped back up Ledru Rollin to work.

If getting a job at the warehouse was Luke's first stroke of luck it proved also to be his second. Nothing came of the apartment Miles had heard of but, through Matthias, he was put in touch with a photographer who was going to spend a year travelling. He had sub-let his apartment to an American but at the last moment this arrangement had fallen through and he needed to find someone else.

The apartment was on the second floor of a shabby block only fifteen minutes walk from the warehouse, less than ten from where Alex lived. Most of the buildings in the street – and a couple of vans – were the site of turbulent political discourse: 'Le Pen' and 'FN' had been scribbled on walls, crossed out, rewritten and sprayed over. The building next door had been demolished so the outside walls were patterned with squares of wallpaper: ghost rooms where families had slept and eaten and died.

The apartment itself was small, a studio, but there was little furniture cluttering up the place. The floorboards were stained a pale, woody colour. Some of the photographer's photographs were on the walls. Black-and-white: street scenes. One showed a crowd of demonstrators confronting police. They were good photographs and the apartment, though small, suited Luke perfectly. He said yes on the spot and paid two months' rent in advance. The photographer left him the key to his bicycle so that Luke could use that too. Luke bagged up his belongings and dropped off the key to his old apartment with Madame Carachos. He considered abusing her for renting such a dump to him, decided against it, and moved into his new apartment the day after going to look at it.

Now that they were both 'colleagues' – as Luke put it – *and* neighbours, he and Alex saw a great deal of each other. They were both English, both new – or newish – to the city, and both single. With the exception of Miles and the guys at the warehouse, Luke knew almost no one. Alex knew a few people – most of whom had been at the Petit Centre that night – but, together, he and Luke were set to get a far better purchase on the city than either of them could have done alone. Meeting each other marked the beginning of the phase in their lives when all the elusive promise of the city could be realized. They flourished in each other's company, their intimacy increased as they met more people. Things Alex said in groups were always addressed implicitly to Luke; other people were used as a way of refracting back something Luke intended primarily for Alex.

You know what a downer it is when you meet someone for a drink or dinner and almost the first thing they say is 'I don't want a late night'? To Alex, Luke was the embodied opposite of that kind of remark. Evenings with him had a quality of unfettered potential. This was exactly the feeling engendered by the city in which they found themselves and many of the qualities Alex saw in Luke could just as accurately have been attributed to the shared experience of a place and time. Alex also ascribed to his new friend an exalted version of the traits which – in quieter, passive mode – Luke saw in him. Alex used Luke as a kind of probe, an extrapolated mirror of himself. Which meant that from Alex's perspective Luke was a special person, to be admired, to measure himself against. The difference, I realize now, was that Alex had a theory – an *idea* – of Luke whereas Luke simply liked his friend, liked being with him. Ultimately this difference would generate another: Luke would never be disappointed by Alex.

There was an additional incentive for playing football at passage Thièré: the women who each day passed by, carrying books, talking or pushing bicycles. They were on their way back to offices or to lectures at the university after their lunch break, just strolling, or eating ice cream when it was hot. Men walked by too but that was just an accident whereas the girls, we liked to think, came by deliberately. Just a slight preference for this route back from the café rather than another one, a simple suggestion by one of a group of friends – 'Let's walk past the playground at Thière' – that was always approved by the others. No more than that. And even if it was not the consequence of any kind of preference, even if it was just a short-cut that extended their lunch break by five minutes, we preferred to think that they came by primarily because of us. Certainly there were other places we could have played football; even if they didn't come by because of us, *we* played there because of them.

Luke noticed one woman in particular. She was tall with a mass of black hair that fell down below her shoulders. One day, when he was over that side of the yard retrieving the ball, he smiled, 'Hi', and she smiled back briefly before walking on. Contained in that look perhaps there was the seed of another meeting of eyes when, weeks later, undressing each other for the first time, his fingers in her hair, their eyes flicked open at exactly the same moment.

Luke watched her walk away, wondering if she would look back. Her legs were tanned, she was wearing tennis shoes, there was something floaty about the way she walked. A lightness. She didn't look back.

As we traipsed back to work, Luke said that the next time she came by we should kick the ball to that side of the playground so that he could talk to her. Thereafter, whenever we were playing and she walked past, the rest of us gestured to Luke to let him know she was there but kept passing the ball in the other direction, luring him away from her. Either that or we eliminated him from the game completely, refusing to pass to him as he inched his way towards her side of the playground. Then, when she had walked past, *then* we would kick the ball over that way – 'Go on Luke, now's your chance!' – leaving him to retrieve the ball and gaze after her retreating form.

One day, though, after we had got Luke running round like a dog, I relented and floated an inch-perfect pass across the yard, landing a metre or two in front of her so that Luke could catch her eye, smile, kick the ball back and wait for her to draw near. When I next looked over he was speaking to her, hanging on to the wire diamonds. We only granted him a few seconds of repose before booting the ball over his way and shouting to him to kick it back, making her conscious of the way we were all standing around, watching and waiting while Luke trotted after the ball and curled it back to us. We let them have a couple of peaceful minutes and then Matthias blasted the ball over that way again, smacking it into the wire a couple of feet from her head like a cannonball. She jumped, Luke turned round and saw us all laughing like yobs while he was obviously trying to impress on her that he was not devoid of sensitivity and actually spent a great deal of time reading, maybe even dropping a hint that he was not without literary aspirations himself. And at the same time that he was annoyed about us louting up his chances you could see he also enjoyed it, the way that we imparted a hint of the ghetto to his wooing.

There was no sign of Lazare when we got back to work and so we sat with our feet up on the packing tables, eating sandwiches, gasping after sips of Orangina, crunching chips.

'Did you see Luke after all that running around, legs buckling—'

'Breathing hard, unable to speak—'

'Coughing up blood – "Just let me get my breath back, you see I'm not like the others" – then BAM! the ball smacks into the fence about an inch from her face.'

'What she say Luke?' Matthias wanted to know. 'What she is like?'

'She's nice.'

'What is her name?'

'Nicole.'

'Oh Nicole! Horny name. And what does she do, horny Nicole?' Matthias pushed his tongue into his cheek, moving his hand back and forth in front of his open mouth. Luke shook his head. Matthias belched and tossed his empty can, clattering into the bin.

We would happily have spent the whole afternoon like that, grilling Luke about his attempted courtship but, hearing Lazare's decrepit Renault scrape through the gate ten minutes later, we leaped to our feet. By the time he walked in we were hard at it, as if we had been so busy packing orders that there had scarcely been time to grab a sandwich.

A few days later, when Nicole next passed by the playground, we decided to let Luke go over and talk quietly, without the ball thudding into the fence, like we were on our best behaviour. She was wearing a dress and a quaint mauve cardigan so that he could not see her arms which one day soon would be around his shoulders as he kissed her, which one day he would grip hard in his fists, shaking her, leaving ugly bruises. I can still see them over there, separated by the fence, wondering what each other was like. She was holding some books in front of her. The sun flashed out from a cloud, the wire fence threw angles of shadow over her face. She held up a book for him to see and he bent towards her and conceded that he had never read Nietzsche or Merleau-Ponty or whoever it was she was reading. Not that it mattered: the important thing about the book was that it served as an intermediary, a bridge between them. Luke watched her looking at him through the fence, sweat dripping from his hair, breathing hard. His sleeves were pushed up over his elbows, the veins stood out in his forearms. Strands of her hair breezed free. She fingered them back into place, over her ear, and he noticed her hands, her woman's hands holding the large book of philosophy.

They were running out of things to say. Luke asked if she would like to meet up sometime if . . . His voice trailed off, he looked to the floor, at the sun-catching grit, making it as easy as possible for her to say 'Well, that's difficult.' He was still gripping the fence, separated from her like a prisoner or an animal. When he looked up again he saw her pausing, weighing things up, knowing the hurt a man has the power to inflict on you. But that pause was already giving way to a smile of assent.

She smiled at him and he looked into her eyes which, at that moment, held all the promise of happiness the world can ever offer. He suggested Tuesday which was no good for her.

'Thursday maybe . . .'

'Thursday I have dance class.'

'Oh . . .'

'I could meet you afterwards.'

'After your dance class?'

'Yes.'

'This is what it means to be a man,' said Luke, glad he was saying something clever-sounding. 'To be a man is to meet women after classes. After dance classes, after Spanish classes, after acrobatics. Women go to classes, men meet them after their classes. After your dance class would be perfect. What time?'

'At nine?'

'Yes. Where shall I meet you?'

'My class is at the Centre de Danse, in the Marais. Do you know it?'

'Yes,' said Luke (he didn't). 'Shall I meet you there?'

'OK.'

In the road a delivery truck was holding up traffic. Cars began honking.

'I should be going,' she said.

'They're not honking at you,' Luke said.

She smiled, turned to leave. Luke started walking back towards us. Daniel floated up the ball for him to volley, with all the force of his happiness, into the top corner of the segment of fence we called a goal.

'And the crowd go wild,' shouted Luke.

The Centre de Danse was in a cobbled courtyard off rue du Temple. Luke arrived at nine o'clock exactly. The building was old, soot-blackened, subsiding so badly that it looked rubbery. Such was the efficacy of dance, it seemed, that even glass and concrete were susceptible to rhythm, supple. Bicycles were lined two deep against the walls. Classes were in progress on three sides of the courtyard. Piano and tap-dancing came from one window, jazz-funk from another. The windows on one side of the courtyard held warped reflections of those on the other. Through these reflections Luke could see the lunge and surge of leotards and limbs inside rooms with huge ceilings and mirrored walls. Men and women, Luke's age and younger, came out carrying bags over their shoulders, all looking pleased. Nicole came out at five past nine. Oh, and she was gorgeous, in a green linen dress and tennis shoes. She carried a green and yellow bag over her shoulder. It would have been impossible to dress more simply, or to have looked more beautiful. Her hair was wet, she smiled. She wore no make-up. Luke held out his hand.

'You look lovely,' he said.

'Thank you.'

'How was your dance class?'

'It was hard,' she said, letting go of his hand.

'Hard?'

'Yes, but was OK.'

'What kind of dance do you do?'

'Oh, is jazz or something.'

'Jazz?'

'Disco.'

'Jazz disco?'

'Tango.'

'Tango too?'

'Ballet.'

'Ballet?'

'Techno.'

'Flamenco?'

'A little flamenco, yes.'

Luke could not think of another form of dance. They were standing in the courtyard. Mopeds were revving into life. Nicole waved at a man – gay, surely – who blew her a kiss as he cycled off.

'Are we standing here for a reason?' said Luke.

'I am standing here because you are.' She folded her arms: ironically determined to stand her ground.

'Shall we go?'

'OK. Where would you like to go?'

'We could have a drink. Have dinner. That's what people do isn't it? Whatever. We can go dancing if you like.'

'Shall we walk a little first?'

'Yes, sure. Let's walk.'

The traffic on rue du Temple was jammed solid, the air heavy with fumes. They turned into rue des Haudriettes which was quieter: a few restaurants, clothes shops, and a cobbler's with a pink neon sign in the shape of a shoe, tins of polish in the window. The tables at Cohn's were all full: Americans mainly.

'Where are you from?' Luke said.

'Belgrade. Have you been there?'

'Once. I saw the Danube. Is it the Danube in Belgrade? There was a sunset. Quick, let's cross.'

Sometimes it is difficult for people who have only just met to cross roads together: unsure if the other person prefers to dash or wait, they somehow do both, stepping into the road and then hesitating, mid-lunge.

'Now is my turn to ask where you are from,' said Nicole, after they had hurried across rue de Rivoli.

'London. Have you been there?'

'Once. I saw the Thames. Is it the Thames?'

'In London? No.'

'There was a sunset too. A great sunset.'

'Maybe that was the Danube too.'

'Or the Nile.'

'Perhaps the Tiber.'

'Maybe the Mississippi.'

'The Amazon even. The conversation is flowing.'

'Seine, actually,' she said, pointing because they had come to the river. A bateau-mouche was going by, throwing light at the buildings behind them. They walked to the middle of the bridge, watching the oil-black water calm itself in the wake of the boat's passing. Lights were on in apartments that commanded beautiful views of the river. In one of them they saw a man standing on his balcony looking out: contentedly watching the river, soothed by the certainty of its being there day after day; in despair, tormented by its passing (it is no good looking to views for consolation). Luke stared at the river, his gaze passing through the quiver-glint of the surface, merging with the body of water itself.

'Stay there. Don't move,' she said. 'I can see the river in your eyes. Perfect.' She had a way of saying 'perfect' that seemed perfect to Luke. 'Can you feel it?'

'The river?'

'Yes.'

'Flowing through my head, yes.' For a moment he could: a dead weight of liquid, purposeless, pressing its way to a destination that never varied; always, eventually, the sea. Reds and greens flashed and squirmed on the surface. He looked at her, feeling as if he had stood up too quickly.

'In Oxford, in England,' he said, 'students jump off a bridge and break their legs because the river is full of – guess.'

'Trolleys from supermarkets.'

'How did you know?'

'It is always shopping trolleys.' A dog padded up to them and went on its way. Nicole said, 'Once I crossed this river fourteen times in a single day.'

'In 1922 a pilot flew his plane underneath the central arch of this bridge that we are now standing on.'

'On the day I crossed the river fourteen times I used six different bridges.'

'In some century, I forget which, let's say the fifteenth, the river, swollen with melted snow from the mountains, burst its banks and flooded the entire town – even though the region was in the midst of a terrible drought.'

'A whale once swam up it as far as the Pont d'Austerlitz, a bridge which I did not cross on the day I crossed the river fourteen times.'

'Is that true?'

'About the whale?'

'Yes.'

'No.'

At a bar on the Ile St Louis they ordered a beer and a small bottle of intense apricot juice. The beer was served in a glass so slim and elegant it was almost a vase. Nicole sat very straight in her chair, tempting Luke (who managed to sprawl on his as if it were a sofa) to compliment her on her posture. A rose-seller offered him the whole bunch for thirty francs. A slight altercation between two dogs threatened to turn nasty. At the next table a woman was listening, spellbound, as an American told her about the deal he was on the brink of clinching. Nicole sipped her apricot juice.

'You have beautiful posture,' said Luke. 'And the ability to sip. I admire that. I gulp.'

'Gulp?'

'The opposite of sipping. I don't even try to sip anymore. I prefer to gulp and then just sit here wishing I had sipped. Is it OK like that, by the way, or would you like some ice?'

'It's fine. Are you comfortable, "by the way"? You don't look it.'

'Oh, I am, yes.'

'It's bad for your back to sit like that, "by the way".'

Luke sat up and said, 'How did you come to be called Nicole? That's not a Serb name is it?'

'Was my grandmother's name. She was French.'

'And are you studying in Paris, by the way?'

'I came here to study.'

'What?'

'Oh, I don't know. Architecture . . .'

'Architecture?'

'Mathematics.'

'Ah, maths.'

'Philosophy. Et cetera.'

'It sounds vague.'

'Vague? What is that? Comme une vague? A wave?'

'Yes. Your study sounds wavy. You study waves. I mean it sounds like a lot of study.'

'I don't really study anything now. I came here on a scholarship. Now I just need to finish off a dissertation I have no interest in. Is nearly finished. I just need to add a comma here and there.'

'What is it on?'

'The same thing all dissertations are on. Nothing at all.'

'You don't want to be an academic?'

'I thought I did. Once. Now, no.'

'What do you do for money though?'

'Translating and other things. Like everyone in Paris. And you? Why did you come here?'

'To become a different person. Or at least *more* of a person.'

'What were you before?'

'An Englishman living in England.'

'*Who* were you before?'

'Someone I'd lost interest in.'

'And now you're an Englishman living in Paris?'

'Put like that it sounds even less interesting.'

'How would you make it more interesting?'

'I'm here because the bars stay open late.'

'Are you learning French?'

'A little.'

'You have to. To become someone else that is essential. When I was little girl my father was very insistent that I learned other languages. He said, "The more languages you speak, the more people you can become." '

'I'm speechless.'

'What is the work you do here?'

'I work at a warehouse. Near passage Thièré.'

'And do you always play football?'

'Yes, although I didn't study it. I play every day. Rain or shine. As long as it's not raining.'

'My brother plays football.'

'You have a brother? I mean how old is he, your brother?'

'Twenty.'

'Ah, a fine age for a brother,' said Luke, pleased, for some reason, to hear himself say this. 'You have just the one brother?'

'Yes. And a sister.'

'Did you have pets?'

'A lovely golden retriever.'

'You had a brother, a sister, and a golden retriever?'

'And two cats. What about you? Do you have brothers and sisters?'

'No.'

'Nor pets?'

'No. In fact I've just realized something crucial about myself. I was an only child. No brothers or sisters. And I had no pets. No cats or dogs. So although I had my parents' love focused on me I had nothing *to* love. I loved them, of course, as little children do, but parents don't count really. My whole experience of love was being on the receiving end of it. A present that was always being given to me. It never occurred to me that *I* might love something. Except my toys. I loved my toys.'

'So, not to beat around the hedge—'

'Bush: beat around the bush.'

'Ah thank you. You must correct my English when I make mistakes,' said Nicole, but Luke was already wishing he had not done so. A hedge was a much better thing to beat around than a bush.

'So,' Nicole went on, 'not to beat around the bush, you are very selfish. What is the word? Spoiled?'

'Yes, but not just spoiled. Ruined.'

'Ruined? What is that word? What does it mean?'

'Ruined. As in ruins. Ruination. It means to fall into disrepair. Through neglect perhaps. But that's only half the story. It's also something to be aspired to, worked towards. Buildings do not just fall into ruin. Something in them wants to achieve the condition of ruination. Any truly great building will achieve its destiny only as a ruin—'

'You are trying to be clever.'

'Yes, I am. It's true. It's a weakness. It will be my ruin.'

'There is a good thing about only children though,' said Nicole.

'What is that?'

'If you have brothers and sisters you learn to lie. If you don't have them then you don't know how to lie.'

'Except to yourself.'

'Yes, but that's not much fun is it?'

She had finished sipping her apricot juice.

'Shall we go?'

'Yes.' Nicole pulled out her spectacle-case.

'I didn't know you wore glasses.'

She opened the case which was full of banknotes and coins. 'Is my purse,' she said.

'I'll get this,' said Luke. She watched him stand up to pay. He wore no jewellery. No rings, no bracelets or chains, no watch. He didn't even carry a wallet: he kept his money screwed up in his pockets. He didn't wear after-shave. He didn't drum with his fingers on tables, didn't whistle or doodle on napkins, didn't chew gum or his finger nails. She noticed the things he didn't do.

They came to the river again: a different bridge. A man and a woman passed. They were walking with their arms around each other. Across the river were the broken walls of old houses that were being torn down. They crossed over into the Marais, passed the corner shop where the old hand-painted sign – 'Boulangerie' – had been preserved even though it was now an expensive clothes shop called Le Garage. Their shoulders bumped when they walked, sometimes. A Dalmatian padded up to them while they stood looking in a shop window. Nicole patted its head and when they walked on it followed them as if it were their dog. She slipped her arm through Luke's. Her arms were bare. There was only his shirt sleeve between their skin.

At the Bastille the streets were gridlocked with pedestrians. The Dalmatian disappeared, which was a shame.

'Perhaps we'll find him again.'

'I hope so.'

'I felt he was our dog,' said Luke.

'He *is* our dog,' said Nicole. They had both said 'our'. They turned into rue Duval and, in moments, were away from the crush of people. They went to the Café Saigon.

'What would you like?' Luke asked.

'You choose.'

Luke ordered, in faltering French, but she liked the way he spoke to the waitress, his smile. He had nice manners.

They shared a portion of satay, followed by plates of vegetables, stir-fried. Nicole ate slowly – a slice of carrot at a time – and drank little wine.

'You eat,' Luke said, 'at the speed of your hair.'

'What does that mean?' said Nicole.

It took an effort of will not to say, 'It means I want to spend the rest of my life with you. I want to be with you when you are old, when your hair is grey . . .' What he actually said was: 'I don't know. It just seems true.' His plate was empty. He watched her eat, looked at her hair. He is in love with me, Nicole said to herself. She looked up again. Their eyes met. It felt as if they were kissing. Luke poured another glass of wine for himself.

'Gulp,' she said, touching his hand. 'Gulp.'

They walked back to his apartment, holding hands. Their hands grew moist. Luke made coffee, lit a candle. Asked if she was warm enough. She studied the photograph of the demonstration.

'Is this of Belgrade?' she said.

'I don't know.'

'I think it is. Do you know when it was taken?'

'I don't, I'm afraid.'

Neon from the café opposite glowed on the walls, reddish. Nicole used the bathroom. When she came back they sat on hard chairs, drinking the coffee neither of them wanted. While they talked, their fingers touched, then their hands. Their fingers became intertwined. He spoke quietly. In order to hear she leaned her head towards him. He breathed in the smell of black hair, his breath a warm shiver in her ear, her spine. She traced the line of his jaw from his ear to his chin. He looked at her mouth, her full lips. She caught a glimpse of herself in his eyes. He ran his fingers through her hair. She touched his neck. She said something he could not hear and when she spoke again her lips were almost touching his cheek. She touched his fingers. His nails were clipped short. She felt his wrists, traced the bones and veins in his arms, his thin arms. He touched the ring on one of her fingers which, for all he knew, could have been the finger on which wedding rings were worn. He looked at her eyes, the deep, deep colour. She smelt the coffee on his breath. A breeze entered the room. The candle flame persisted. He breathed in the smell of her hair again. As she spoke a narrow strand of saliva stretched momentarily between her lips. He touched the mole on her cheek. She ran a finger along his lips. His lips touched her eyelids, the flutter of her eyelashes. Her fingers moved up his forearm until she came to the crook of his elbow. He did the same, moved his hand higher to feel the slight swell of her bicep. His fingers met round her arm. Their lips almost touched, then they did, for a second, and then, a few seconds later, they did so again. She kissed him, slightly – only the sound proved it *was* a kiss – then moved her lips away. Their lips touched again. They were kissing. His hand was on her back, feeling her spine, moving, bone by bone, up to her neck, under the mane of hair through which he ran his fingers, pulling it slightly, then harder, tilting her head back so that he could cover her throat with his mouth. He felt her hands on his back, on his skin, pulling his shirt free, surprised how thin he was. He moved his hand under her arms, feeling the sweat gathered there. Her breasts were very small. Her hands were on his shoulder-blades, running down his ribs, moving to the small of his back. They slid off the chairs so that they were kneeling, facing each other. She undid the top button of his shirt, then the second. He moved his hands around the hem of her dress, moving it slightly up her thighs, brushing the outside of her legs and then touching the inside, the softness, the unbelievable softness.

'Come inside me.'
   'Is it safe?'
   'My period is tomorrow.'

They woke early, took it in turns to shower and then, enjoying the feel of each other's clean skin, made love again. Nicole took another shower while Luke shaved. She walked out of the bathroom, wrapped in a towel, leaving wet footprints on the floor. In the mirror Luke watched her looking intently at the photo of the demonstration in Belgrade.

   'This is very strange,' she said.
   'What?'
   'You have no idea when this photograph was taken?'
   'No. Why?' Luke came and stood by her. There were a couple of bloody nicks on his jaw.
   'Look,' she said, pointing to a woman near the front of the photograph. She had long black hair.

'No!' said Luke. 'Can it *really* be?'

'I think it is.'

'I think it is too,' said Luke, looking closely, shielding his eyes to stop sunlight reflecting on the glass. 'It *is* you.'

'It's a coincidence, isn't it?'

'It's incredible.'

Luke continued staring at the picture; reflected in the glass he could see Nicole dressing behind him. When she was ready they went out for breakfast, holding hands. A group of youths parted for them. It was market day on Richard Lenoir, the boulevard given over, normally, to baggy skateboarders. Stall holders were calling out the names of fruit, filling the air with the sound of strawberries, figs, raspberries, cherries. The sky was the colour of pale stone, as if, over the centuries, it had taken on the tones of the buildings below.

They walked to the Café Rotonde which everyone always referred to as the Kanterbrau because the sign advertising beer was larger than the one displaying the name of the café. An Alsatian stood guard, that is, it lay in the doorway, on the brink of sleep. When Luke was a boy Alsatians were regarded as vicious, dangerous: the man-eaters of the dog world; now, in the wake of the savage ascendancy of the Rottweiler and pitbull, they seemed dopey, loving. The only thing you had to worry about was stepping on their tails and disturbing their rest.

The waiter took their order and came back with orange pressé, café au lait, croissants, water.

'Drinking coffee, eating one croissant and looking forward to having a second,' said Luke. 'That's what I'm doing now.' His eyes felt taut from lack of sleep. There was a tension between his relaxed body and the strained, gritty feeling of his eyes, but mainly he was aghast at the metamorphosing power of their having made love. It changed everything. Not just him and Nicole but the world around them. The smallest actions – the garbage collectors loading poubelles on to the back of the truck, the waiter carrying trays of coffee, the guy drinking a glass of red wine at the bar – celebrated the happiness of the world as it converged on the couple who had just spent their first night together. Luke looked across at a young man busy writing in a notebook and felt sorry for him: he had only his book for company – even his coffee-cup was empty.

'I have to go,' Nicole said, gesturing for the waiter. She had an uncancellable appointment at the university.

'I can't believe it,' said Luke, touching her hair. 'You are the most beautiful woman I have ever seen, and last night we made love, on our first date. I can't believe my luck.'

'Maybe it's not luck.'

'What then?'

'I don't know.' She ran the two words together, as in 'dunno'. Luke was a little disappointed: at that moment, especially in the wake of Nicole's finding herself in the photograph in his apartment, even a word like 'destiny' or 'fate' would not have embarrassed him.

'I have to go,' she said. 'Are you leaving too?'

'No, I'm going to stay here a little while.'

'Then what do you do?'

'I'm going to sit here and watch you walk away. Then I'm going to sit here and have another coffee which I shouldn't have and which I'll probably regret having. I'll think about you, and then, just in case last night was a dream, I'm going to go home and lie in bed and hopefully fall asleep and dream it again.'

'What will you dream?'

'Of me pulling your dress over your head and seeing you naked for the first time, of you taking me in your mouth, the way you tasted when I first pushed my tongue into you, and how, as soon as you came, I came in your mouth too. Kissing you afterwards, then being inside you for the first time . . .'

'What a rude dream!'

'Can you come tonight as well?'

'In a dream?'

'No, for real. Can I see you tonight?'

'Yes.'

'We'll stay in. I'll cook. We'll go to sleep early. We'll sleep for ten hours.'

'OK.'

'The code is C25E,' said Luke. Nicole wrote down the number. Her pen was white, decorated with dots that matched exactly the dark green ink. Love someone, thought Luke, love their possessions.

'Are you not working today?'

'I don't have to go in till later. There's very little to do.'

'No football?'

'I'm too tired. Aren't you tired?'

'Yes.'

She kissed him on the mouth, stood up and slalomed through the thicket of café chairs, shoving one with her hip, only slightly, once. He watched her go. Tennis shoes. Tanned legs. Lime green dress. Bare arms. Long black hair. Her.

He would always love watching her walk away, seeing her disappear into the Métro, around a corner or becoming lost in the crowd. Her floaty walk. Even when, years later, they parted for the last time, he would be the one to watch her walk away. It would be up to her to stand, to look at him and walk away, feeling his eyes on her: a final concession.

A bicycle messenger wearing a luminous bib – Speedy Boys – came in and ordered a coffee. The sun squeezed between clouds, flooding the café terrace with hot light. A bus shuddered to a halt and passengers began spilling out. Spotting a gap in traffic, a little dog wagged across the road. Luke remembered the utter passivity of the previous night, how neither of them had needed to make the slightest move towards each other, how, instead, they had simply waited . . .

He finished his second coffee and then returned to the apartment, opening the door slowly as if not to disturb someone who was sleeping. It was exactly as he had left it but it was changed, utterly, from how it had been the morning before, from any morning except this one. The curtains were open. Sun streamed through the dust-patterned window. One of the two towels was hung over the bathroom door, the other was in a lump on the back of a chair. The coffee cups were on the floor. Nearby were his socks. Wax from the candles had solidified in a saucer. There was no sign of her clothes. She had taken them all with her. The quilt was piled up at the end of the bed. The sheets were wrinkled, the pillows still bore the dent of their heads. Luke went into the bathroom and saw, in the basin, two hair grips: hers.

The door-bell jolted him out of his sleep. He opened the door. Her hair was tied up. She held a bike light in each hand. She was wearing a suede jacket, a loose skirt.

'Did you dream there was someone at the door?'

'As it happens, yes.'

He stood aside to let her in, closed the door behind

them. She put her arms round him, kissed him, pressed the
rear light to his left ear and the front to his right. Then she
turned them on, like electrodes.

'Bzzzzzzz!'

'You cycled.'

'It was a little chilly. I should have worn trousers.'

'I'm glad you didn't. Would you like the heating on?'

'No, I'm OK.'

'How are you?'

'Tired.'

'Me too. I was asleep when you rang the door. I fell
asleep, I mean. I'm still waking up.'

'I brought some nice wine.'

'How kind. Would you like a glass?'

'Yes.' She kissed him on the mouth. 'Your mouth tastes
sleepy,' she said.

'Not nice?'

'Yes, is nice. Nice and sleepy.' He had his hands on her
hips. She kissed him again and he kissed her back. He undid
the buttons of her blouse. She was wearing a bra. He
unclipped it and pushed her against the wall. She tossed the
bike lights on to the bed. They were turned on still. She
reached between her legs, moved her knickers aside and
guided his fingers into her, kissing him hard.

They felt bewildered afterwards, by this fundamental breach of
etiquette: screwing before they'd even unwrapped the wine –
let alone opened it – while the lasagna was still baking. Nicole
took off her wet knickers and they lay on the bed, not speaking until Luke said:

'Would you like some wine now?'

'Yes.'

'Stay there. I'll get it.' His jeans were around his ankles. He took off his socks as well, turned down the oven and came back with wine, glasses, a corkscrew, olives and a bowl to put the pits of the olives in. She was still wearing her suede jacket.

'What about the heating? Would you like the heating on?'

'Is OK.' Luke opened the wine. They clinked glasses and sat with their legs entwined. The light was fading. Occasionally there were shouts from the street. There was a silence in the room. She was at the centre of the silence, he was at its edge, constantly on the brink of saying things: *It's lovely wine. It's a lovely evening. You look lovely.* If he could have thought of a sentence which did not have the word 'lovely' in it he would have said something. Instead, he waited for her, watched her chew away the olive and then, discreetly, put the stone in a bowl. After a while, she said:

'It's lovely wine.'

When it had grown dark he put on a light and took the lasagna from the oven. He served it and brought it to the bed where they ate off their knees. Nicole had half a plate left when Luke served himself a second portion.

'What do your parents do?' he asked.

'My mother was a professor. Now she is retired. My father was a doctor. He's dead.' Immediately, instinctively, Luke thought, *she is the first woman I've been to bed with whose father is dead.* This seemed to explain everything even though he was unsure what it explained. 'He died when I was eleven.'

'What happened?' said Luke, unsure, even as he asked, if this was a question he should have avoided.

'He had a heart attack.' Matter-of-factly. 'What about your parents?'

'They split up when I was sixteen. My mother remarried but it was my father who left.'

'He met someone else?'

'No. That's the strange thing. He went to live on his own. He died when I was twenty-two.'

'Were you close to him?'

'Not really. I hardly saw him after he left. He was nice when I was young but, well, he made my mother incredibly unhappy. *She* met someone else but I think she never really recovered from my father's leaving like that. He ended up very twisted, bitter. An alcoholic. He was a disappointed man.'

'Disappointed by what?'

'By everything, I think, but himself mainly. I have a friend here, Alex. You'll meet him. His parents are still alive but they're old. He doesn't see them much and he's worried about their dying. He asked me if I wished I'd told my dad I loved him before he died.'

'Did you?'

'No. But I wished I'd told him I hated him.'

'That's terrible.'

'I know, I really missed my chance.' She hit him on the arm, not sure if he was joking. Luke had already polished off his second plate of food; Nicole had not yet finished her first.

'You know that picture,' she said, 'of me in Belgrade?'

'Yes.'

'You have a picture of me before we met. I'd like one of you.'

'I don't know if I have one.'

'You must have.'

'Actually, maybe I do. Does it matter when it was taken?'

'No. As long as it's you.'

He took the plates away and began trawling through the box file in which he kept his papers.

'Here you are.' He handed her the photograph. It showed a little boy wearing a cowboy hat, standing in front of a car, pointing a toy gun at the camera.

'Is it really you?'

'Of course.' The picture *was* of Luke but it was no different from any number of pictures of little boys. There are hundreds, thousands, of pictures like this and they are all the same. From a selection of such photos there is no telling which little boy might become a famous footballer or painter, which ones will grow up to have families and take pictures like this of their own children. Then someone tells you that this photo is of a boy who died, aged twenty, in a car crash, or killed himself before he was thirty, or became a down-and-out, or a painter or a well-known footballer. And nothing changes. It remains indistinguishable from the hundreds of other pictures of little boys in shorts, hair cut straight across their foreheads, pointing toy guns at cameras.

While Nicole looked at the photo Luke lay on the bed again, his head in her lap. She stroked his head. He turned over so that he was looking up at her face. A police car wailed past. Music began in the apartment next door: five minutes of Techno, intense, pounding, then it stopped and the door slammed and there was silence. It was Friday night, the neighbours were going out.

'What would you like to do?'

'I don't mind.'

'Do you want to go out?'

'I don't mind.'

She held up his head slightly and tilted wine into his mouth, as if it were water from a canteen and he was an actor who had been shot. He moved around on to his side, facing away from her and again he caught the smell of sex which he wanted to smell more closely, more deeply. He raised his head from her lap and crawled back under her knees, his face towards her cunt.

'Open your legs,' he said, and then lay there, breathing in her smell. He breathed on her, hard enough for her to feel, enough to make her push herself towards him. He wriggled back so that she could move away from the wall, could lie with her knees steepled over him. He pushed his tongue into her. While he licked her he also pushed two fingers inside her. She was on the brink of coming for a long while and by the time she did his left arm was almost numb. He rolled on to his back. She moved around, touched his prick which was not quite hard. She masturbated him and then, as he was about to come, moved her face over him so that his semen sprang into her mouth.

She took off her blouse, he pulled his T-shirt over his head and they snuggled under the quilt, already almost asleep.

'It's no good,' he said, getting up. 'I can't go to sleep if I haven't brushed my teeth.'

If I were to make a film of this story I know exactly the image I would begin with. An aerial shot, from the height of the middle branches of one of the trees in the park bordering a path on which are painted the words INTERDIT AUX VELOS. Then, from above, we would hear the ringing of a bicycle bell and see pedestrians scattering out of the way of two cyclists speeding over those words: Luke and Nicole.

They had woken at ten, sun streaming through the window. Nicole got out of bed and looked down into the street. Luke wondered if anyone could see her there, naked, saying:

'Do you have a bike?'

'Sort of. The guy I'm renting this apartment from left me his. I haven't used it. Why?'

'We could go for a ride.'

'We could ride the 29.'

'What's that?'

'A bus. My favourite bus. But no, we can do that another day. I'd love to go for a bike ride.' Nicole turned on the radio. A DJ was babbling about the great day that was in prospect. This is what you are meant to do in the mornings, thought Luke. You turn on the radio and receive encouragement. You wake up, turn on the radio and get out of bed. What could be simpler? Why had he never done that? Nicole found Radio Nova and began dancing: exaggerated disco dancing. Her small breasts hardly moved as she danced. You turn on the radio and watch your woman, naked, dancing her way to the bathroom. Then you get up and go for a cycle ride . . .

Except the photographer's bike turned out to be in very poor repair. It was hanging on a rack in the damp courtyard, the tyres were flat, the seat was too low, the back brake rubbed . . .

'Shit!' Luke kicked the front wheel in disgust and disappointment. 'No wonder he left it with me. It's completely fucked.'

'We can fix it.'

'It'll take all day. And I hate getting my hands all oily.'

'I'll do it,' said Nicole. 'It takes twenty minutes.'

'I don't have any fucking tools.'

'You swear too much,' said Nicole. 'I have tools. In my bag.' She even had a puncture repair kit. Luke went back up to the apartment to get a bowl of water to test the inner tube for punctures. While he was there he rolled a joint. When he came down again, the bike was upside down and Nicole was taking the front wheel off.

'What's that in your hand?' he said.

'A spanner.'

'Ah, I thought as much. Very evening class. And what are you doing with this so-called spanner? Loosening something I'll be bound.'

'Yes. It's almost ready.' Luke crouched down and watched. Nicole fixed the puncture and eased the inner tube back on to the wheel and into the tyre. Then she fitted the wheel back between the forks. She stood up and swept the hair out of her eyes with the back of her hand, leaving a smudge of oil on her forehead. She flipped the bike over and made some further adjustments.

'You like fixing things,' said Luke banally.

'Things break.'

'Whereupon one throws them away.' She did not look up. 'Bicycle maintenance,' Luke went on. 'It's never been a strong point of mine.'

'What are your strong points?'

'That's the thing. I don't actually have any.'

'The lasagna was nice.'

'Thank you.'

'And you kiss nicely.'

'Don't tell me, tell your friends,' said Luke. 'What are you doing now?'

'Tightening something.'

'Tightening and loosening,' said Luke. 'Such is the dismal life of the spanner.'

'Sit on the saddle,' said Nicole. 'To check the height.'

Luke straddled the bike. 'That's perfect.'

'Sure?'

'Yes.'

'You see, it was easy,' said Nicole, clearing the tools away. 'How long did it take?'

'About two hours. And the saddle is way too high. I can hardly touch the floor.'

'No!'

'Joke. And the repairs only took half an hour. But your hands *are* covered in oil.'

She washed them in a puddle.

Her bike was a red racer, tuned to perfection, stripped to sleek essentials: thin tyres, strapless toe clips, no mud guards, rack or saddle bag. It hummed. Luke's rattled, clanked and rubbed. Nicole said she would fix it properly next week. After they had been cycling for twenty minutes they came to the botanical gardens and sat there for a while.

'Would you like to get stoned?' said Luke.

'Stoned?'

'Smoke dope. Get high,' he said, holding up the joint he had made.

'OK.'

They set off again, cycling aimlessly. Nicole had taken off her suede jacket and tied it round her waist. Everywhere they went they saw green-overalled Africans cleaning up litter and dog shit. Parisians have always been terrible litterers – why bother throwing cans in a bin, or training your dog to crap in a gutter when there are all these silent Africans to tidy up after you? – but now they had an excuse: most of the litter bins in the city had been sealed in the wake of fundamentalist bomb attacks. A poster for Le Pen was overshadowed by an advertisement for the United Colours of Benetton. They were partners of a kind, it didn't matter what either of them said or stood for: all that counted was that the names – Le Pen, Benetton – stuck in people's minds. They spoke the same language, a language in which there were no verbs, only nouns: names and brand-names. Both were dwarfed by the billboard which displayed the global apotheosis of this tendency: 'Coke is Coke'.

Construction work was in progress everywhere. Great swathes of the city were being demolished and redeveloped but wherever they went they saw cafés they intended, one day, to return to. Roller-bladers, solitary or in packs, roamed swiftly through the dream-time of the city. Stoned, Luke found himself looking forward to a time when not having learned to roller-blade would be one of the major regrets of his life. They followed buses, cut through parks, crossed over railway lines, annoyed drivers, skirted traffic jams and orbited churches whose names they made no attempt to establish. After two hours they were hopelessly lost.

'Let's go in here then,' said Nicole, pointing at a shop specialising in maps and atlases.

'How convenient. Like having an accident outside the hospital or getting robbed outside the police station.'

Inside, variously projected maps of the world were

arranged in large V-shaped racks. They turned the polythene-protected posters as if they were choosing a picture of Che or Hendrix in an Athena shop at the dawn of the poster era. The selection was vast: maps showing population density, per capita incomes, political boundaries, mineral deposits, annual rainfall and physical features. In the standard Mercator projection the world looked swollen and robust, bursting with prosperity and confidence. Great Britain was slap bang in the middle of things, about half the size of India. In a newer, alternative projection the world looked sad and thin, dripping towards Antarctica. Little Britain on this projection was barely visible, a streak that looked hardly worth invading.

'Where would we be without maps?' Nicole asked rhetorically.

One rack held only antique reproductions, olde maps drawn in different versions of the same buried treasure aesthetic, zephyrs blowing galleons across the whale-crowded sea towards jagged coastlines of indeterminate exactness. Another held maps of the oceans, great stretches of contoured blueness; in another were maps of space: the Moon, Mars, the stars.

There was also a selection of globes which were immune to the vagaries and distortions of projection. Some were actually lights, contained their own suns, glowed from within. The Moon was uniformly grey, nothing like as nice as the Earth which was greenish and deep blue. Still, it was the Moon and, as such, they felt drawn to it.

'The Sea of Tranquillity,' read Luke.

'Easter Sea.'

'Ocean of Storms.'

'Bay of Dew.'

'Sea of Crises.'

'Sea of Nectar. It makes you wish there were places on Earth with names like that,' said Nicole, but there was no disguising the fact that, names aside, the Moon was a pretty crummy place. 'Look,' she said. High up on one wall was a satellite photo of the Earth seen from space. Flattened out to show the entire planet, it looked exactly like a map of the world.

'That's the only thing the Moon's got going for it, really,' said Luke. 'You get a great view of the Earth.'

'It's the best planet, isn't it? We're so lucky to live on it.'

'None of the others come within a million miles of it.'

They had succeeded in putting the afternoon in a massive, dwarfing context. Re-entering the earth's atmosphere, they went down to the basement where the maps of individual countries were kept, maps showing regions within a country, states and counties, folded street plans of crowded cities – London, Rome, New York, Cairo, Moscow – that showed every avenue and street, every cul de sac and alley of the city they were in. There was even a diagram, on the wall, of the shop itself, a map of maps with a red arrow saying, 'You Are Here.'

'I feel better able to face the world,' said Luke. Better able, he meant, to face the journey home – not the Ancient Egypt section of one of the city's daunting museums.

'Why on earth do we want to see that?' he said.

'It's very interesting,' said Nicole. 'It was a civilisation in which nothing ever happened, a culture which consisted entirely of sitting. Very like Paris in fact.'

Fortunately (for Luke) most of the Egyptian wing was closed, for renovation; unfortunately, they found themselves in an endless collection of armour and weapons from the twelfth century onwards. The earliest guns looked like dark fossils, as if they would have been more use as clubs. Gradually the guns became more ornate with elaborate decoration on the barrels and handles. Fowling pieces, muskets, flintlocks, stand-and-deliver pistols. Then there were the swords, 'the unbelievably boring swords' (Nicole): halberds, pikes, sabres, broadswords so huge that they didn't seem like instruments of violence, just totems of violent intent. That was the attacking side; on the defensive side there was the armour ('the even more unbelievably boring armour'): tons of the stuff, row upon row of breast-plates and helmets, cleaned up to a kind of dull sheen. Suits of armour, evidently, were ten a penny in some army surplus store of museum artefacts. Taken together these paired displays of armour and weaponry foretold the entire history of the arms race: attack and defence cancelling each other out, their interaction becoming more and more elaborate until everything was raised to a level of rhetoric.

The undertow of violent intent lent this section of the museum a certain minimal fascination (for Luke, at any rate) but they soon found themselves in a wing devoted to decorative arts. Luke and Nicole were searching for an exit but all the signs directed them through mile after mile of tables, desks, carpets, chairs, bureaux and beds. They were desperate to get out of the energy-sapping heat but after the carpets and beds came the porcelain: tea-cups, plates, dishes, pots, saucers: anything that happened to have survived from the Ming or any other dynasty.

'This is it,' said Luke. 'The real bargain basement, the flea-market of ancient history.' They were moving quickly, hardly glancing at any of the meticulously labelled bits of broken crockery.

'I'm exhausted,' said Nicole. 'It's like walking across a desert.'

'I've got museum knee, museum back: the works. I don't think I can walk another inch,' said Luke, but there were many miles of bits and pieces to trudge through before they erupted finally into the late-twentieth-century light.

'That settles it,' said Luke. 'One day I am going to open a museum of boredom. A history of tedium through the ages. Global in scope, displaying the full range of boredom, all the culturally and historically specific variants.'

Nicole had claimed she was exhausted but the prospect of being back in the saddle revived her. 'Let's go to the mosque,' she said, unlocking her bike. 'We can have thé à la menthe there.'

Inside, the mosque was crowded, smoky, secular. Luke was ecstatic to be sitting down, free at last from museum-traipsing and pedal-pushing.

'Sitting in the mosque, drinking mint tea, eating delicious harissa, already looking forward to ordering another tea: that's what I'm doing now,' he said. 'That and watching the most gorgeous woman in the world eat her baklava.' Specifically he was watching the bones in her jaw move as she chewed. There was a flake of pastry on her lip which she wiped away with a napkin. Luke did not want to tell her he loved her: they were words which, once spoken, could never again contain the feeling they had once conveyed. But the longing to tell her he loved her was overwhelming. He looked at her and said to himself, as powerfully as he could: I love you, I love you.

Before leaving the mosque Nicole bought some honey because she liked the elegant 'glass tin' that it came in.

'Glass tin?'

'Is that not the right word?' she said, holding up the jar for him to see.

'No, no. That's absolutely right.' Nicole also tried on a pair of pointy yellow babouches that smelt like an animal. Luke bought them for her and she wore them that night as she cooked dinner for them both at her apartment.

Luke was taken aback by the chaos in which she lived. The main space was a living room and kitchen. Yellow walls, orange book shelves. The news was on TV; the TV was on the draining board; the kettle was on the TV, on the brink of boiling. A leg of prosciutto was hanging from a hook screwed into the white-painted wooden beams that were all that remained of the wall that had once divided the space in two. Between these two beams were two filing cabinets, one black one orange. They were ugly things, filing cabinets: most people tried to hide them away in corners, but displayed prominently in the centre of the room like this, they had a kind of battered glamour. Propped against the back of one of them was an old mirror.

Luke had bought beer. The fridge was full so he broke up the pack and arranged the bottles in whatever nooks and crannies he could find and then put two glasses in the freezer. Nicole said,

'Would you like some prosciutto?'

'Um, no thanks.'

'I don't like prosciutto either. A relative brought it from Italy. I don't know what to do with it.'

There was a bed at the far end of the room. Her bike – which she had carried upstairs – was propped against the wrought metal of the headboard. Papers and ill-treated books were all over the floor. There was even a piano. Luke lifted the lid and asked Nicole if she could play.

'It's just here because it's too heavy to move. It's hopelessly out of tune. Let me show you the rest of the place.' She ushered him out of the main room and along a short corridor and into the bathroom. A pale green bath and toilet, a round wooden mirror. Lotions. Shampoo. Candles. She led him out into the corridor again.

'That was the bathroom, obviously. And this,' she said, archly, 'is the bedroom.' There was a single mattress on the floor, true, but it bore a closer resemblance to a vast walk-in wardrobe. Except it was almost impossible to walk in. A rail was crammed with coats and dresses. Shirts, trousers, socks lay in heaps on the floor or were piled on chairs.

'Actually,' she said, 'although this is officially the bedroom, we don't sleep in here.' (He loved that 'we'.) 'Mainly because there's not actually any room.'

'You could do with a chest of drawers.'

'I hate drawers. I always stuff them too full and they get stuck so I have to saw them open.' Luke followed her back into the kitchen.

'Would you like a beer?' he said.

'Please.'

He rummaged in the fridge, decided that the bottles were not cold enough, took the glasses out of the freezer, crammed the bottles in there instead and found room for the glasses in the fridge.

'Put a record on,' she said. He played the record that was already on the turntable, 'Bonnie and Clyde' by Serge Gainsbourg, duetting (somewhat absurdly) with Brigitte Bardot. While that was playing he looked at her LPs which were stacked on top of each other so that any dust became wedged in the grooves. He pulled out a recording of Bach's

Well-Tempered Clavier – at least that's what it said in the cover. Inside was a Chet Baker record. He put it on anyway.

'Where's the lid to the record player?'

'It got broken when I tried to make cheese in it.'

'Ah yes, of course.' He opened the fridge, took the beer out of the freezer and poured two bottles into the chilled glasses which they clinked before drinking. Still holding her glass, Nicole crouched down and looked in the oven. Chet played some trumpet and then began singing 'There Will Never Be Another You'.

'Did you see that mirror by the filing cabinet?' said Nicole.

'Yes. It's nice.'

'It's from Belgrade. Very old. So old that it doesn't work properly.'

'What do you mean?'

'Sometimes is slow to work. Like an old wireless. It takes time to warm up. Come. I'll show you.' They walked around the filing cabinet and stood to one side of the mirror. 'Usually it works normally. Sometimes not. We'll see.' Nicole took Luke's hand and they moved in front of the mirror which, for a second, showed only the bed. Then their reflections moved inside the frame and looked back at them. They stepped aside but, for a few moments, the mirror continued to hold their images.

'I don't believe it,' said Luke.

'We were lucky. It is only very rarely that it happens.'

'Isn't it spooky?'

'It's just old.' Luke moved back in front of the mirror, in synch with his image. He repeated the action several times and each time the mirror worked absolutely normally.

'Did it really happen, first time?'

'Oh, yes. Sometimes there is a very long delay. You can never tell.'

'And you don't think it's scary?'

'It's just old,' said Nicole. 'We can eat soon if you like.'

'OK,' said Luke, stepping in front of the mirror once more: again it worked normally. Nicole put on oven gloves and began tugging the roast chicken out of the oven.

'Oh we need some big plates. Could you get them? They're in the – what's it called? That thing. The cupboard that washes.'

'The dishwasher?'

'Dishwasher, yes.'

'Cupboard that washes is much better,' said Luke. He kissed her neck while she served the food.

'You're supposed to correct my English.'

'Your English is perfect. But how come you have one of these things, whatever it's called?'

'A misunderstanding. The person who had the apartment before said she had a washing machine and if I wanted it I could have it. I said yes but what she called a washing machine was actually—'

'A cupboard that washes.'

'Yes. You see, that is why you must correct my English.'

Nicole carved, sort of, and they sat down to their plates of oven-dried chicken, raw roast potatoes and peas.

'It's awful isn't it?' said Nicole, watching Luke chew.

'The peas are fine.'

'I'm sorry.'

'I'm not that hungry anyway.'

'I can't cook.' She looked as if she might cry.

'You should have said. I love cooking. You can maintain the bicycles and I'll cook.'

'OK.' She reached for his hand.

Luke pushed his plate away. 'That really was fucking disgusting.'

'Have some prosciutto,' said Nicole. 'There's lots.'

They went to bed early. Nicole moved the TV to the end of the bed and they watched a thriller they had both seen before. The main segment of the film featured a famously devastating car chase. Nicole claimed that car chases took place only on film, never in print, never in books. She was wearing a green and white striped robe that made Luke think of toothpaste. A bowl of fruit was on the floor close by. Luke reached for an orange and began peeling it.

'Don't spurt in my bed,' said Nicole. He passed segments to her, dripping. The car chase had come to a standstill. Half the vehicles in the city had been destroyed or damaged. Nicole's period had started. They fucked with a towel under them, in the blue blaze of TV, their faces inches from the screen. Luke mouthed the words silently into her ear: I love you, I love you. She pulled her face away and pressed her mouth to his ear. He felt her lips moving, forming words he could not hear.

On Sunday night Luke met Alex at the Petit Centre. It was normally quiet on a Sunday but, for some reason – maybe everyone had spent the weekend with their new lovers and had been unable to get there until now – the Centre was packed. Luke was ecstatic, glowing in the way that women are said to when they are in love. He was not the only one with romantic news, though. Alex had met Sara, an interpreter.

'Where did you meet her?'

'At Steve's house. The gay guy you met here that first night after work. I went there for dinner. Then I bumped into her last Thursday, just quickly, at an opening. And then I saw her again – though not to speak to – the following night.'

'What does she look like?'

'Short hair, black. Brown eyes, dark skin. And, crucially, she doesn't smoke.'

'She's not French then?'

'American, I think.'

'You need to move quickly. Non-smoking women in this fucking smoke-filled pit of a city are hard to come by. Have you got her phone number?'

'I hardly need it. I keep running into her.'

'D'you know if she's got a boyfriend?'

'I don't think so.'

But when she turned up in the bar half an hour later she *was* with a man. She was wearing a dark sweater, leather jacket and narrow, pale trousers. The guy she was with was called Jean-Paul. To hide his disappointment at seeing Sara in the company of a man, Alex bought them both a drink. Jean-Paul may have been the same age as Luke and Alex but, since he appeared successful, had an implied sense of direction, of purposefulness, of money, he looked considerably older. They stood at the crowded bar, Alex monitoring the movements of Jean-Paul and Sara, trying to establish the state of their relationship. It was obvious they didn't know each other well – and equally obvious that Jean-Paul was aiming to remedy this situation. Sara's attitude to him was more difficult to decipher. She was friendly to everyone but she retained some essential loyalty to her date. They had been to the cinema together.

'What did you see?' Alex said. 'More precisely, which Cassavetes film did you see?' There was a Cassavetes season on. You could not move for Cassavetes films.

'*Faces*.'

'*Faces*? I can't remember whether I've seen that one or not. It's the one that's exactly like all the others, right?'

'That's the one. Have you seen it?'

'Yes. Or maybe it was one of the others.'

'Actually they're beginning to get on my nerves, Cassavetes films. I don't think I'm going to see any more.'

'Why's that? I agree, but why is that? For me it's because the characters are always wearing dinner jackets. I hate films where the characters are always wearing dinner jackets. I hate James Bond films for the same reason,' said Alex, glad to have got a quick purchase on the conversation. Jean-Paul also wanted to get in on it but Luke, spotting Alex's chance to engage Sara, immediately set up a conversational barricade to keep him from her. If Jean-Paul wanted to have his say about the film they'd just seen he would have to say it to Luke.

'He's too indoors,' Sara said to Alex. 'There are outdoors films and indoors films. His are indoors films. I only like out-doors films.' Alex was stopped in his tracks. He saw immediately that she was right: all great films were *outdoor* films. He searched rapidly through his memory but could not think of a single exception to this rule.

'You're right,' he said. 'That is absolutely it. It's as simple as that. Dinner jacket-wearing is just a whatever the word is of indoorness.'

'Metonym?'

'I guess.' Jean-Paul lit a cigarette. Alex could sense him

monitoring their conversation: everyone, it seemed, was monitoring everyone else's conversation. 'Are there no exceptions?'

'None,' she said, with absolute certainty.

How they change, the faces of our friends, of the people we love. When they had met at Steve's dinner Alex had not noticed Sara particularly. They had been sitting at opposite ends of the table and had not spoken to each other. Then, when they had met at the gallery opening, he had begun to study her face, which changed, became attractive to him, as if it took on the qualities of what she said. Now he looked at her with longing.

Jean-Paul too. He broke through the cordon of conversation Luke had thrown around him and started in on his opinion of Cassavetes. That's how it was at that time: no evening was complete unless everyone had their say about Cassavetes, his directorial style, his limitations, his influence. Jean-Paul was speaking French but Alex was hardly listening. He was watching Sara to see how she responded to what Jean-Paul was saying: was she listening to him with the same fascination that he had listened to her? No, he ventured to think, no. Alex was so preoccupied by this question that it scarcely occurred to him to wonder if she could be attracted to him. Even if Sara had not been attracted to Jean-Paul then Alex was sure it was Luke she would be drawn to. This was an essential part of Luke's power: not the *fact* of his attractiveness to women but Alex's belief – an assumption, almost – in that attractiveness. On this occasion there was a circumstantial logic behind that conviction: you are never more attractive to women, it seemed to Alex , than when you have just got out of bed with a woman. The corollary of this

was depressing: the longer you went without sleeping with someone the less likely it was that you ever would. After a year, forget it. They can see the moss growing on your dick . . .

Sara went to the toilet. Jean-Paul said he had to make a phone call.

'What do you think?' Alex asked Luke.

'She's great.'

'What about him? D'you think they're together?'

'Definitely not.'

'How can you tell?'

'He's the kind of man who knows how to seduce women. That's all he knows about women, how to seduce them. Plus, he smokes and she doesn't. She couldn't put up with that.'

'Do you think he'll seduce her?'

'Probably, yes.'

Sara rejoined them. Alex wanted to ask for her phone number but Jean-Paul returned from making his call. A few minutes later they left. Jean-Paul had a smirk of triumph about him. Sara kissed both the Englishmen goodbye, leaving Luke and Alex on their own again. Luke bought Alex a 'consolation beer'.

'I really like her,' said Alex.

'I think she likes you too.'

'I don't know.'

'No, she does. We have come to believe French men are great lovers, romantic and so forth. But who do we keep hearing that from?'

'French men?'

'Exactly. More specifically, French men who smoke. But here is a little known fact. Women actually like English men.

The Englishman is universally derided for being unromantic, bad at sex, uptight, mean, not washing his underpants enough – all that stuff. But it turns out that women actually quite like English men.'

'I see. Just because you got down some Bosnian bimbo's pants on your first date you're now an authority on all matters erotic. Because you happened upon the one woman on earth who was willing to chow down on your cheesy English schlong, you think all women are attracted to all English men.' Alex was joking, obviously, but the crudity of his words was the result, also, of a rumbling jealousy, anxiety about how Luke's meeting Nicole would affect their friendship.

'Not *all* English men,' said Luke. 'Not some no-hoper who looks like spending the rest of his life working at the Garnier warehouse.'

'Someone like you, you mean?'

'You're just feeling bad because Jean-Paul is going to fuck her tonight. French-style. While smoking.'

'Very funny.'

'You should have got her phone number. You could call her first thing in the morning. If Jean-Paul answers you could ask him what it was like.'

'Fuck you, Luke.'

As it turned out Alex had to wait less than forty-eight hours to ask her in person. He saw her on Tuesday morning but she was hurrying for a bus and they had time only to exchange greetings. Then, later that afternoon, he saw her coming out of a shoe shop on rue de la Roquette. She was adjusting her bags of shopping and did not notice him – which meant that he had a few moments to compose and prepare himself for a

spontaneous greeting. It could not have worked out more con-
veniently if he had been stalking her. She was wearing
sunglasses (it was not sunny), walking towards him. She saw
him just as he prepared to call out her name.

'How *weird*,' she said, taking off her glasses. She looked
pleased to see him, he thought.

'What?'

'You won't believe it.'

'Oh I'm sure I will. I'm one of those people who believe
anything.'

'I set my alarm clock for eight fifteen—'

'No!'

'—I woke up and looked at the clock – eight fifteen –
and turned off the alarm before it could go off. I forced myself
to get up straight away. It was dark, very quiet. I showered and
got dressed. Then I looked at the clock: six thirty. When I'd
set the alarm I'd left it showing the time that I wanted it to go
off at. It was only by turning off the alarm that I had revealed
the real time. And so, having woken myself up and got up, I
then got back into bed and tried to sleep. Then, an hour and
a half later, I had to get up again. So all through the morning
I was thinking to myself that this would always be remembered as The Day I Got Up Twice.'

'I don't believe it.'

'There's more. I met Jean-Paul for a coffee.' Alex was
both galled and relieved: galled to hear his name, relieved
that they had evidently not spent last night together. 'He
went in and ordered the coffees. Then, a little later, I went in,
ordered two more, and paid for all four. Only to discover that
Jean-Paul had already paid for the first two. Effectively I had
paid for them twice. Suddenly it seemed that this was not

only The Day I Got Up Twice, this was The Day Everything Happened Twice.'

'And then you bumped into me twice.'

'Exactly.'

'Tell it me again.'

'I set my alarm clock for eight fifteen . . .'

Alex pointed at her shopping bag. 'What did you buy?'

She hauled a shoe from her shopping bag: an ankle-length boot actually: black, with elasticated sides.

'And you bought two of them. A Pair. Effectively you bought the same boot twice as well. They look great,' said Alex. 'Would you like a coffee? I mean, shall we go for a coffee?'

She glanced at her watch. Alex found himself thinking, *she is the kind of woman who wears a watch.*

'I really haven't got time. I'm late.'

'Right, yes, right,' said Alex, wind emptying from his sails. 'I'm kind of in a hurry myself.' She looked at him. 'Well no, I'm not actually, but I know the feeling. There have been occasions when I have been. In a hurry, I mean. Perhaps I could call you. If you wanted to go out one evening. As opposed to just bumping into each other.'

'You mean we could *arrange* to bump into each other?'

'Yes.'

'I'd like that.'

'Would you? I mean, great. And, incredibly, I have a pen.'

'Four four, six oh, six two, four three.'

'OK.'

'Call me. OK. Ciao.' With that she was hurrying across the street, waving, cars snarling around her.

*

He timed his call carefully. To have telephoned the next day would have appeared over-eager; the following week too casual. So he called after three days – exactly, as Sara calculated, when someone romantically inclined would do so. At the first attempt he got an answering machine: her voice, in French and English, with no music and, encouragingly, no mention of a flat-mate or live-in lover. Abiding by the manly notion that if you leave a message and she doesn't call back then you have used up one of a very limited number of message-lives he hung up without speaking. He called back an hour later and this time – convinced suddenly that she was in her apartment, screening calls and guessing who was calling and hanging up like this – he left an agnostic message, asking her to call him. As soon as he put the phone down a tepid despair overcame him: the ball was out of his court now, he was no longer an active agent in his own life. Torn between staying in and waiting for her call (intolerable) and going out and missing her call (equally intolerable), he spent the next hour preparing to go out.

As it happened, Sara *was* in when Alex left his message. She was in the shower, didn't hear the phone, and when she got out didn't even glance at the answering machine. She only noticed the blinking red light later, when Jean-Paul rang. As soon as she hung up she played back Alex's message, twice, trying, second time around, to assess the coded intent behind its abbreviated form: 'Hi Sara, it's Alex. I would love to bump into you one night, if you're free. Give me a call if you can. Bye. Oh, my number is . . .' The crude innuendo of 'bump into you' was probably accidental, the tone might have been matter-of-fact, but this – especially,

coming as it did, three days after she had given him her
number – was certainly a romantically loaded call, one of the
few, in recent months, she was pleased to receive. She called
back immediately. He was about to go out – as he had been
for the last hour – but resisted the temptation to snatch up
the phone on the first ring. If I pick it up now, he reasoned,
it will be my mum. If I wait one more ring . . . it'll still be my
mum.

'Hello.'

'Is that Alex?' It was *her*!

'Yes?'

'It's Sara. I got your message.'

'Oh hi! How you doing?'

'Hi. How are you?'

'I'm fine. How are you?'

'I'm fine.' There was a pause. Then Sara said, 'We can
have another round of that if you like.'

'No, no,' laughed Alex. 'I think I'm ready to move on to
the next phase of our conversation . . . Well, um, would you
like to go out one night?'

'Yes, of course.'

Alex had devoted considerable thought to the issue to be
addressed next, namely *which* night. Friday and Saturday were
too charged: if she did have a boyfriend they would be ruled
out, and even if she didn't have a boyfriend and was free there
was no point squandering these nights on a first date. Sunday
and Monday had no charge at all: they were non-nights: they
would both be preoccupied with thoughts of bringing the
evening to an end and going home, separately, and watching
an hour of TV before sleeping. With any luck she would be
free on Wednesday or Thursday.

'What about Wednesday?'

'Wednesday is no good.'

'You don't have a dance class by any chance do you?'

'No. Why?'

'Oh nothing,' he said, adapting what Luke had repeated to him. 'It's just that, like all men, I've spent a lot of my life meeting women after classes. Dance, Spanish, Self-defence . . .'

'So you spend your life meeting women?'

'Well, trying to. But they're always in classes. I sometimes think it would be nice if someone could meet *me* after something.'

'It will happen.'

'Really? Could it even happen after work on Thursday?'

'It certainly could. What would you like to do?'

'Shall we meet at the Petit Centre?'

'Oh let's not meet there. What about the Café Pause on rue de Charonne? Do you know that?' She was sounding impatient, eager to get off the phone. Alex wondered if he'd irritated her.

'Yes. Let's meet there. Then we can have dinner. OK?'

'At what time?'

'Eight?'

'OK.'

'Ciao.'

'Ciao.'

Alex was waiting for Sara when she arrived: more handsome than she remembered, hair even shorter (he'd had it cut the day before), sitting at the bar. She was wearing a black polo neck, check slacks and the boots she had bought when they

had met on rue de la Roquette. She angled her cheek for
him to kiss. It was chilly outside, her face felt cold. He had on
the shirt he had been wearing at Steve's dinner and a black
jacket.

'I have a present for you,' he said and handed over a
rolled-up poster, battered slightly at the corners.

'What is it?'

'Have a look.'

She unrolled the poster. It was huge, for a film: *Shadows*
by Cassavetes.

'Do you like it?'

'Very much. Thank you.'

He asked what she wanted to drink. She said red wine
and began rolling up the poster. Here we are, she thought, as
he went up to the bar, here we are on the boring outskirts,
the suburbs – the parts that are always the same – of . . . Of
what? Seduction? Incompatibility? Friendship? (Who needs
it?) She liked him, as far as she knew him at all, was
attracted to him, but in a sense the whole evening was taking place in a kind of anticipated retrospect. Its purpose was
to find out what it led to, if it would lead to anything. They
were on a date.

Which made it all the more surprising that, two sips into
her wine, they were joined by Alex's friend – the one he'd
been with that night in the Petit Centre – and his girlfriend.
For a moment Sara thought they had turned up by chance
but, as Alex introduced them and began arranging more
chairs round the table, she saw that it was to be a group
evening. She was disoriented, a little disappointed. How
would he have felt if she'd invited friends along? Had she mis-
understood the situation entirely?

No. Only Alex's handling of it. It was precisely because they were on a date that Alex had asked Nicole and Luke along. What Sara had felt only faintly, momentarily, as she arrived – that sense of first date as preliminary survey – Alex experienced with something akin to dread. He hated the serve and volley, the I-say-something-you-say-something-back of the one-to-one. The problem, as he saw it, was that, unless you got mugged or sprained an ankle, the typical formula for a first date – drinks, conversation, dinner – was designed for an exchange of histories but offered no opportunity to begin racking up some shared history. Dinner together involved two people cocooned separately in a vacuum of expectations and desires. Whereas this format – four friends having dinner – meant that, from the word go, they were caught up in events, in one another's lives. They were gathered round a table, they all had drinks. Alex said how pleased he was to meet Nicole, said he had only seen her through the fence at passage Thiéré.

'Luke said you were the one that kicked the ball at my head that day.'

'No, that was that yob Matthias. I was the one that kicked the ball over that way so he could talk to you.'

'What! It was deliberate?'

'Of course. Didn't you know?'

'No. Is that true Luke?'

'I'm afraid so,' said Luke, not displeased at having his cunning revealed.

'What about you?' Sara said to Alex when he had told her the story. 'Were you waiting for me on rue de la Roquette the other day?'

'He's always waiting on rue de la Roquette,' said Luke. 'Stalking his prey.'

Thinking it best to move the conversation on, Nicole asked Sara where she lived. As soon as Sara had told them Luke plunged into a diatribe about a café he happened to have been to on that street, a fucking awful place where the barman . . . Alex didn't need to listen: he saw straight away that Luke was wired up on his behalf, so desperate to make sure that the evening was a success, to speed through the preliminaries of getting to know each other, that he was quite happy to serve as pace-maker. Mouthing off like this was actually part of being good company. Let Sara think him a fool, an egocentric, loud-mouthed idiot, anything just to speed things along, to generate the energy the evening needed. He was still in mid-rant when Nicole placed her hand on Sara's and said,

'Take no notice. He likes to think he's all the Ms: mean and moody, but he's actually all the Ns: nice and normal.'

'I'm sure he has hidden shallows,' said Sara. She was hungry. They were all hungry but deciding where to eat took them into another round of drinks. Several places were proposed and rejected. Alex wanted to go to a Vietnamese place around the corner.

'Is it cheap?' said Sara.

'Oh yes,' said Alex. 'If we're being absolutely frank, I don't do expensive.'

'I appreciate your telling me.'

'I've always thought it a shame that miserliness is not considered a more attractive quality in a man.'

'It is pretty low on the list.'

'You mean there is something lower? That's reassuring.'

'Well, there's a whole bunch of things. All clustered at the bottom together.'

'What are the others?'

'I wouldn't know where to start. What about you Nicole?' said Sara. 'What are some of the thousands of unattractive qualities in a man?'

'Men with hubbies.'

'*Hubbies?*'

'Have I got the word wrong?'

'Possibly. It depends.'

'You know, like something he does all the time. Like making aeroplanes or collecting stamps, or—'

'Ah *ho*bbies!'

'Don't you think it depends on the hubby, though?' said Luke. 'Alex, for example, has lots of hubbies and some of them are quite harmless, even potentially endearing.'

'Have you, Alex?'

'Oh don't get him started on his hubbies. We'll be here all night. What else though? What are the other unattractive qualities in a man?'

'Men who bite their finger-nails.'

'He's a compulsive nail-biter,' said Luke.

'Pot bellies.'

'He's got one of those too.'

'Hairy backs.'

'It's like you're *describing* him,' said Luke.

'Stained underpants,' said Sara.

'Now you're getting really personal.'

'Men who look in their handkerchiefs after they've blown their nose,' said Nicole.

'Oh come on. It might not be nice but it's not gender specific.'

'Also, how many men do you know who have handkerchiefs these days? This is the age of the tissue.'

'Men who can't dance.'

'Men who put their socks on before their trousers.'

'Men who smoke.' Luke shot Alex a *what did I tell you?* glance.

'And women who smoke,' he said.

'Smoking generally.'

'Men dancing badly and smoking in their socks and stained underpants.'

'Yes.'

'Men who can't cook.'

'I'm a brilliant cook,' said Luke.

'Men who boast.'

'*English* men,' said Nicole and Sara together.

'What about attractive qualities? What do women *like* in a man? I think that's the kind of angle Alex and I are more interested in.'

'Definitely,' said Alex.

'Seriously?' said Sara.

'Of course.'

'Broad shoulders,' said Nicole, putting her arm around Luke's thin shoulders.

'Strength.'

'Kindness.'

'Yes, kindness is a lovely quality,' said Sara. 'Often over-looked.'

'Men who dance well.'

'Tanned ankles.'

'Men who don't have holes in their socks.'

'Speaking of socks,' said Sara, 'there are men with a foot in both camps, so to speak. Damaged men. There are women who like damaged men. That is, women go through a phase of liking damaged men. They think they can mend them, like socks. Then, hopefully, they come to their senses and realize that a damaged man is actually just a boy.'

'Damaged,' Luke said to Nicole, 'is not the same as ruined.'

'Apart from that, it's very simple and not at all mysterious,' said Sara. 'Women like in men exactly the things men like in women. Attractive faces, nice bodies, intelligent, generous, sexy, funny.'

'The most important thing,' said Nicole, 'is that women like men who like women.'

'*I* like women,' said Alex.

'One out of six is not bad going,' said Luke.

'That still leaves the question of where we're going to eat,' said Sara.

'Actually, we could eat here.'

'Shall we eat here?'

'Let's eat here.'

'Here is good.'

'Let's eat here then.'

When they had ordered, Sara told them about her work as an interpreter: French, Italian, Spanish, English; consecutive, simultaneous . . . The latter – translating into one language at exactly the same time the words you were hearing in another – seemed an unimaginable skill. Especially to Luke whose French, according to Alex, was 'lamentable, pitiful'. This was unfair and inaccurate, though not as inaccurate as Luke's own verdict ('fluent'). Nicole was nearer the mark with 'coming along'. Alex was keen to gloat because, in the language hierarchy, he was second bottom with two (including English). Nicole had four; Sara had five, six if you included the smattering of Arabic she remembered from her childhood in Libya. She had spent her childhood there (because of her father's work) and her teens in Chicago. Singapore (where she had seen several cobras) also figured in the picture. There was a lot of information to take in, much of it confusing. Her name, for example, was not Sara but *Sahra*.

'How long have you been in Paris?' asked Luke, seeking clarification.

'Three years.'

'Do you think you'll stay?'

'I feel at home here.'

'Me too,' said Nicole.

'But I have a great urge to go back to my roots,' said Sahra. 'To Libya.'

'Ah Libya,' said Luke.

'El Alamein,' said Alex.

'Tobruk.'

'The Desert Fox.'

'*The Rat Patrol.*' By mutual consent Luke and Alex abandoned this bewildering – to Sahra and Nicole – riff before it had properly got going.

'Roots are overrated,' said Luke, backtracking. 'I couldn't care less where my roots are. I've got no interest in them. So what if my grandfather was illegitimate? So what if he was born in Senegal?'

'Was he?'

'Actually he was born in Hertfordshire. But he could have been born on Mars for all I care.'

'It's different if you move around a lot when you are growing up,' said Sahra. 'You grew up in England, right?'

'Yes, ma'am.'

'You see, we were always moving. My father would come home and say that he had been posted somewhere new. He'd get out the globe and we'd all sit down and look to see where we were going—'

'Sounds fantastic.'

'So I was always leaving my friends behind and starting at a new school in the middle of the term in some place I'd not even heard of. I'd have to stand at the front of the class while the teacher said, "This is Sahra, she is blah blah . . ."And all the kids would be looking at me and I'd have to start making friends over and over, and no one could get my name right. Not unlike now, come to think of it. . .'

'Except we're all new here,' said Nicole.

'We're all new kids in this class, honey,' said Luke.

'This is the first time I've lived out of England and I feel totally settled here,' said Alex. 'So settled, in fact, that I wouldn't mind trying somewhere else, to see if I could feel even more settled there.'

'The paradox of nomadism,' said Sahra. 'You keep moving because you're searching for a place to stay. Once you realise you *can* live in other countries you can never quite settle anywhere again. You can never feel quite content.'

'Contentment,' said Luke. 'A word which should never be spoken, only spat.'

' "Every day spent in the country you were born is a day wasted," ' said Nicole. 'That's another of his favourites at the moment.'

'Speaks the man who has lived in Paris, right next door to London, who has spent his time entirely with English-speaking people, for all of three weeks: a man called intrepid.

Intrepid with a small i! God knows what would have happened if I hadn't taken him under my wing,' said Alex.

'The ideal is to feel at home anywhere, everywhere,' said Sahra.

'Perhaps it's a question of being at home in time as well as space,' said Nicole.

'That's it,' said Luke. 'That's it absolutely. Whatever it means.'

'What *does* it mean?'

Nicole shrugged. A clock in one of the churches nearby began to strike.

'Listen,' said Luke. 'That's what it means: now, now, now!'

'I love being alive now,' said Sahra.

'And me.'

'Moi aussi,' said the waiter, bringing their food.

'The final thing of all,' said Sahra as the plates were being set down. 'To be at home in yourself.' Already shovelling food into his face, Luke grunted.

'It's not just his French,' Alex said to Sahra. 'His manners also need a bit of fine tuning. But what does *that* mean, being at home in yourself?'

'It means it doesn't matter where you live or what happens to you,' said Sahra.

Luke looked up – a rare event when he was eating – as if chewing over this idea. 'When I came here,' he said, 'I felt I was inhabiting the fringes of my life because for me the centre had always been England. Now I can feel myself, almost physically, moving towards another centre. One which I chose and made – am *making*, rather – as opposed to one I was just issued with.'

'And when you've made it you'll see that it is exactly the same as the one you were issued with,' said Sahra. Luke resumed his scoffing. After a few minutes Sahra looked at him again and said, 'Do I remind you of your sister?' It was a weird question.

'No. Actually I don't have a sister. Why?'

'It's just that you remind me of my brother,' said Sahra. 'He eats like that.'

'Like a pig?' said Nicole.

When the pig had finished eating – the others were still in the middle of their meals – he said he wanted to go back to something they had touched on earlier.

'We saw that film *Homicide* a few days ago. Have you seen it?'

'I think so,' said Alex. 'Years ago.'

'Me too,' said Sahra.

'OK,' said Luke. 'Do you remember the scene at the beginning, when the Feds burst into that apartment?'

'Not really.'

'It doesn't matter. But before they burst into the apartment they unscrew the light bulb in the hall. Now why do they do that? And it's not just FBI agents. Intruders, assassins always do it too. Why not simply switch it off? Surely the noise of the click is too slight to be heard.'

'What's this got to do with anything we touched on earlier?'

'It's to stop someone – a neighbour – accidentally turning the light on again at another switch,' said Sahra, ignoring Alex's question.

'Is it really as simple as that? I was hoping there was no practical reason for it. That it existed in the realm of pure convention. I love the way they always have a handkerchief for exactly that purpose.'

'Ah,' said Alex. 'The link is handkerchiefs.'

'If they didn't have a handkerchief they would use a sleeve,' said Nicole.

'Yes but they always *do* have a handkerchief. That's unusual don't you think? Like we were saying earlier: how many people do you know who carry a handkerchief now?'

'Weird isn't it?' said Sahra. 'The way the same questions keep coming up.'

'A handkerchief seems like a leftover from another era of hygiene. Basically if someone has a handkerchief in a film they're either with the FBI or they're about to assassinate somebody.'

'To whack somebody. The word is whack,' said Alex.

'You're right, the word is whack,' said Luke. 'But have you noticed the way the bulb is always a screw rather than a bayonet fitting? That's a factor. If it was a bayonet fitting they'd have to use two hands – thereby raising the problem of what to do with their gun. They couldn't put it back in the holster at a moment like that. And they can't have it dangling from their trigger finger. It would look ludicrous and, besides, it might knock against the lampshade – even though there isn't a lampshade, of course. Essentially this is a bare-bulb scenario. And I'll tell you another thing that bothers me: what do they do with the bulb when they've taken it out? Presumably they put it in a pocket but it's still hot, of course. It could burn a hole. These little details, they're the only things in the cinema that interest me now. Tropes, I suppose you'd call them.'

'Ah, he does love his tropes,' said Alex.

They paid the bill and went to a café across the road. Nicole and Luke squandered twenty francs on an apocalyptic pinball machine. It was like flipping balls into the jaws of a shrieking, flashing hell. Sahra and Alex stood at the counter, helping themselves to sugar from a silver bowl with a long silver spoon.

'Even something as simple as dispensing sugar in cafés is not straightforward,' said Alex. 'As I see it, there are three main options: shaker, cubes or bowls, each with its own disadvantages and advantages.'

'Shakers are prone to clogging.'

'Cubes can be too big.'

'A bowl and spoon is messy,' said Sahra, pointing to the spray of crystals on the counter.

'We've only listed disadvantages,' said Alex. It was true.

Luke and Nicole came back from playing flipper. Luke was all for going somewhere else – another bar, a club – but the other three were sleepy, ready to leave. Luke was never tired (unless, as Sahra would later point out, he was doing something he didn't want to do). The four of them stood outside the café, saying goodbye.

'We're having a dinner on Saturday,' Nicole said to Sahra. 'Would you like to come?' She and Luke had hatched this plan with Alex while Sahra was in the toilet.

'I'd love to.'

'It's at my apartment,' said Nicole. 'I'll give you the address.'

Luke watched Nicole write it on the receipt for the coffees, which she then handed to Sahra. Love a woman, thought Luke, love her handwriting: neat (surprisingly), bold, the A a triangle, the I dotted with a small circle, the E three horizontal lines, unjoined.

*

Although the dinner was at Nicole's apartment it was Luke who was doing the cooking. He was peeling, boiling, chopping and frying when first Alex and then Sahra arrived. Nicole was laying the table. Music was already playing loud. This, claimed Luke, was one of the secrets of the successful dinner: no background music but, from the start, pounding music at a volume that meant the door-bell could only be heard in the breaks between tracks. The other secret was to get everyone high and drunk as soon as possible. The final secret was that the first two weren't secrets at all, that people knew exactly what they were in for, so that there was no question of people arriving for an evening of chatting and eating rather than a fully-fledged head bang. It worked. Even Miles – who arrived with three bottles of red wine but without his wife – claimed that the previous night he had deliberately stayed in (unusual), drunk nothing (unbelievable) and gone to bed early (unheard of) so that he could be on top form for this evening. Ahmed arrived with a new girlfriend – Ahmed always had a new girlfriend – called Sally. They were both taken aback by the leg of prosciutto hanging on a hook, still untouched. Ahmed picked up a pair of mirror sunglasses that he found on one of the filing cabinets.

'Try them on,' said Nicole. They turned out to be mir-rored both ways. All he could see was a magnified reflection of his eyes and eyelashes and, at the edges, the distended outline of the window behind his head. There were always things like that in Nicole's apartment: weird things, fun bits and pieces she'd come across that no one else would have bothered with. The big mirror, the one from Belgrade, had been turned against the wall. The guests took it in turns to try on the pointless glasses and to ask Luke if he wanted 'help' but by now the cooking had reached such a frenzy of activity that he scarcely had time to answer. If Luke was into something he was into it *totally* – and cooking was definitely one of the things he was into. Nobody cooked like him. He had pioneered an idiosyncratic version of fusion cuisine or world food, combining ingredients, herbs and spices from distinct culinary territories, flinging them into meals that were endlessly diverse but which were always immediately, recognizably his. Like many good cooks he was a kitchen fascist: weeping, Nicole chopped the odd onion, but Luke preferred to do everything himself, manufacturing incredible meals at high speed and minimal expense. Eight people, he said, could eat like kings for only twenty francs a head when he cooked.

There was only just enough room around the table for seven people. Nicole served the first dish, a green papaya salad. As they were about to eat Luke leaped up and asked if everyone was warm enough, turning up the heater before anyone had a chance to reply.

'Have you noticed how he loves to regulate temperature?' said Alex. 'It's one of those charming little idiosyncrasies that we hate about him.'

'It's true,' said Nicole. 'I've never noticed before but it's true. "Would you like a little more ice in that?" "Shall I warm that up a bit?" The first time he came here he spent the entire evening rearranging beers in the fridge. All he said was, "Hmm, they're not quite cold enough yet." '

Luke nodded in happy acknowledgement without ceasing to trowel food into his face. Despite being the last to serve himself he was the first to finish. He got up from the table and went back to the cooker. He handed plates of the main course to Nicole who carried them to the table.

'It looks great Luke,' said Alex. 'But what is it?'

'Something midway between Malaysian Reng Dang and Moroccan Tajine. Stew to a savage like you.' By the time Luke sat down again the talk was of England, a country everyone had visited.

'It was freezing when we were there last December,' said Miles, opening more wine (Miles was *always* opening more wine). 'People kept dying trying to rescue their dogs from frozen lakes. The dogs lived. The owners died. The pathos.'

'I was fourteen when I went,' said Sally. 'I remember the names of pubs. The Dog and Duck. The Fox and Hounds. The White Horse. I thought it was a law that all pubs had to be named after animals.'

'I was fifteen,' said Sahra. 'Everywhere seemed to be called something Hampton: Littlehampton, Minchinhampton, Wolverhampton.'

'I had to visit my aunt in Alton,' said Nicole. 'She said it was exactly fifty-five minutes from London. I spoke hardly any English. So I got on my train and I waited and waited and nowhere called Alton came up. Eventually, about two hours later, the train stopped at Southampton—'

'You see, I was right,' said Sahra. 'Another Hampton—'

'Yes, exactly. So I asked the station manager and he was very kind and said the train had divided and I was on the wrong half of the train. What I had to do was go back to some other station – I forget the name, something else Hampton – and then take the train that went along the other branch. So I waited for a train back to wherever it was, went there and waited for a train to Alton. Before I got on I asked the station manager which train to get on and *he* was very kind as well and pointed me to a train and I got on. And this train went past exactly the same places as the last one and I ended up in Southampton again and saw the original station manager. "What are you doing here again?" he says. "You're supposed to be in Alton." I told him what happened and he said I had to do the same thing again: go back to the station where the train divides and then make absolutely sure I got on the train to Alton. By the time I got there my aunt was distraught. The police were looking for me. The fifty-five-minute journey to Alton had taken seven and a half hours.'

'That's England in a nutshell,' said Alex. 'Trains dividing, places called Hampton, kindly station managers. Simple journeys taking all day.'

'When I was twenty-one I spent Christmas with my boyfriend's family in Hampshire,' said Sahra. 'We had lunch. The afternoon seemed to last all day. His mother was very polite. The father hardly said a word. Every now and again she would say to him, "Are you still with us, Trevor?" Then he'd drift off until she asked him again: "Are you still with us, Trevor?"'

'*That's* England,' said Luke.

'Deep England,' said Alex.

'The other thing I remember was the television,' said Nicole. 'Nothing but snooker.' This got the biggest laugh of the evening: it was the first time anyone had heard of this game that rhymed with hooker.

Everyone had finished eating. Luke took the plates away and Nicole brought in a bowl of fruit. Sahra undid a banana, badly bruised, 'just as I like it'. She has perverse taste in fruit, thought Alex. Miles asked Nicole if there might be 'another drop of wine hidden away somewhere'. There were still two open bottles on the table but he was getting worried. Nicole was reassuring him – there was an assortment of bottles, she said, in the bottom drawer of the filing cabinet – as Luke reappeared with seven lines of powder spread neatly on a CD case.

'Dessert!' he beamed. We didn't earn much at the warehouse. Cocaine was an expensive luxury, the kind of thing you kept hidden away if there were lots of people around, but Luke was not like that. Either generosity was not something he had needed to learn or it was something he had learned before I met him, before he came to Paris.

Nicole didn't want her line which was shared by Alex and Luke ('yes, always yes') even though coke sometimes made him jittery. Everyone started gabbling at once. Nicole turned up the music. She and Sally began dancing. Ahmed was flicking through records and when he found one he liked he got up and danced too. Sally had smoked a lot of dope in the course of the evening and had laughed often. She had said very little but she was a terrific dancer. With the music turned up loud it was necessary to shout. Luke began dancing in his seat while talking and then got up to join the others, leaving Alex and Sahra and Miles talking at the table. The music became louder. Alex and Sahra joined in the dancing and Luke turned it up again and then announced – or suggested – a change of plan. Instead of staying in and dancing and annoying the neighbours, why didn't they go to The Select? Five minutes later he was locking up the apartment while everyone else trooped downstairs.

They walked through the crowds of young people from the suburbs who had come to the quartier for Friday night and were hysterical, drunk. Even the roads were full of people strolling. At one point Luke and Nicole found themselves on opposite sides of the road. A young guy who was walking in the middle of the street looked at Nicole. His eyes lingered on her and then he looked over at the opposite pavement, at Luke – who was yacking away to Miles – and knew, instantly, that they were together. An energy linked them even when they were not standing together or looking at each other.

Miles told Luke he was too old for dancing and slipped off to a bar before they got to the club. The others joined the queue. It was an essential part of the experience, queuing. People were frisked thoroughly. No one was allowed to bring drugs into the club; the only people not expected to were those who had taken them already. You could feel the throb of the bass outside but the music hit you as you went in, as you passed into another world, where the rules of outside ceased to exist. It was packed. The throb felt outside was not simply the bass: it was also the pulse of all the energy confined inside. Everyone began dancing. No one wanted drinks – what a relief not to have to queue for over-priced beer at the bar – and in minutes they were consumed by the music. Luke was a terrible dancer – his arms were too long, he neglected to move his hips; Nicole said he looked like a giraffe having a seizure – but in this environment it was impossible not to dance perfectly. Everyone was a spectator, everyone was a participant. Luke (thought he) was dancing like Nicole who danced wonderfully. Her eyes burned blue in the ultraviolet, her teeth cackled. Luke's T-shirt was drenched with sweat. They knew some of the tracks, recognized, now and again, the samples that had been used to make these new tracks which were themselves segments of one enormous piece of music, endlessly mixed and remixed, lasting seven or eight hours.

Ahmed and Sally left at about four. Luke, Nicole, Alex and Sahra left later, their ears buzzing with noise. The city was at the quietest point in its day. The only people around were the garbage men and a few other strays who had been up all night. A single car circled the Bastille. It was too early and too late to go anywhere else: Lavigne's was closed tight, and they were stacking the tables outside Lila's. Sahra had to go in the opposite direction to the other three. Alex offered to walk her home but she was fine. They waved goodbye. Nicole and Luke said goodbye to Alex at his apartment.

Luke and Nicole showered and lay in bed. 'It's so lovely to go to bed and not have sex,' Luke whispered. 'Isn't it?' Nicole was already asleep. He lay on his back, unable to sleep, drifting. There will come a time, he thought, when I will look back on this night, when I will lie in another bed, when happiness will have come to seem an impossibility, and I will remember this night, remember how happy I was, and will remember how, even when I was in the midst of my happiness, I could feel a time when it would be gone. And I will realize that this knowledge was a crucial part of that happiness . . . The same thought went through many remixes as he lay there, drifting, alert, sort of asleep.

They woke late but not late enough to feel rested. It began to rain. Nicole had to work. Luke washed up and meandered to his apartment. He passed a fountain he had not noticed before, struggling to hold its own in the rain. Alex came round in the late afternoon, miserable about Sahra.

'I can't work her out,' he said to Luke.

'Nor me.'

'I mean, what does she want?'

'Who knows?'

They were playing records, taking it in turns to flick through *Pariscope*, convinced that if they went through it one more time, there would be a film to go to.

'This is the best city in the world for films—'

'Correct.'

'—and there are still not enough films on.'

'Also correct.'

'In fact it's useless for films.'

'The truth is we probably spend too much time at the cinema. If we went less there would be more to see,' said Luke. 'Pass me *Pariscope*, could you?'

'There's nothing left to see,' said Alex, handing it over. 'We've reached saturation point.'

'I can't believe *Strange Days* isn't on. Have you seen it?'

'No.'

'Now *there's* a film for you, there's cinema.'

'I thought it was just a rehash of *Blade Runner*.'

'Are you kidding? It's the ultimate. The last word in cinema.'

'Right up there with *Chariots of Fire*, yeah?'

'*That's* what I'm in the mood for this afternoon. Something English.'

'You're right, it's the kind of afternoon that makes you wish you were back in England, watching telly.'

'What would you watch? Ideally. Apart from *Chariots of Fire*, I mean.'

'Good question.' Alex paused. '*Colditz*, I think.'

'Any particular episode?'

'They were all great episodes.'

'Basically you can't go wrong with that genre.'

'*Albert R.N.*'

'*The Wooden Horse.*'

'*The One That Got Away.*'

'Which one's that?'

'The one about the German fighter pilot escaping from a prisoner-of-war camp in England or Scotland.'

'I remember asking my dad about that. About why so many English prisoners-of-war tried to escape and only one German. He said it was because they liked it in England. Good food, pleasant scenery.'

'They're always idyllic, POW camps.'

'Especially Colditz, the TV one, I mean.'

'The place in *The Great Escape*, that was the real Club Med of POW camps. There was so much to do there: tunnelling, getting rid of the sand, choir practice to cover up the noise of digging . . .'

'Forging papers, making escape suits out of blankets.'

'Growing vegetables in the thin soil outside the hut.'

'And football, always football.'

'Elaborate systems of knocks, folding newspapers, whistling and tapping pipes to warn of approaching guards.'

'Goons. Not guards, goons.'

'Goons, right.'

'Red Cross parcels.'

'The commandant: basically a good sort.'

'Studied in Oxford before the war. Hence his good English. Editions of Goethe on his bookshelf. Emphatically not a Nazi. Considers Hitler a vulgar little corporal, a man with no culture.'

'The Geneva Convention.'

'Simply a loyal officer of the Wehrmacht. Doing his duty but already resigned to Germany losing the war.'

'But always, in the background, the shadow of the SS: the snake of threat in this carceral paradise.'

'Still pretty nice though: a public school with the officers as prefects—'

'The escape committee.'

'And the odd Welsh—'

'Taff!'

'Or Scot—'

'Jock!'

'Or chirpy Cockney—'

'Blimey!'

'As fags, running errands. A little microcosm of England where everyone knows their place but all the classes, all ranks, muck in together.'

'So why bother escaping? They're home already.'

'It's the duty of every officer to escape.'

'Thereby diverting troops that might otherwise have been used at the front.'

'Plus the obligation to escape reinforces the pleasantness of being there. Without that there'd be nothing to do. Time would weigh as heavily on your hands as tunnel dirt. The purpose of escape is to make you cherish your time there, like last orders in a pub, to make you realize it's not going to last for ever, this little public-school Eden.'

'To escape. It's an existential need.'

'Plus it's not *really* home. There are no women for a start.'

'That's not a problem. All sexuality is sublimated in the act of tunnelling. No women and no gays.'

'There's no boozer.'

'Basically it's not Civvy Street.'

'Exactly.'

'When I was young I used to think Civvy Street was this street in London where everyone worked and then went drinking afterwards.'

'The border. Switzerland.'

'Neutral Switzerland.'

'Heading for the border, for neutral Switzerland, on the train.'

'Sweating in your escape suit. Double-breasted, pinstripe. Trilby pulled down over your eyes, trying to hide behind your newspaper.'

'Praying you don't bump into that old bore Charles Bronson.'

'Banging on about all the tunnels he's dug. A real one track mind. Either that or throwing a tantrum about being claustrophobic.'

'Half the passengers on the train are escaped POWs.'

'Rush-hour on the Switzerland Express. Standing room only.'

'The Gestapo getting on the train.'

'Brown leather overcoats. Buttoned up. A creaking sound as they move up the carriage, checking documents, peering.'

'Sweating even more in your escape suit, so much so that the makeshift dye is forming a small blue pool at your feet.'

'Clutching your forged inter-rail pass.'

'Wishing to God you hadn't flunked German O level.'

'And he says to you in his Rommel German: "Guten Morgen, can I see your papers?" Trying to catch you out by throwing in a bit of English.'

'You're about to make a run for it —'

'Then you realize *he's* an escaped POW as well, disguised as a member of the Gestapo, winding you up.'

'Hissing at him as he sits next to you: "You're a *damn* fool Hargreaves!" '

'Ah, I feel better.'

'I don't.'

'Me neither.'

Alex got up and looked out of the window. It was still raining.

'I can't make her out,' he said.

'More to the point,' said Luke, 'you can't make out with her. Ho ho.' He had his feet on the coffee table. No lights were on in the room. It was growing dark. The streetlights were on. Neon squirmed in the street.

'Maybe we *should* go to a film,' said Luke, picking up *Pariscope* again.

'Maybe we should dig a tunnel.'

'You're right. We're wire happy.'

'Are you seeing Nicole tonight?' said Alex.

'Yes. Do you have plans to see Sahra?'

'I guess I'll call her.'

The music started, drowning out the rain.

It was still pouring when Luke set out for Nicole's. Just outside his building he bumped into Miles.

'How lovely to see you, Luke!' he said, unperturbed by the rain. He was taking his Labrador for a walk.

'Shit, Miles, you look like you've been tramping round in the rain ever since we said goodbye.'

'Not at all. I was tramping round *at home* until half an

hour ago. How was the dancing?' They stood talking in the rain. Miles asked Luke where he was going, said he'd walk with him part of the way, show him a shortcut.

'I've often wondered where this led,' said Luke as they came to an alley.

'That was your mistake,' admonished Miles. 'In this world there is one unique path which no one but you may walk. Where does it lead? Don't ask: take it.'

'You always sound like you're quoting, Miles.'

'Nonsense! Anyway, I must be getting on,' he said, holding out his hand to say goodbye.

'You don't want to come to Nicole's for a drink?'

'Must go. Phone me. Turn right at the end of the alley and you're there.'

'OK. Bye Miles.'

'Ha!'

Nicole had washed her hair, was wearing her toothpaste-striped robe, sitting cross-legged on the floor, pulling apart a book of sepia-tinted photographs of the New Mexico desert. She had salvaged the book from a skip full of water-damaged books. One by one she held up the pictures and tried them in a frame with a circular picture window.

'What about that one?' The circular mount made all the photos look as if they were of the same brownish planet.

'It's OK.'

Luke saw Nicole and himself in the Belgrade mirror. She sipped from a mug of tea, yellow, and tried some more pictures. Eventually she chose a photo of the wind-filled sierra, clouds in the distance. She taped the frame together and held it up. She was in a dreamy state.

'Lovely isn't it?'

'Not really.'

'It is. You see, I love things that are disappointing.'

'Is that why you like me?'

'Probably.' She kissed him. Luke moved behind her and kissed her neck.

'I bumped into Miles as I was walking here. He had his dog with him, a lovely Labrador.'

She turned her head and kissed him. 'And?'

Luke kissed her neck again and pushed the robe up her back, to her shoulders. 'I stroked its head. I looked in its eyes. And I remember thinking: if I concentrate hard now I will learn the difference between a dog and a human being. Imagine that. All I had to do was concentrate. But of course I didn't bother, because of the rain. But something came out of it: a kind of residue of ungrasped illumination.'

'What a stupid story.' Luke knelt behind her and licked down her back. She lay still, looked at the mirror, waited. He bit her buttocks lightly, licked up her back again, almost as far as her shoulders, and then down again. She lay still, waited. He traced the valley between her buttocks with his tongue, not pressing. She moved, almost imperceptibly. He licked more deeply between her buttocks, almost touching her. She pushed up at him. His tongue brushed her anus. She opened her legs more, pushed herself at his face. He touched her again with his tongue, wetting her. He stiffened his tongue, waiting, until she eased back on to it. His hands were on her buttocks, pulling them apart. He pushed his tongue into her and then, when she was wet, circled her arsehole with his finger, slid it into her.

'Wait,' she said. She stood up and walked into the bedroom. Luke undressed. She came back and passed him a pot of moisturising cream. She felt the cream on her, cool; in the mirror she saw him dip his fingers into the pot, watched them disappear between her buttocks.

'Is that too cold?' he said.

'Even here,' she said, 'he has to regulate the temperature. It's cool. It's nice. Look at the mirror.' Everything they saw lagged fractionally behind what they felt. He slid his finger into her more easily, began masturbating her arsehole. He felt her tense, relax, tighten, relax. She reached back, pushed her own fingers into the pot and smeared cream on to him.

He moved towards her, began pressing gently. In the mirror she was still rubbing lotion on to him. His penis slid up between her buttocks. She reached back and guided him. He pressed. She gasped.

'Did I hurt you?'

'Yes.'

'I'm sorry. Shall I stop?'

'No, try again.' She pulled her buttocks apart. He could see her arsehole, dark, smudged with white cream. He leaned forward, pressed.

'Yes, there . . . No, there. Yes.' She felt him enter her. 'Ah, gently. Wait, wait.' His prick was in her now. 'OK.' He pushed a little more, could feel the head of his prick inside her, gripped tight. In the mirror she saw him pressing, not yet inside her.

'Yes.'

'Is that nice?'

'Yes, yes. Do it harder, deeper,' she said, touching herself.

'I'm going to come soon.'

'Wait,' she said. 'Wait.'

'Come, come soon.'

'Yes, now, yes.'

Luke collapsed on top of her. In the mirror they were still locked together, tensed on the brink of coming. They lay as they were, not speaking, then Luke moved on to his side.

'Is it . . . is it clean?' said Nicole. Luke looked down at his penis.

'Yes.'

'What a relief.'

'It wouldn't have mattered if it wasn't,' said Luke. 'But I'll go to the bathroom anyway.'

Luke pissed and then washed his penis in the basin while Nicole sat on the toilet. He touched her head and left the bathroom. It was raining harder. He opened the door to the balcony, startled by the noise of the rain. They lay in bed, listening to the rain, watching it pour past, angling in and bouncing off the floor of the balcony. Lights across the road were blurs and streaks.

'Did you like that?'

'What?'

'Me in your arse.'

'Yes. You're so tender, Lukey. You were in my core. Is that the word?'

'Yes.'

'It was, I don't know, primitive.'

'Had you done it before?'

'Why?'

'I don't know.'

'Yes. Have you? No, don't tell me. If you have I don't want to know.' She turned away. Then she faced him again and said, 'I ask you something else instead.'

'Anything.'

'What is it you want to do, Luke?'

'How do you mean?'

'With your life.'

'I'm doing it.'

'Ultimately.'

'Ultimately I want to keep on doing it. Keep on living it. My life, I mean. You just said I was in your core, yes? Well, I feel the same. That I'm close to the centre, the core, of my life.'

'What about work?'

'As in a career?'

'Yes.'

'I don't think I want to spend the rest of my life working five days a week at the warehouse.'

'What would you like to do instead?'

'I'd like to go part-time.'

'Then?'

'I'd like to retire.'

'You're strange, Luke. When I first saw you, at passage Thiéré. I thought . . . There was such yearning in you.'

'I was yearning for you.'

'No, it was more. I see it in you still. It's part of you. It *is* you. And then in other ways you seem almost not to want anything, not to care.'

'I care about you. And I really want a beer. I'm yearning for one.' Luke walked over to the fridge and opened the door. 'Actually,' he said, rummaging around for a beer, 'I yearn to be exactly where I am now.' Nicole said nothing. Luke turned and found she was gone. The room was full of the hiss of rain. He walked by the bed and peeked round the door of the balcony. She was leaning with her back against the balcony rail, the rain flooding over her. Her hair was soaking black over her shoulders. Her eyes were closed. The rain was falling so hard that it must have been on the brink of hurting. Luke watched the ricochets and darts of rain like electrical charges leaping around her.

She opened her eyes and looked at him.

Ahmed turned up for work on Monday with a broken nose and a black eye. He looked like he'd been in a fight. He *had* been in a fight – or at least he'd been on the receiving end of one. He and Sally had left the club together. She had to get up early the next day and had taken a taxi home. Ahmed had begun walking. There was never any trouble in clubs and Ahmed had carried that safe, friendly atmosphere out into the street with him. It was late, there was hardly anyone around. A guy asked him the time. Ahmed said he didn't have a watch. The guy punched him in the face. The blow knocked Ahmed to the floor. He felt a couple of kicks in the ribs and the side of the head but was able to scramble to his feet and run. The guy who'd hit him didn't bother giving chase. Ahmed walked straight to the hospital and stayed there till nine in the morning, getting his cuts stitched, having X-rays.

'Why didn't you telephone?' said Luke.

'It was too late.'

'Too late?'

'And I was sort of embarrassed. Sunday I slept almost all day. I called Sally and she came over.'

Lazare said Ahmed could go home, he'd pay him for the day anyway. Ahmed preferred to work. He didn't want to sit at home moping about what had happened. Lazare was in excellent spirits: a consignment sent to Marseille had gone missing so he was able to spend the whole morning calling people up and abusing them. When I went into the office I heard him use the word 'cocksucker', a sure sign that he was enjoying himself.

In the afternoon Luke went out for ten minutes and returned with a box of Arab cakes.

'For everyone,' he said, 'but make sure you leave some for Ahmed since he's not capable of fending for himself . . .'

Sahra called Alex before he had a chance to phone her, on Monday night. His heart leaped when he heard her voice.

'How've you been?' he said. 'What did you do yesterday?'

'Sunday? Oh, I didn't leave the apartment. The Day That Wasn't Even A Day. What about you?'

'I can't remember. Maybe the same.'

'There's a party,' said Sahra. 'On Friday. Would you like to go?'

'Sure. Yes.'

'It's quite a smart party. We'll have to dress up – *you'll* have to dress up.'

'Great. I love to dress up.'

'And Nicole and Luke. Do you want to ask them as well?'

'Yes, sure.'

'Is that your idea of a conversation: "Yes, sure?"'

'Yes, sure,' said Alex, glad at the chance to sound laconic.

'See you Friday then,' she said – and hung up.

Nicole was still getting ready when Luke called for her. He was wearing his suit.

'I've never seen you look so smart,' said Nicole, kissing him. 'You look so . . .'

'So what?'

'So *manly*.'

'What do I normally look like?' he said, watching her leave the room.

'I'm not quite ready,' Nicole called back. 'Put a record on.'

She tried on various outfits but was happy with none of them (Luke liked them all). Eventually she tried on a sleeveless dress, pale yellow, short.

'What do you think?'

'You could make a dead man come,' said Luke.

'Always charming,' said Nicole, and disappeared into the bathroom. When she came out she had made up her eyes and put on lipstick.

'What's the matter?' she said. 'Why are you looking like that?'

'Like what?'

'Like you've lost a pound and found a flyover or whatever that stupid English expression is.'

'Lost a fiver and found a pound,' said Luke, grinning.

'Something must be wrong if you correct my English. What is it?'

'It's just that I've never seen you wear make-up before.'

'So?'

'I think you look nicer without it.'

'What if I want to wear it?'

'Fine.'

'So, are we ready?' She picked up her bag, her keys, a tube of mints.

'Sure.'

'Why don't you want me to wear make-up?'

'Because you look so much nicer without it.'

'You just don't want other men to fancy me.'

'Actually, like most men, I like it when other men fancy the woman I am with. As it happens, nobody could fancy you with all that shit on your face.'

'What did you say?'

'You look like a doll. I hardly recognize you.'

'I don't tell you how to dress, or how to look.'

'If you did I wouldn't mind.'

'*I* mind you telling me.'

'I just hate make-up. Lipstick makes me want to throw up. I've never seen you wearing make-up before so I was shocked. The only people who need to wear make-up are people with something wrong with them.'

'You should wear it then, you bloody fucker!'

Luke laughed: Nicole rarely swore and never sounded convincing when she did. She threw her bag at his face. He ducked. The bag hit the wall behind him. Nicole strode into the bathroom. Luke picked up the bag and its scattered contents, waited. A few minutes later she came out of the bathroom with no trace of make-up to be seen.

'You look beautiful,' said Luke. He put his hands on her shoulders, kissed her.

'I hate lipstick too,' she said. 'I knew you wouldn't like it.'

'How did you know that?'

'I don't know. I just did.'

'Does that count as our first quarrel?'

'I suppose. Even though we were quarrelling about something we agreed on.'

'So, you're a temper-loser rather than a sulker.'

'What is sulking?'

'You know, after you've quarrelled you refuse to speak for ages.'

'Oh yes, I hate sulking. Life is too long for that.'

'Do you mean too short?'

'No, too long.'

'You're right,' said Luke, hugging her. 'But we should get a move on. We're meant to meet Alex and Sahra in ten minutes.'

The four of them arrived at the party at the perfect time: just late enough to make them wish they had arrived earlier. Sahra had been invited by the husband whose wife was using her birthday as a chance to exhibit her paintings: large, skin-coloured nudes of her husband. In the flesh, the husband was clothed in a white shirt, patterned waistcoat and dark trousers. He helped Sahra off with her coat. She was wearing black jeans and a white, sleeveless blouse. It was the first time Alex had seen her arms. The wife, the artist, was wearing a shimmery top and an ankle-length greenish skirt with a long slit up one leg. It was an outfit that declared a mature understanding of parties, of the need to lend the evening a slight erotic frisson which, at around midnight, would give way to a franker, tipsy flirtatiousness. It was the perfect outfit for a hostess. Alex and Luke handed over shopping bags full of wine and beer. In return the husband poured glasses of champagne. It was amazing champagne. Luke helped himself to a beer. The bell went again and the husband left them to toast his wife who made the four of them feel as welcome as if they had all been invited. She introduced Sahra and Alex to a painter who was also a writer and then went off to accept gifts from the latest arrivals. They moved into the

main room, stood near a piano, listening to the painter who
was also a writer talk about painting and writing. There were
about forty people in the room and except for the walls
which were lined with paintings of the naked husband, it did
not appear crowded. The bell to the apartment was ringing
frequently. Everyone was drinking champagne except Luke
who preferred canned drinks, beer essentially. In the kitchen
a table was loaded with food, red serviettes and plates.
Having finished his first glass of champagne, Alex, as hungry
as he was thirsty, loaded tabbouleh and other salads on to a
plate. Aware of a desire to hang, puppy-like, around Sahra,
he made a special effort to do the opposite, introducing himself to strangers, levering these introductions into
conversations that gradually took him away from her. Every
time he looked back she was talking to someone else. Nicole
came and stood by him, complimented him on his suit, asked
how it was going.

'The party?'

'No. Sahra.'

'Who knows. What do you think?'

'I think,' she said, 'that you missed an important chance
when we arrived.'

'Really? What chance?'

'You could have helped her off with her coat.'

'That kind of thing always seems a bit too attentive, too
gallant.'

'No. You don't understand. Helping a woman with her
coat is a perfect, formal way of establishing some kind of physical intimacy.'

'Jesus, that's right! I've never thought of that before. I'll
help her on with it at the end.'

'That might be even better. Helping her on with her coat is a little more formal. Helping her take off her coat might be a bit too – a bit too like undressing her.'

'Shit, I wish I *had* helped her off with it!' laughed Alex. 'Now I can't wait for the party to end so that I can help her on with her coat.' When in pursuit of a woman, Alex thought, your friend's girlfriend will always be your best co-conspirator. Nicole took a sip of wine and immediately began coughing, spluttering.

'It went down the wrong throat,' she said, her eyes suddenly wet with tears.

In another corner of the room a grinning German passed Luke a joint.

'Does it have tobacco in it?' he asked. The guy thought it did. Luke said he would pass. He also declined the offer of champagne when a bottle was angled towards him. He saw Nicole leave Alex's side and make her way to him across the room. A few moments later he saw Sahra touch Alex on the shoulder.

'Are you ignoring me?' she said.

'Hi. No. How are you? I was . . .'

'Looking at that woman's stomach.'

'Yes, I was. There's no denying it.' When Nicole had moved away he'd found himself doing exactly that: contemplating the bare stomach of a woman standing a few feet away from him.

'Do you like that? The ring through her navel?'

'I don't know.'

'I have one like that.'

'Do you?'

'But not in the same place.' Embarrassingly, Alex was

sure he was blushing. He felt hot. 'You're supposed to ask where,' said Sahra. Alex took a gulp of champagne but there was nothing left in his glass.

'Where?' he said, sure that the next word he was going to hear would be 'nipple' or 'clitoris'.

Sahra shook her head: 'Joking. And you're blushing.'

A woman with long Spanish hair sang a couple of songs, accompanied by two men who played guitars. The guitarists were grey-haired, neatly dressed in sports jackets and ties. Luke loved this tradition – and anything he loved automatically became part of some 'tradition' or other – of the soberly dressed guitarist in polished shoes revealing a slight gap of pale flesh between turn-up and sock. In the instrumental break the guitarists sparred with each other before the singer returned for the last verse of the song. It wasn't exactly flamenco but it appealed to the spirit of flamenco. Sahra translated for Alex who listened intently. The first song was about separation, parting and blood. The second was about betrayal, faithlessness and blood. The third was a mixture of the preceding two. There were no songs about reconciliations, meetings and returns. When the last song had finished the two guitarists shook hands and the singer kissed them both and everyone applauded. Later a woman in a white blouse read out some poetry that turned out to have been by Verlaine. More joints were smoked. Luke was stoned. The music on the stereo was jazz.

'Too jazzy,' said Sahra. 'I hate jazzy jazz. The more like jazz it is the less I like it.'

'I like it,' said Alex.

'Der-*iv*-ative! der-*iv*-ative!' sang Sahra, syncopating the word, holding out her glass to a woman pouring champagne.

People danced a little to the jazzy jazz and then the music changed and they started dancing to rock 'n' roll.

Taking the opportunity to start airing preferences of his own Alex said he hated rock 'n' roll – but this particular preference was lost on Sahra: Jean-Paul had arrived, had walked straight over to her. They kissed, began talking, leaving Alex with only his drink for company. He found Luke who was grumbling about the music: he wanted to dance but the music, he claimed, was 'undanceable'.

'I've actually got a tape with me. Maybe I can seize control of the stereo,' he said.

'That might not be such a good idea, Luke.'

'You're probably right. But it's a party with no clear musical policy,' he said. 'I'm going to get another drink.'

'Jean-Paul's arrived.'

'Who's he?'

'That guy who was with Sahra at the Petit Centre.'

'The guy she was with at the Petit Centre?'

'That's exactly what I just said,' said Alex. 'They're over there. Look.'

They were laughing together. Sahra had her hand on his shoulder.

'What am I going to do?'

'You may as well leave now to avoid further humiliation,' said Luke. Sahra looked over their way, Jean-Paul too. They came over. Sahra re-introduced them. Jean-Paul was formal, friendly in a not so friendly way. He wasn't sure exactly when they had met.

'Au Petit Centre,' said Alex.

'Ah, le Petit Centre,' said Jean-Paul, lighting a cigarette.

'Yes, the Petit Centre,' said Luke. Sahra left the three of

them together. Luke did most of the talking. After a few minutes Jean-Paul excused himself. Luke and Alex watched him
cross the room, heading towards Sahra.

'I'd like to fight him,' said Alex.

'Sure, champ.'

'Smash his face in.'

'Break his nose.'

'Bust up his kidneys.'

'Make him piss blood.'

'Kick fuck out of him.'

'Fuck him up bad.'

'Hurt him.'

'Hurt him and fuck up his face. That's it, champ,' said
Luke. 'Forget it, champ. Look at him. He's finished.'

'You think?'

'Sure. It's over between them. Probably nothing even
started. And now even that nothing is over with. He's out of
the loop. He is out of the fuckin' loop, man. OK?'

'Sure.'

'Now I'm going to get a drink.'

'OK.'

'Hey champ. You're OK yeah?'

'I'm OK.'

'You sure you're OK, champ?'

'I'm OK.' Alex stayed where he was. Jean-Paul was talking
to a guy Alex didn't know and Sahra was dancing with someone
else he didn't know. After three indifferent songs, 'Get Back' by
the Beatles came on and Sahra stopped dancing and went over
to Nicole. Alex saw Luke on his own and the four friends seg-
regated themselves by sex. The two pairs could see each other
talking. More exactly, the men leaned against the wall, wearing

their manly suits, saying nothing, watching the women talk. Nicole had her hand on Sahra's arm. Luke and Alex could not hear what they were saying but they saw them giggling.

'Man, what are those bitches talking about?' said Luke. Seeing the men watching them Sahra whispered to Nicole who then glanced at Luke, held up her hand, thumb and forefinger a couple of inches apart, before they both doubled up laughing. Luke mimed a sardonic belly laugh.

'Right, we'll show them,' he said to Alex. 'We're going to have a conversation about the vampire film I saw on TV a few nights ago.'

'What about werewolf films? The way the escalation of terror is always indicated not by atrocity but lexicographically, by consulting a dictionary. An old, heavy dictionary. A dictionary of the arcane. "Lycanthropy: here we are . . ." '

'That's a *werewolf* conversation. I'm talking about a vampire conversation. Talking about trying to make sense of that convention whereby the traveller is on his way to Castle Dracula.'

'Wind, wolves, rain, lightning. The coachman lashing the horses,' said Alex, getting in the groove.

'And after lashing the horses the coachman sets down the traveller at an inn—'

'A lonely inn.'

'Called something like The-Creaky-Sign-Blowing-In-The-Storm-Arms and everyone in the pub turns hostile when he tells them where he's going. A lightning flash fills the window at this point, obviously. But why, instead of explaining to him that he'd be better off going somewhere else, why do they suddenly turn all sullen and virtually show him the door? It doesn't make sense.'

'It's because they realize the whole cycle is about to start all over again,' said Alex. He saw Nicole put her glass neatly on a table and walk down the corridor. There was no sign of Jean-Paul but another man came over and began talking to Sahra.

'But if they just let him stay a couple of nights till the storm died down and he then got the coach back to England, to his fiancée, everything would be fine. From time to time he could send them a postcard, thanking them for their hospitality. I would prefer that to the whole dismal bit about Dracula. Basically by the time he gets to Castle Dracula it's all pretty well downhill. What I like is the cosiness that the prospect of horror builds up.'

'You wouldn't get that cosiness without the horror.'

'Just the prospect of horror would do. I'd happily sit through two hours of jovial scenes in a Transylvanian pub. Culminating with him stepping outside into the storm-washed landscape, nursing a killer hangover, squinting at the terrible damage outside: uprooted trees, broken branches, omens of an obscure catastrophe narrowly averted. And there, in the background, in plain view, framed by the blue sky: the castle. What do you think?'

'I think I'm dying for a piss,' said Alex.

He went into the bathroom just as Nicole came out. She smiled at him, a little hurriedly. As he locked himself into the bathroom, Alex understood why: the smell of shit was heavy in the air. Probably her shit smelled just as bad as a man's but in this context – an expensive bathroom with gleaming mirrors and towels of hotel whiteness – it mixed with the strawberry scents of oils and lotions in a way that, as Alex pissed into the white bowl in which no trace of excrement could be seen, seemed specifically feminine, not unpleasant, almost exotic.

The other three had all gone out on to the balcony. Alex joined them. An apartment opposite was filled with the blue lurch of television. It had started raining. Luke and Nicole put their arms around each other, alerting Alex to the way that he was not at liberty to put his arm around Sahra. The music changed: a track Nicole liked. She led Luke back into the party to dance, leaving Sahra and Alex alone. We are on our own on the balcony, Alex said to himself. He thought about trying to kiss Sahra but was aware of the rancid dryness the champagne had left in his mouth. She had been drinking champagne too, but she had also been chewing gum which – if advertisements were anything to go by – had rendered her mouth fresh and kissable. On the one hand the thought of her gum-fresh mouth made him *want* to kiss her, on the other it made him still more conscious of the parched sourness, the *un*kissability of his own mouth. He took a gulp of beer. Sahra was leaning with her forearms on the balcony rail, a glass held loosely between her fingers, staring through the rain. Alex was on the brink of kissing her – on the brink, rather, of plucking up the courage to do so – when the painter who was also a writer joined them on the balcony. He was carrying a bottle of champagne and filled Sahra's empty glass with over-flowing fizz that subsided almost to nothing. He was drunk but Sahra was adamant,

'If you're a painter you should just paint.'

'Nonsense,' said the painter who was also a writer.

'There have been no painters who were good writers.'

Alex tried to think of one who was, but the painter who was also a writer beat him to it. 'What about Van Gogh?' he said. 'His letters are superb, some of the greatest letters ever written.'

'Yes,' said Sahra. 'But have you seen the paintings?'

That was the moment that Alex knew, without question, that he was in love with her. He suspected that the artist who was also a writer had fallen in love with her too: he rocked back on his feet, held out his hands – bottle in one, glass in the other – and called out to the street: 'This woman: she is too much for me. Ha! Too much for the world.' With that he headed back inside, chuckling, shaking his head and saying, 'Too much'.

Rain fell out of the darkness, becoming purple as it passed through a belt of neon and then glowing yellow in the lights of cars whose wipers greeted it mechanically. Sahra held out her glass into the night, letting the rain bounce into it. Alex leaned on the balcony and looked down at the couples hurrying for shelter, disappearing beneath the red awnings of the café across the street. Sahra's arm was shining wet, the glass filling with coloured sparks of rain. They stayed like that for several minutes, hearing the music behind them and the cars swathing by below. When there was half an inch of water in the glass she brought it to her lips and drank. Now he will kiss me, Sahra thought to herself, turning her face towards him, wiping rain from her lips. More people came on to the balcony, bringing bottles and laughter. Tossed out into the street, a cigarette butt fell like red tracer through the rain. An elderly couple appeared on one of the balconies opposite, watching the rain, waving back to the crowd of young people who greeted them noisily.

Sahra and Alex moved into the kitchen. Hummus-smeared plates were piled up on the draining board. On the

table were the remains of a cake, and a bowl shaped like a lettuce leaf, full of grapes and stalks. The music in the living
room had changed: dance music, louder than anything else
that had been played. Above the table was a framed poster for
an exhibition of Diebenkorn paintings: pale blues, squares of
yellow, the same yellow as Nicole's dress.

'Perhaps you'll frame the poster I gave you,' said Alex.

'I hate frames,' said Sahra. Then, after a pause: 'Actually,
I hate posters too.'

'You're on good form tonight, Sahra,' said Alex.
'Vehement.' She was eating grapes, her back to the fridge
which was covered with coloured magnetic letters. Over her
shoulder, on the freezer compartment, Alex saw a blue B, an
orange O, and a red R which had been used to clamp a postcard of a Scottish loch in place. Jean-Paul came into the
kitchen.

'Est-ce qu'il y a encore de la bière?' he said, awkwardly.
Sahra moved aside. The multi-coloured words CHEVAL and
ELANE loomed into view as Jean-Paul opened the fridge door.
After rooting around for a moment he emerged holding a bot-
tle of German beer.

'T'en veux, Sahra?'

'Non merci Jean-Paul.'

'Et toi, Alex?'

'Oui, s'il en reste encore une, Jean-Paul,' said Alex. Jean-
Paul passed him a bottle but was unable to find an opener.

'Laisse, je l'ouvre,' said Alex. Jean-Paul passed him his
bottle. Holding that bottle in one hand he used his own to flip
the top off Jean-Paul's. He did it as quickly as if he'd been
opening a can of Coke. 'Voilà,' he said, passing the bottle to
Jean-Paul.

'Merci,' said Jean-Paul, taking it.

'Je t'en prie,' said Alex, taking another beer out of the fridge and using that to lever open his own bottle.

Jean-Paul left the kitchen. 'He is out of the fuckin' loop,' said Alex, suddenly exultant.

'Sorry?'

'Nothing. A line from a song.'

'Pretty impressive, I have to admit,' said Sahra. 'The bottle-opening, I mean. Where did you learn that?'

'Zimbabwe.'

'Zimbabwe?'

'Well, a friend who'd been to Zimbabwe taught me. In London.'

'I'll just go to the bathroom,' said Sahra.

'Sure,' said Alex, intent on scanning the letters on the fridge door. He couldn't find a Y but by the time he saw Sahra coming back along the hall he had arranged the letters into a rough draft, hiding his preparatory work by taking up the position she had occupied, directly in front of the fridge.

Sahra poured a glass of water and helped herself to the last grapes. While she was doing this Alex nudged a few more letters into place, completing his little sentence and then moving aside. Sahra watched absently and then saw, in blue, orange and green letters:

I WANTO GO
BED WIV U.

She looked at Alex, who stood uncertainly, wondering if he should smile.

'You must be a good Scrabble player,' she said. The atmosphere in the kitchen had changed. Alex leaned on the fridge which began to rumble. Having drunk half of his bottle, Alex poured the rest into a glass and studied the foam. Was it just the fridge he was leaning against, or had he begun to shake very slightly?

'Is it my turn now?' said Sahra.

'Sure.'

She slipped her finger into the orange O from GO and moved it into a space of its own. Alex watched, preparing to see her precede it with an N. Instead she reached down and added a K.

The volume of music in the living room diminished. Luke and Nicole came into the kitchen. Luke poured glasses of water which he and Nicole gulped down. They were sweating.

Luke whispered in Alex's ear, 'I've just seen Jean-Paul leave. Like I said: out of the mother-fuckin' loop.' Aloud, triumphant, he said, 'I got my tape on!'

'For about ten minutes,' said Nicole. 'Then they took it off.'

The party began to thin out. Nicole and Luke were ready to leave.

'Shall we go soon?' Alex said to Sahra when they were alone again.

'Yes.'

'And can I come home with you when we do go?'

'No, not tonight.'

'Why not?'

'Now I'm tired and drunk.'

'I want to,' he said.

'So do I.'

'So?'

'What are you doing tomorrow afternoon?'

'Nothing.'

'Will you be at home?'

'Yes.'

'I'll come by tomorrow afternoon.'

'Would you like lunch?'

'Yes.'

'OK.'

'So I'll see you tomorrow, yes? At about two.'

'OK.'

'Perfect. Now I'm going home,' she said, kissing him briefly on the mouth and turning away.

'I'll get your coat,' said Alex, remembering.

He was actually vaguely relieved that they were not going home together tonight. He had said – or at least he had written – that he wanted to go to bed with Sahra which was true but as yet he felt no lust for her. He wanted to go to bed with her so that he could begin lusting after her. He knew immediately when he fancied a woman but what did it mean, this fancying? It meant he wanted to sleep with her, become her lover, fuck her – but lust played no part in it. He only lusted after women he had already slept with. He lusted after his old girlfriends but Sahra, he looked at her and felt . . . what? A longing. An ache – not even an ache really, something more abstract than that, an abstract ache if that was possible: an absence. He felt incomplete, insubstantial without her. And yet, at the same time that there was no lust in this feeling, it contained the seed of what, once they had begun sleeping together, would become overwhelmingly focused on sex. He had to sleep with her so that he could begin wanting to sleep with her.

Sahra arrived at two o'clock on the dot, when Alex was still preparing the salad. He greeted her at the door, holding a bowl of lettuce, just washed.

'Punctuality,' he said. 'A great quality in men and women alike.' She kissed him on the mouth, exactly as she had the night before.

'Let me take your coat,' he said, standing behind her.

'You're very gallant all of a sudden. Thank you.'

'You got home OK?' said Alex, hanging up her coat.

'No. I was raped and murdered actually. How about you?'

'Are you in a bad mood?'

'Just playing.'

'I walked. Ten minutes, that's all. I was quite drunk.'

'Me too. Do you have a hangover?' she asked.

'No. Surprisingly. You?'

'No. A little. We're speaking in short sentences. Have you noticed?'

'Yes. Why? I mean why do you think that is?'

'Because we are due to go to bed together, probably.'

'That was a longer sentence,' said Alex. Sahra was standing at the window, leaning with her back to the light. She would have been silhouetted had the room not been filled with light from all sides. It poured in.

'It's a nice apartment,' she said. 'Very light.'

'Would you like a drink?'

'Of water, yes, please. Tap water is fine. And you have a lovely view.'

'Almost down to the Bastille. Yes, I love it.' The water

took a while to run cool. He handed her a glass. She was wearing slacks. He supposed that's what they would be called. Light, tight-fitting around the ankles: difficult to take off, he thought.

'What is this music?' she said. She was looking along his shelves, at his books and stuff. 'Do you mind if I look?'

'It's the radio. No, you can look.' He dried the forks and knives he had just washed, put plates and bowls on the table.

'Why are you so tense?' she said.

'I'm not tense,' he said. 'Except now I am, of course. That was an unfair remark, guaranteed to make me tense. You said it because you're tense.'

'Well yes, I am tense. I thought I wouldn't be but I am.'

'Why?'

'Because of this fucking sex thing, I suppose.'

'We can eat if you like.'

'Yes, I'm hungry. Actually I'm starving.'

They sat opposite each other. He broke the loaf of bread in half.

'It was fun last night, wasn't it?'

'Yes, I enjoyed it.'

'In spite of the music.'

'The music was bad.'

'Let's eat. Add oil. Pepper, too, if you like. Then it's just a question of chewing.'

The tomatoes were over-ripe, as Sahra liked them. The basil was dusty with its own scent. Deep Purple were on the radio. Alex turned up the volume, played a little air guitar. They duetted on the chorus:

'Smoke on the water . . .
Fire in the sky.'

By the time the song had finished Sahra was mopping up

the tomato-pipped residue of olive oil on her plate with a piece of bread. When there was nothing else to mop up she poured in some extra oil.

'There's more salad if you like.'

'No thank you.'

'Fruit?'

'Do you have any?'

'I can get some.'

'Oh don't bother going out. Shall I go?'

'It's no bother.' He seemed eager to procure fruit.

'What would you like? An orange?'

'An apple would be great.'

'I'll get you one.' Sahra followed him as he walked across to the open window.

'Hey, Louis,' he called down to a man working at the fruit stall across the street. 'Passe moi une pomme. Je te paierai plus tard.'

'Pour la demoiselle?'

'Oui.'

Louis reached back, selected a good apple, held it up.

'Celle-là va bien?'

'Parfaite.'

Louis threw it up and Alex caught it in both hands. He gave the apple to Sahra and the thumbs-up to Louis. Sahra smiled down at him, waved.

'Was that off the cuff or up the sleeve?'

'Ideally I would have caught it in one hand.'

Sahra peeled her apple, quartered it, cut out the pips, handed Alex a piece. They munched noisily.

'How is it?'

'Quite good.'

'Not crisp enough?'

'Too crisp. I like soft apples. The sort they give to pigs.'

'No one likes apples like that.'

'That's why they give them to the pigs. But I love them.'

After they had finished chewing Alex went to the bathroom. When I get out I must kiss her, he said to himself over and over. When he got out, she had gone. Then he looked over at the bed. She was under the duvet, making exaggerated snoring noises. He looked over at the chair to see if she had taken her clothes off. He saw her trousers and top, he wasn't sure about her underwear.

'Nice clean sheets,' she said. The sheets were pulled up to her neck. Only her head was visible.

'If we're being absolutely frank I changed them specially.' He wasn't sure what to do.

'You can get in too, if you like. It's your bed, after all.'

'Yes,' he said. 'Except that would involve me taking off my clothes, in broad daylight. Crucially, I wouldn't know whether to take my underpants off. Are you wearing your underwear?' It would be inappropriate, he felt, to lift her clothes off the chair to check.

'No.'

'Basically, not to beat about the hedge, you're naked.' Disseminated by Luke, Nicole's almost correct English expressions were becoming standard.

'Yes,' said Sahra.

'I see. So that would involve me taking off *all* my clothes in broad daylight.'

'Yes. And I'll watch. To see how you cope. Like this I don't feel so nervous. In fact I don't feel nervous at all now. How about you?'

'Oh I'm pretty nervous, yes. So I think first I'll draw the blinds.' He walked over to each window in turn, lowered the blinds and tilted them so that the walls and floor were lined with gold stripes: the kind of lighting effect seen in commercials. The large window was still open, the blinds clinked in the breeze. The atmosphere in the room thickened, as if the sky had suddenly become dense with rainclouds. Sahra watched Alex take off his T-shirt and toss it on to the chair where her clothes were piled. He removed his socks.

'Well remembered,' said Sahra. 'No pot belly either.' Alex unbuttoned his jeans, climbed out of them, wobbled slightly. Without taking his boxers off he walked over to the bed and climbed in beside Sahra. She put her arms round him. 'And no hairy back,' she said. 'A perfect specimen in fact.'

'Weren't there some other things as well?'

'I forget.' They lay beside each other without speaking. It was the kind of silence in which they could both feel just content enough not to speak. They kissed.

'It will take me a while to get used to you, Alex.' Her eyes were open, watching him.

'And me you,' he said.

On Tuesday we had a semi-official (i.e. floodlit) football match on a full-size pitch near Belleville. The regular players from the warehouse joined forces with some friends of Matthias's to take on a team from the local art school. The game ended six–five (the defenders of both sides really wanted to be attackers) and afterwards a group of us went and drank at a bar in Belleville. We stayed till midnight and then walked towards the Bastille. There were five of us, slightly drunk, exhilarated rather than drunk. As we turned into passage Beslay we saw a man up ahead, walking towards us. We thought nothing of it. Then Ahmed hissed: 'C'est lui.'

'C'est qui?'

'Le type qui m'a attaqué.' We looked down the narrow passage. He had seen us, but continued towards us.

'What shall we do?' said Luke. The guy was drawing closer. When he was within a few paces of us we stopped walking and he stopped too.

'Tu me cherches ou quoi?' It took us by surprise, his speaking first, and it alerted us to the fact that, yes, perhaps we were looking for him, for trouble.

'Tu me reconnais?' Ahmed said

'On aurait déjà été présenté?' he sneered. He was drunk, heavily built, with small scars on his forehead and chin. Tough people always look like that, like they've spent their lives getting beaten up.

'Disons que tu t'es fait connaître,' Ahmed said, pointing to his nose which was still swollen. There was a small purple mark beneath his left eye.

The guy spat. 'Pas moi.' He was smiling, indifferent, not frightened.

'Si. Toi.' We were standing close to him, close enough to smell the booze on his breath over and above the beer that was on ours. Tacitly incriminating, the letters FN were scrawled on the wall behind him. He looked round and realized that he was cornered. It wasn't that we had him cornered – we wouldn't have known how to do such a thing – but it happened that he was cornered. He looked at us, tried to gauge our intentions, noticed that we had none. We were all hoping that the matter would be taken out of our hands, decided for us. If we thought we sensed his nervousness, fear even, that was just a magnified reflection of our own. My heart was beating harder. He smiled again, becoming more certain that, although there were five of us, we were incapable of a descent into violence. We didn't know how to go about it. It was all down to him. We were four or five feet away and I was starting to tremble, a kind of vertigo, an awareness of being close to the edge of something. Even so, maybe nothing would have happened – I think we all realized that none of us, in spite of the loathing we felt for him, was capable of making the first move, not even Ahmed – if he had not forced it to happen. He saw us faltering and decided this was the moment to make a break for it. If he had waited for us to get closer, until we were a foot or so from him, perhaps nothing would have happened. Probably we would have ended up talking to him. But he couldn't wait that long, his experience of fighting told him that once a group closes in on you like that you're finished. And so he charged at us, fists flailing, trying to burst through the loose cordon we had formed.

It almost worked. Fear is the instinctive response to aggression and abruptly all our encroaching menace had been flung back at us. We flinched. Even as we tried to block his escape so, simultaneously, we were trying also to move aside. He ran at us and hit Luke in the side of the face, elbowed Matthias. He kept his knees high and dangerous like a rugby player making a lunge for the line. Daniel was directly in front of him and the guy swiped a fist at him. Daniel swayed back to avoid the blow, leaving a path clear for him. Suddenly there was no one to stop him getting away and the sense of how pathetically easy it had been made him pause, turn slightly

and aim a punch at Ahmed, to show us how feeble our shuffling threat was in the face of someone who understood the
reality of pain and violence. He could not only get away, he
could dish out some hurt in the process. Luke grabbed his fist
as he was preparing to smash it into Ahmed's face and at that
same moment Daniel dived into his back, almost knocking
him over. Then we were all scrambling over each other. He
was lashing out wildly, without thought, trying to remain on
his feet, oblivious to the blows that caught his face and shoulders. He had his hand around Luke's throat. Matthias hit him
hard on the ear and he swung around, scattering us all. His
legs and arms were flying everywhere. He was not aiming at
anyone now, but was trying to create a centrifugal force of violence so great that no one could approach him. Again he
almost succeeded. We had all fallen back when Daniel kicked
him in the small of the back. He pitched forward, stumbled,
was about to regain his balance. Then Ahmed brought his fist
down on the back of his neck. He was still on his feet but suddenly we were swarming all over him, sometimes catching
each other with an elbow in our eagerness to get at him. Fists
and feet were flying everywhere, we were oblivious to the
pain of punches. For a few seconds everything was in the balance and then, for the first time, he was on the defensive,
using his arms increasingly to protect himself, allowing us to
move closer to him. Able to get to him with next to no risk
we all piled in. I was hit twice by glancing blows from
Matthias or Luke. Less from any particular blow than the
chaos of our attack, he began to go over, arms curled around
his head as we flung our feet at him.

It lasted only ten or twenty seconds but I remember those
seconds as being some of the most charged of my life. I think

we all felt the same way. It was like something had been unleashed. A latent part of our being, our species, that, until then, none of us had ever directly experienced, suddenly made itself felt. It was as if we had been granted a violent insight into a fundamental flaw in the process of evolution. Everything was a blur and everything was perfectly clear. I remember my foot thudding into his ribs at exactly the moment that Matthias called out: 'Arrêtez les mecs, arrêtez!'

We stood for a few seconds, the alley dense with the fog of our breath, gazing down at the huddled figure on the floor. Luke kicked him again in the back, very hard, several times. I pulled him away. Then we ran back down the alley.

Back on avenue Parmentier someone said it was best to separate and meet up again at Matthias's place in a quarter of an hour. It seemed a good idea though no one was sure why.

Suddenly Luke was on his own. His heart was pounding. The shutters of shops were covered with elaborate snakes of graffiti. Broken glass glittered in the gutter. A puddle held the reflection of the moon, pale as ice. Two people walked towards him and he immediately felt vulnerable and alone, bristling at the threat but ready to defend himself against anyone, indifferent to everything. They walked past nervously, aware, it seemed, of some volatile presence.

Luke was the last to arrive at Matthias's. We were all panicked and scared but mainly we were excited, excited and dangerous, ready to go out and fight again. Matthias noticed his hand was hurting, Luke's face throbbed where he had been hit. Matthias poured drinks which we inhaled quickly. We talked about the fight over and over, listened attentively to each other's account of what had happened, how we had felt, what we had done. We wondered what kind of damage we had done to him and reassured each other that, at the very worst, he had maybe lost a few teeth and broken his nose: injuries like this had suddenly become no more significant than grazes. We had not even knocked him out but, had I not pulled Luke off, I don't know if he would have stopped kicking him.

Years later Nicole told me that one of the things that had surprised her about Luke was how tender he was. But that night, in passage Beslay, I glimpsed a capacity for cruelty, for inflicting pain, that he would later turn on himself.

Matthias said we should go back and give him another helping. Everyone laughed but, beneath our exhilaration, there was some small element of shame which made itself felt more and more powerfully as the violence drained from us and left us weak. We parted, each of us a little scared of what had happened and what might happen, frightened that we had been initiated into a spiral of violence and reprisal, a vendetta from which we might be unable to extricate ourselves.

It was not a big thing morally and, looking back now, of all the things that happened to Luke and the rest of us, it would be among the very last that I would trade back if I had to start pawning the events in my life. A whole dimension of human existence opened up and became plain in those few moments. It changed us in some way; violence lost its mystery. There was a huge gulf separating the world of fighters and non-fighters and we had crossed it. We were different now. We could see the attraction of being violent men in a gang, could see the pleasure of violence and the self-respect and satisfaction it gave you – but at the same time this was tempered by a sense of how foolish and pathetic this was. It was for this reason as much as any fear of getting caught that we all agreed to tell no one else – not Nicole, not Sahra, no one – about what had happened.

I asked Luke about this incident when I saw him in London, many years later.

'You remember when we beat that guy up that night?'

'Yes.'

'Did you ever tell Nicole about it?'

'No.'

'How come?'

'How come what?'

'How come you didn't tell her?'

'Well, we agreed didn't we?'

'But you know how it is. You make all sorts of promises not to tell your woman this or that – and nine times out of ten you tell her.'

'Well. I didn't tell her.' He was sitting very still. Then, for the first time since we had been sitting there, I saw the life return to his eyes.

'It was great wasn't it?' he said, smiling.

In the days following the fight Alex was often on the brink of telling Sahra about what had happened but always, at the last moment, he restrained himself. It was difficult to keep things from her. Partly because she was so open herself, but mainly because, for the first time in his life, Alex found that he had formed a close friendship with the woman he was going out with. In the past the women he had been involved with had never been his friends: almost, sometimes, never quite. He had liked his girlfriends, loved them, but eventually their romantic involvement had always curtailed or over-ridden the relationship's potential for friendship. This simple, apparently common experience of being friends with his girlfriend was entirely new to him, so new that, for a time, he was not even aware of it, or at least was aware of it only in terms of unexpected compatibilities, a system of reckoning which actually plays no part in friendship.

She was the only woman he had ever met who, exactly like him, preferred to leave restaurants as soon as she had finished eating. They asked for the bill while they were still chewing and, ideally, left while still swallowing. In terms of the cinema they shared the same middle of the road – more accurately middle of the auditorium – taste. Going to the cinema with Luke was always something of a strain – a neck strain – for Alex because Luke insisted on sitting at the front with the screen looming over them. Alex liked to sit slap bang in the middle of the middle; Sahra was neurotically obsessed with doing so. Invariably these perfect seats were already occupied and they often had to sample four or five pairs of seats before selecting the ones – usually those they had originally opted for – that offered an acceptably compromised combination of centrality, unobstructed visibility and leg room. They also discovered that they were great cinema-leavers. Ten minutes, half an hour or an hour into a film, Sahra would gesture with her thumb towards the exit and they would be up and out. On one occasion they were within minutes of the end of a film when Alex turned towards her, moved one arm over the other and, without any hesitation, they gathered their things together and stumbled out of the darkness. There was never any disagreement: they always wanted to leave at the same time.

It wasn't simply a question of compatibility. Even their divergences and disagreements were a source of harmony. On the subject of Luke, for example. Sahra thought he was funny, clever, good company . . . What she found hard to take was Alex's 'need to idolise him, to make him into something more than he is'.

They were lying in bed, tipsy, after a dinner at Nicole's.

'I don't *idolize* him.'

'You do. It's not enough for you to be friends with him. You have to look up to him. And to do that you have to make him into something he's not. Which means, weirdly, that you're not doing justice to him.'

'I don't idolise him but I do see him as—'

'What about what you *don't* see him as?'

'What don't I see him as?'

'Look, I love them to death too, both of them. Luke is terrific. But I can also see that he's a complete waster. You don't notice it because he's so thin but in many ways he's just greedy. A consumer. He doesn't really have emotions. Just appetites. At the moment he's happy as a sandboy because there's so much still to gobble down. But what's he going to be like when he's tried it all, when there's nothing left to gobble, or when he gets fed up gobbling?'

'I don't know. You tell me.'

'He'll be exactly like my brother.'

'And what's your brother like?'

'Dead.'

'No!'

'No, that was a lie. He's a fat, idle pig,' said Sahra. 'Honestly, he's like a greedy only child—'

'Your brother's an only child? Now we're really getting to the crux of the matter.'

Sahra laughed. 'I mean Luke. But they're both oblivious to everything outside their own desires. It's like he hasn't been weaned. The world is just a breast to be sucked.'

'How can you say that when he's just cooked yet another incredible meal for us?'

'Easily. The fact that he's very generous doesn't stop him being totally selfish.' Alex kissed her. Whatever he thought of his friend it was always pleasing to hear him denounced like this. He was less keen on what came next.

'Or maybe what's going on is that you project your own desires on to him, that you like imagining you're him.'

'How d'you mean?'

'Maybe it's not Luke at all,' said Sahra, slowly. 'Maybe it's Nicole. You worship Luke because you want to fuck Nicole.'

'Very clever,' said Alex, quickly. 'I think it all comes down to you and this only-child brother of yours. How old were you, by the way, when you first sucked his pig-dick?' Sahra punched him on the shoulder. 'And while we're on the subject of selfishness,' Alex went on, 'you are the most selfish sleeper I've ever shared a bed with.'

It was true. During her waking hours Sahra was considerate, thoughtful; asleep she sprawled, hogging the duvet and mattress as if he were not there. At first, forced into the chilly fringes of the bed, he lay awake, fascinated by the sea-change that came over her. Then it became a source of irritation. He started shoving her back into her half of the bed, tugging the duvet over his way, dragging her – as he hoped he would – out of the depths of her sleep.

'You're always waking me up,' she whined.

'You're always taking the duvet,' he whined back.

'You're always nagging me about the duvet.'

'You're always nagging me about leaving drawers and cupboards open.'

'I nag you about the cupboards and drawers because I'm always hitting my head or knees on them.'

'I nag you about the duvet because it's always leaving me in the cold.'

'Well that just goes to show doesn't it?'

'What?'

'We both like nagging. It's fun to nag.'

'You're right. What's wrong with nagging?' said Alex and they both settled back to sleep.

It may have been fun to nag but to be able to do so in several languages seemed, to Alex, an awesome achievement. Any pretensions to sophistication – a comprehensive knowledge of opera, say, or the capacity to discriminate between various recordings of Beethoven's quartets – were nothing compared with the ability to chat with grocers and taxi-drivers in four or five languages. Sahra didn't know the first thing about classical music – nor did Alex for that matter, nor Luke (Nicole did) – but her linguistic resourcefulness meant that she had even improved Alex's hitherto strained relationship with his concierge. A Portuguese whose duties consisted, in the mornings, of looking miserable and, in the afternoons, of hanging out at a miserable bar with other miserable men, he had several times complained to Alex about petty infringements of the building's non-existent rules. Since Sahra had begun chatting to him in Portuguese (which she did not even count as one of her languages) his behaviour had changed entirely; on one occasion he had even signed for a registered letter and brought it up to Alex later that day.

Alex admired and loved Sahra's languages but what he loved more than anything were her *habits*: the way she folded her clothes away, the way she still used a pen that her father had given her ten years ago and still wore a hat (fluffy with coloured hoops that looked tartan from a distance) that she had been given for her seventh birthday. He liked to think of her when she was fifty, still wearing the same hat, using the same pen.

Alex was used to drawing up litanies of quirks like this. He was aware, likewise, that he and Sahra had grown close, that their relationship had evolved a pattern and rhythm of its own but the most important, the defining part of its development, was the invisible, unremarkable fact of their friendship.

Sahra was equally unaware of this – for precisely the opposite reason: she could not conceive of her lover *not* being a friend. To Sahra her lover was, above all else, a friend, her best friend. Alex came to realize this only negatively: he found himself thinking of Sahra as a friend rather than lover. They had known each other only a short time, they were in love, but something was missing. The first time they had gone to bed together they had said it would take time to get used to each other. Now they had got used to each other, but getting used to each other also meant getting used to there being something missing between them – and what was missing was so subtle that it was almost impossible to isolate or talk about. It wasn't Sahra's fault, it wasn't Alex's, but even in their moments of greatest arousal they were still there, still themselves. Sahra had had many lovers: was it always like this for her? Alex knew that it had not always been like this for him. Alex could talk to no one about this: to have talked to Luke would have been to have betrayed Sahra; the only person he could talk to was Sahra and he couldn't talk to her. How did she feel? Was she feeling the same? He didn't know. He didn't know because she did not know how to ask him if he too felt as she did: namely that there wasn't that perpetual flow of longing between them – that flow which anyone could sense passing between Luke and Nicole.

Who existed in a trance of longing, inhabited a state of constant wanting. Everything had been perfect from the first night they spent together. Neither of them knew why. It had just happened like that. And it continued happening like that.

'There's a bun for every burger,' was the best explanation Nicole could come up with.

'Where on earth did you pick up that expression?'

'I heard it somewhere. I forget.' She went on crunching her salad. Luke – who had finished his salad and loved reminiscing about their first date, their first night together – tried another tack.

'Don't you think it's strange that we didn't have safe sex that first night?'

'I don't know.'

'Don't you normally?'

'I don't normally sleep with people.'

'How many men have you slept with?'

'Why?'

'I don't know. It's just a question that is there, waiting to be asked or not asked.'

'But it's not not being asked is it? You *are* asking.'

'So . . . How many?'

'Three,' she said, finishing her salad.

'Three!' Luke laughed. 'You're kidding. Is that including me?'

'Yes.'

'Wow!'

'Why you laugh?'

'Because,' he tittered, 'it's so few.'

'And how many women have you slept with?'

'More than three.' Her face went blank with hurt. He put his arm around her, laughing still. He kissed her cheek, her ear.

'Why you laugh?'

'Because . . . Well, I mean. How did you learn so much about sex?'

'I didn't learn anything. You think it's like exams? You think you passed lots of exams?'

'No. It's lovely. You're lovely.'

'So how many?'

'How many what?'

'How many exams you have passed?' Her English deteriorated quickly when she became angry.

'Oh I don't know.'

'Many?'

'Not that many,' said Luke. 'But more than three!'

Her eyes blazed with anger. She pushed him away, walked to the bathroom and shut the door quietly: a tacit slam. Luke tried the door: it was unlocked.

'Get out!' She raised her fist and, for a moment, Luke was sure she was going to hit him. Instead she focused her rage on the toilet seat. She gripped it with both hands and – whether accidentally or deliberately was impossible to tell – tore it free of the bowl and threw it out of the door.

'That was the most bizarre display of temper I have ever seen,' said Luke. He went out to retrieve the toilet seat. When he came back she was sitting on the cold porcelain, knickers around her ankles, crying.

'Interesting. You're one of those women who can cry and piss at the same time.'

'I'm not pissing. And I'm not crying. I'm sort of cry-laughing.'

'I brought you a present,' he said, handing her the toilet seat. She stood up and he slid it beneath her.

'Let me feel you piss,' he said, putting his hand between her legs.

'No!'

'Listen, the reason I find it funny that you've only slept with three people is, well, because I've never met anyone sexier than you.'

'So it's not just about passing exams. You get grades as well.'

'Nine out of ten.'

'Only nine?'

'You only get ten if I can feel you piss.' He touched her.

'I'm still angry.'

'Piss through my fingers.'

'I can't.'

He kissed her cheek. Then pressed his mouth against her ear, shaping once again the words they had never said aloud to each other. Aloud, he said, 'You really do have a temper.'

'I hit my brother over the head with my uncle's trumpet once.'

'Why?'

'It was the only thing within reach.'

'I meant why'd you hit him?'

'He stole my sweets and wouldn't give them back.'

'Not like me. I didn't have a brother to steal my sweets. Or a sister. So I gorged myself on sweets all day long.'

They kissed. She moved her hands under the sleeves of

his T-shirt. He pulled her dress up so that he could see her stomach, her pubic hair.

'I can't see you. I want to see you piss.'

'How?'

'In the bath.' They undressed. Nicole stood with one foot on each side of the bath and lowered herself down, using her hands for support. His prick reached up towards her.

'Now.'

'I'm trying,' she laughed. 'It's too ridiculous.'

'Doesn't it turn you on?'

'Hmm. I don't know.' He raised his hips so that his prick was touching her. 'Don't,' she said. 'If you do that I can't. I have to concentrate.' She shut her eyes. A few drips sprang from her, on to his prick and stomach.

'More.' There was another pulse of urine and then she was flooding over him. He pushed up and into her. Her balance was precarious. Luke's back and shoulders began burning with the strain of keeping himself arched up like this and it was only by concentrating on that pain that he could stop himself coming and then he could hold back no longer. His arms gave way. Nicole collapsed on to him. He fell back into the tepid wash of piss at the bottom of the bath. In the space of a few seconds urine had reverted to its customary lavatorial character.

'I didn't come,' said Nicole, clambering off him. 'And now I don't think I want to.'

'Perhaps we should have a bath,' he said.

In November Luke received a letter from the photographer saying that he was obliged to return to the city, would have to move back into his apartment 'sooner than anticipated'. The letter was phrased like this in order to suggest that their arrangement had been vague, flexible, even though the photographer had been adamant about renting his place for a year. In different circumstances Luke would have refused to budge. As it was it made little difference because he and Nicole were spending almost every night together, usually at her place which was bigger, nicer. Luke wrote back to the photographer and claimed that he was being severely inconvenienced. He'd counted on being there a year, he said, had even spent money on having the bike repaired. The photographer phoned and offered to let him off three weeks' rent. And Luke could keep the bike, he said.

'Actually,' said Luke, 'there is one other thing I would like, if that's OK.'

'What's that?'

'A print of one of your photographs. The one of the demonstration.'

'You like that picture?'

'I love it,' said Luke.

'I'm flattered,' said the photographer.

'When did you take it, by the way?'

'I can't remember exactly. But I'd only been in Bucharest a day—'

'Bucharest?'

'I'd just got in and this demonstration blew up and I shot off a whole roll of film. There were a couple of good shots but that one on the wall was far and away the best. Anyway, I can get you a copy no problem,' said the photographer

'That would be great,' said Luke. 'Thank you.' He hung up and called Nicole. 'You know that picture?' he said. 'The Belgrade one.'

'Yes.'

'It was taken in Bucharest.'

'No!'

'I just spoke to the photographer.'

'I did go to Bucharest once.'

'How old were you?'

'Ten.'

'It's funny isn't it, how we persuaded ourselves that it was you?'

'Perhaps it is me. A Romanian me. There might be several of me.'

'There could never be another you,' sang Luke.

A few days later he moved into her apartment. Luke's only concern about this change in circumstances was that he now had little or no chance of protecting his property. Nicole had a knack of filling her apartment and life with things that delighted Luke – love someone, love their possessions had become something of a motto for him – and there were times when Luke would see her spectacle-case (i.e. her wallet) or her red string shopping bag, or one of her hats or shoes lying on the floor of her apartment and be so overcome with love for her that he felt like weeping. They were *her* things. Everything she touched became suffused with her personality. Nicole herself was aware of this capacity she had to lay claim to objects.

'I only need to have something for two minutes and it's completely mine,' she said to Luke as they unpacked his few belongings.

'You mean it's completely broken. Broken or lost.'

'That's not true.'

'Robust objects become fragile. Immovable objects disappear.'

'That's not true.'

'It is actually. What about my sunglasses that you borrowed two days ago?'

'I haven't broken them.'

'No. And the reason for that is that you lost them before you had a chance to break them.'

'They're not lost. I just mislaid them.'

'No, you *lost* them. Mislaid means you know where they are but you can't put your finger on them.'

'Exactly. I've mislaid them somewhere in the city.'

The days grew shorter. It became cold. As promised, the photographer mailed a print of the picture of the demonstration which they framed and put on the wall. Nicole was finishing her studies and had begun applying for jobs. With Christmas deadlines looming the warehouse became busier than it had been for months. Lazare was under a lot of pressure and therefore happy. Luke and Alex worked late. The flu season started. Nicole stayed in bed for three days, coughing constantly. At night the sheets became so drenched and cold with her sweat that they had to get up and change them. Luke resigned himself to catching Nicole's flu and as soon as she felt well enough to get up he began to feel lousy. He still felt bad when he felt better. Alex avoided flu but went down with a cold that, at any other time of year, would have passed for flu. Sahra remained healthy which was fortunate because there was a sudden rush of well-paid interpreting jobs. Christmas decorations went up on rue de la Roquette. A series of power cuts left the quartier in freezing darkness. It was too cold to play football. Sealed in against the weather, cafés became intolerably smoky – even more intolerably smoky than they were the rest of the time. Lazare decided to throw an impromptu – and somewhat premature – Christmas party. We all had to come, he said, and in the unlikely event of any of us having girlfriends or wives they should 'get drunk at my expense too'. Nicole, Sahra and Sally came and were all shocked by Lazare – shocked, that is, by how charming he was. In the presence of women his belligerence was transformed into equally extravagant courtesy. Luke's friend Miles came too, and some other pals of Lazare's. Everyone got drunk and danced and went away happy and those of us who worked there came back the next day, hung over, and cleaned everything up.

The Cassavetes season had finished months ago but an Antonioni season had just begun. The four friends went to see every film, too stunned by boredom and colour and space even to consider leaving. In the black-and-white films there was no colour to be seen, just the space and the boredom and people saying things. Some of what was said was lost on Luke because the dialogue was often in Italian and the sub-titles in French. They were all in love with Monica Vitti, especially her green dress in *Red Desert*. Nicole liked the way the photos in *Blow-Up* became clearer as they were enlarged.

'That was amazing,' said Luke when they came out of *L'Avventura*.

'Amazingly boring, you mean?' said Sahra.

'Yes, exactly.'

At weekends they went dancing. Luke, Sahra and Alex took Ecstasy. Nicole didn't want to and this became an issue between her and Luke. Nicole was adamant that she did not need to take drugs in order to enjoy anything. She was happy to get stoned – which she had done only occasionally before meeting Luke – but she drew the line at anything chemical.

'That's so stupid, Nicole,' said Luke. 'Dancing is much better if you take E.'

'But I love dancing anyway.'

'That's not the point. The point is that everything can always be improved.'

'How can you ever be happy if you think that?'

'How can you ever be happy if you don't?'

'What does *that* mean?'

'It means everything can always be improved by drugs. It's just a question of fitting the substance to the activity in question. Or finding the right activity for the substance. You admit that listening to music is much better if you're stoned, right? And dancing is much better if you take—'

'For you, yes.'

'For everyone.'

'But I don't *want* to take it. I don't try to persuade you not to. So why do you try to persuade me to?'

'Because you're missing out on something great. It can get to the point where there's nothing but lights and music. You can feel yourself dissolving as an individual. You can feel yourself not existing.'

'I love my existence.'

'And we could do all that kissy-feely stuff you see people doing.'

'We can do that anyway,' said Nicole. 'We can do it now if you like.'

Eventually Nicole was persuaded – by Sahra, who loved it – to try a half when they went to their favourite club, The Coast, as this near-derelict space bizarrely called itself.

The evening began at the cinema. *Strange Days* was showing and, as the lights went down, the four of them passed a bucket-sized Coca-Cola – 'small' by the gigantic standards of cinematic refreshment – along the row and swallowed their pills. Luke had seen the movie twice before but this time it blew his mind, totally. Coming up, he began to feel – in the film's millennial argot – like he was wire-tripping, not so much seeing the film as jacking into it, living the experience of a movie which was a commentary on all the movies it had come out of: a pastiche of everything, even itself. Oh, it was perfect, perfect as the playback of Faith in her T-shirt and black bikini bottoms, teaching Lenny Nero how to roller-blade, and then heading back to the apartment and undressing in front of him. 'So,' she says, 'you want to watch or you going to do?' And Nero, sitting in his lousy apartment, looped into the past, feels and hears and sees himself say, 'Watch and see.' 'I love your eyes Lenny,' she says, moving beneath him. 'I love the way they see.'

The apocalyptic party at the end of the film made them so desperate to get to the club that they practically ran there. As soon as they checked their coats they were like dogs let off a leash. The dance floor was crowded, the music pumping. With every track the surge of the music deepened. The lights poured into their faces. Under Nicole's tuition Luke's dancing had improved to the extent that he was no longer, in Alex's words, 'quite the embarrassment he used to be'. If it still seemed like he was having a seizure it was at least a rhythmic one. Luke looked at Nicole and Sahra. They had their arms round each other, laughing. Sahra moved over to Alex and they began dancing together. Nicole danced over to Luke and kissed him. She was wearing a sleeveless white dress, plimsolls.

Her eyes were wet with laughter. Luke touched her arms, still dancing. The music surged and returned and paused, surged even while pausing, paused and surged and pumped again. The only light was a strobe: Luke saw Nicole's arms and hair, coming and going, illuminated and vanishing, crackling into view and disappearing. Smoke began pouring on to the dance floor, so thick it was impossible to see. The trance deepened. The light became solid: purple, then green, then gold. Luke could see no one, not even Nicole, not even his own arms. There was no distance or direction, only the impenetrable light, the endless pump of the music.

Their eyes were still as wide as planets when they left the club, just as it was beginning to get light. Being outside made them realize how out of it they still were. It felt less like the city was getting light, more like it was reconstituting itself, as if it hadn't been there in the night, as if it had dissolved and now, in the grey non-light, was becoming substantial again. As it did so they saw things they wouldn't otherwise have noticed: bits of buildings, architectural details whose names only Nicole knew. It became lighter as they walked. At boulevard Richard Lenoir the market stalls were being assembled. Vans were crowded with boxes of fresh produce. Scales were being set up, prices written on cards. The immensity of the effort of getting the produce here – sowing, planting, ploughing, growing, digging up and transporting – seemed out of all proportion to the end results which, when all was said and done, were only versions of the onions, carrots and potatoes they had eaten for dinner the night before. It didn't make sense.

'It would be nice if somewhere was open,' said Sahra.

'We could try the Kanterbrau,' said Luke. The sky was

blue-grey now, birds were already flying in it. The Kanterbrau had just opened. They were the first customers. No one knew what to order, whether to opt for a night-cap or a morning coffee. Luke fancied a refreshing lager. Alex thought he'd have a refreshing lager too. Nicole wanted an orange pressé. Sahra was ready for coffee. Alex changed to coffee and so did Luke. Then he changed to an orange juice and the waiter trudged off, undaunted.

They were still full of chemically engendered expectation but that anticipation was gradually coming to refer to the past, to something that had already taken place. They were wide awake, distracted, glowing. They said things without being sure who had said them. Speaking and listening had become indistinct. Alex paid for the drinks. Their bodies were still full of the pump and colour of the music so they went back to Luke and Nicole's and danced some more. When Alex and Sahra had gone home Nicole took a shower. She came back into the main room, wrapped in a towel.

'Do you want to watch or do?' she said.

After a few hours' sleep the four were back together, still spaced out, tired and not tired, overcome by a lovely nostalgia for events that had taken place only hours earlier. Luke squeezed a jug of orange and carrot juice and then, as soon as they had drunk that, he made another jugful, this time adding a knuckle of ginger. Sahra lay with her head in Nicole's lap, drifting. Alex played records. They danced some more and reminded each other of things they had seen and felt the night before, in the club and in the film, the two parts of the evening becoming more and more deeply intermingled as they did so.

Alex and Sahra left, Nicole went to lie in the bath 'for two or three hours'. Luke tidied up and switched on the TV: rugby. With the sound turned down he forgot he was in France. He sat facing the screen, feeling suddenly alone, worn-out, dejected. The door-bell rang: Alex, back for something Sahra had left behind. As Luke opened the door to let him in he felt a surge of déjà vu. When Alex had retrieved Sahra's bag Luke returned to the TV, trying to locate the origin of that sensation, the original experience of which he had just felt the tantalising echo.

He couldn't, of course, you never can, because although that misleadingly named sensation sends you scurrying into your past, the moment it urges you towards is *that* moment itself. And at that moment you glimpse the Eternal Recurrence as a potential fact, as a mechanism, rather than a metaphor. That is the solution contained in the riddle of déjà vu. All memories are premonitions, all premonitions are memories.

For her part, Nicole was converted; after that weekend the four of them always took E when they went out dancing.

They also decided to spend Christmas together – without having any idea of what they would do or where they would go. Ideally they wanted to find a house in the country and spend the holiday there. Sahra had an uncle who, she thought, owned a house somewhere. She wrote to him the next day but heard nothing back. Staying in the city seemed a dismal option but, they agreed, if the worst came to the worst they would do that. They would cook a huge meal, get high, and let the day ripple over them.

In the meantime, in various permutations, they went

shopping for Christmas presents for each other. Sahra and Alex went looking for presents for Luke and Nicole; Nicole and Sahra went looking for gifts for Alex and Luke. Luke didn't go with anyone because he hated shopping.

'We've tried to do it a couple of times,' Nicole said to Sahra as they drifted round Magasin. 'But then, after about ten minutes, before we've even tried anything on, he starts moaning about how expensive everything is. We always end up just going for coffee or to a film. The only thing he likes doing is looking at records.'

'We go all the time,' said Sahra. 'I try on expensive cocktail dresses and Alex tries on expensive suits. Sometimes we even buy things. Not expensive things. Oh, let's go into lingerie.'

'Actually, that's one of the things Luke *does* like to buy. Or at least to look at.'

'Alex too.'

'We'll probably bump into them.'

The first displays were of night-gowns. Then girdles, substantial brassières and large comfortable undergarments. As they walked further into lingerie, the items became progressively skimpier, more revealing, so that the shop seemed to be undressing itself. Then, gradually, lingerie gave way to shimmery evening wear.

'What now?' said Nicole.

'I'd like a coffee.'

'You're as bad as Luke! Actually I'd love a coffee too.'

They went to a café on rue Saint Honoré. The waiter brought their coffees and a handful of sugar cubes. The wrapping of each cube was illustrated with the flag of a different country. Nicole held them up one by one and Sahra tried to guess which country was represented. First was a tricolour: a white stripe bordered by two greens.

'Nigeria,' said Sahra.

'Good,' said Nicole. She held up another tricolour: red white and green, with a tiny emblem in the middle of the white.

'Mexico.'

'Very good,' said Nicole, picking up a red flag with a yellow star in the centre.

'Vietnam.'

'You'll never get this one.' It was an absurdly crowded flag: four horizontal bands – blue, white, green, yellow – a red stripe running down the middle and a yellow star in the top left-hand corner.

'Central African Republic,' said Sahra without hesitation.

'How did you know that?'

'Alex and I were at a place with the same sugar last week. The same ones came up.'

'Cheat! What a coincidence though.'

'Not really. They're only the flags of coffee-producing countries.' Nicole threw the Central African Republic at Sahra. 'Alex wanted to get Luke to come to a place where they have the same sugar and bet on how many countries he could name,' said Sahra. 'He knew Luke wouldn't be able to resist it and he'd make a fortune out of him.'

'He would have, I'm sure.'

'I don't think I'm in the mood for serious shopping today,' said Sahra.

'Me neither.'

'Shall we go to a film instead?'

'What would you like to see?'

'I don't know, we'll have to look in the paper.'

'It's a shame Luke's not here. He spends so much time checking the times of films in *Pariscope* that he knows them off by heart.'

'And Alex.'

'They're funny aren't they, these English men?'

'Nothing they say is serious.'

'And everything is.'

'Yes.'

'Still, at least they dress nicely.'

'Too bad they look like working at that warehouse for the rest of their days.'

'They love it there.'

'I know. But it's strange not to have *any* ambition, don't you think?'

'Luke is so lazy. He claims he came to Paris intending to write a book. I think he wrote about half a page. If that. And he has this idea of doing some stupid film about the 29 bus but he never will, I'm sure. He *has* learned some French but basically as long as he can play football, sleep with me, get stoned, go for drinks at the Petit Centre with Alex and go dancing at the weekend with the three of us he's perfectly happy.'

'Alex is the same.'

'At least he can speak French. And he's not *obsessed* by those things.'

'Only because he's got Luke to do his obsessing for him.'

'Actually, do you know what I think Luke is really obsessed by?'

'You?'

'No. Happiness. For most people it's incidental, almost a side-effect. But all of Luke's energy – and that's why he's so unambitious in other ways – is focused on living out his ideal of happiness.'

'Then I *was* right,' laughed Sahra. 'You're the embodiment of that ideal.'

MC Solaar came on the radio or jukebox or whatever it was. The two women knew the song well and sang the first line together: '*Le vent souffle en Arizona . . .*' Then they drank their coffees, tapping the table, listening.

> '*Il erre dans les plaines, fier, solitaire*
> *Son cheval est son partenaire*
> *Parfois, il rencontre des Indiens . . .*'

'*Alex* est son partenaire,' laughed Nicole.

'They're like that aren't they?'

'*Et nous sommes les Indiens.*'

'Actually, that's been a big breakthrough for Alex. *We're* partners. Which is a very new thing for him. A few weeks ago he came across something in Saint-Exupéry about how love means not looking *at* the other person but looking in the same direction. He's taken to that like a religious conversion. I sometimes think we're more like friends than . . .'

Sahra paused because Nicole appeared distracted. She was thinking about Luke and, for the first time, was troubled by the way he looked at her, the way he was so obsessed by her beauty, by having the proof of his happiness before his eyes.

'I'm sorry,' said Nicole. 'I was thinking about something you said. Go on.'

'No, it was nothing. Nothing important.'

'Really?'

'Yes.'

'Do you ever think about the future?'

'Funny question. Why do you ask?'

'Because I never do.'

'I don't either. I think that's one of the things about taking E. It becomes impossible to think about the future. The present becomes all-consuming. Or at least the past extends back only as far as the weekend before.'

'And the future as far as the weekend to come.'

'Yes. It's actually a stupid drug, don't you think? You never have any thoughts at all when you're on it, let alone interesting ones.'

'That's probably why the boys like it so much.'

'No thought, only sensation.'

'It *is* bad for your head though, don't you think? It takes so long to get over it, and even when it's over it's not over. Two days later you mean to say one word and another comes out. You want to say chair and you say table.'

'You do that anyway Nicole!'

'That was only in English. Now I'm doing it in French too.'

'Maybe we *should* think about the future,' said Sahra. 'Shall we try it now?'

'OK.'

'Ready?'

'Yes.'

'Go.' They shut their eyes and thought hard for several moments, holding hands as if at a badly attended séance.

'Well?' said Sahra.

'Nothing.'

'Me neither. Unless you count Christmas presents that we still haven't bought.'

'That's better than me. When I try to think about the future I always end up thinking of the past. As if they were the same thing, as if the future had already happened.'

'How do you mean?'

'Well, Luke and I slept together the first night we went out and I think that's why. Although I hardly knew him it was as if I already knew him, as if we already *had* slept together. It wasn't like he seduced me – I don't think he'd know how to seduce anyone – or I seduced him. It was the most unsurprising thing that has ever happened. In some ways I feel I've always known him.'

'I know what you mean,' said Sahra. 'I can't imagine you not being with each other. Maybe it's because I met you both at the same time.'

'I can't imagine not being with him either,' said Nicole. 'But I *can* imagine him not being with me – but I can't imagine him being with anyone else. Whereas although I can't imagine me not being with him, I can imagine me being with someone else. Does that make sense? I'm not sure I followed it myself.'

'The really difficult thing to imagine is Alex without Luke.'

'Or vice versa.'

'It's like: buy one and get the other free.'

'Luke says they're like brothers.'

'That's because he doesn't *have* any brothers,' said Sahra, more sharply than she'd intended, as Solaar came to the end of his rap:

'Toujours à contre-jour, c'est bien moins héroique
Dans le monde du rêve on termine par un "happy end"
Est-ce aussi le case dans ce quel l'on nomme
Le nouveau western . . .'

The café was filling up with people and smoke. It was lunch-time.

'What shall we do now?' said Nicole. 'Shop?'

'Shall we not bother?'

'I'd love to not bother. Let's go to the cinema. If we see presents on the way we'll buy them.'

They paid for their coffees and left. As they waited to cross boulevard Sébastopol a car pulled up beside them. The women were looking at the lights, waiting for the illuminated red pedestrian to turn green. The driver waved, catching Sahra's eye. The women looked into the car: two men, young guys, both laughing. The men smiled. The women smiled back. The driver pointed at himself and raised his eyebrows as if to say, 'Moi?' Nicole shook her head. He pointed across at his passenger, looked at Sahra, and raised his eyebrows again: 'Lui?' Sahra shook her head. 'Non, lui,' she mouthed silently, pointing at the green man on the lights, stepping into the road with Nicole.

A week before Christmas, Sahra heard from her uncle: he *did* have a house, and while Sahra and her friends were welcome to use it over the holiday period it was probably best if they didn't. It had always been in fairly bad repair and since he hadn't been there for over a year – and, in any case, only used it in the summer – he had no idea what kind of state it was in now. He enclosed a map with instructions on how to get there and find the place where, if he remembered rightly, the key was hidden: if they were *determined* to go, that is.

Alex and Sahra were undecided. They called Luke and Nicole to see what they thought.

'It's perfect,' said Luke. 'The more decrepit the house, the more exciting the adventure. When shall we leave?'

That was another problem: Sahra's car. She used it almost as rarely as her uncle used the house and it seemed unlikely that it would be up to such a long journey. Alex was the only person who knew anything about cars and he knew almost nothing. He 'looked it over' – checked the water, kicked the tyres, cleaned the windscreen – and pronounced it 'ready to eat up the road'.

They set off early in the morning on the day before Christmas Eve. Sahra's uncle had written that there were no shops nearby and so, on the outskirts of the city, they stopped at a hypermarket and bought enough food and wine to last a week. Everyone else was buying food and wine to last for ever. The scale of consumption defied belief. In such a place it seemed insulting to buy in multiples of less than twelve. The queues at the check-outs – and there seemed an infinite number of them – were immense. Luke waited in line while the others went off in search of Christmas accessories: fairy lights, crackers, decorations. Their receipt, when they'd paid for everything, was almost a metre long.

The boot was already loosely packed with bags, blankets and presents and to make room for this great haul of provisions everything had to be re-loaded. The back seat and the floor around the front passenger seat were crammed with pillows, coats and cartons of food.

'There's no room for passengers. It's cargo only.'

'We'll have to eat everything now, just to make room for ourselves.'

Alex and Nicole clambered in the back. Sahra (who was driving) and Luke (who claimed he had to go in the front because of his long legs) piled stuff on top of them. Then Luke got in and Sahra piled stuff on top of him too.

The hypermarket had been on the edge of the city but this edge looked like continuing right up until the edge of the next city. When they finally hit the autoroute it began drizzling. Theirs was the slowest car on the road and everything that overtook them – cars, vans, trucks, coaches – threw up a grey spray that the wipers could only smear across the screen. The radio, likewise, proved incapable of making itself heard above the roar of the engine. They passed the time playing *Pariscope*: between them Luke and Alex had mastered the entire repertory schedule of Paris cinemas so thoroughly that if the women picked a film, 'any film', they claimed, then they would give the time and place where it was showing.

'*Jules et Jim?*' said Sahra.

'The Accatone, Monday, 17:55,' said Luke.

'Not bad,' said Nicole, checking the magazine. '*Days of Heaven?*'

'Le Champo, Thursday 13:50,' said Alex.

'*Paris, Texas?*'

'14 Juillet Beaubourg, 19:30, daily.'

'Incredible. What a waste of brains.'

'We can do it the other way round too. Give us a cinema and time and we'll tell you the film.'

'Studio Galande, Friday, at four o'clock,' said Sahra.

'Too easy,' said Alex. '*Le Mépris*.'

'Thursday at nine fifteen, Le Grand Pavois.'

'Now that's a difficult one,' said Luke. It was: there were four screens at Le Grand Pavois, showing a total of thirty or forty films a week. 'I'm not sure but I *think* it's *Blade Runner*.'

'C'est incroyable,' said Nicole, throwing *Pariscope* into the front seat.

'Actually,' said Alex, leaning forward, 'I've got a question for you, Luke.'

'Shoot.'

'You're watching television. Suddenly you realize there's a wasp crawling along your arm.'

'I'd kill it.'

'You go into a restaurant, the entrée is boiled dog . . .'

Luke said nothing. His eyes met Alex's in the rearview mirror.

'Tell me,' said Luke, 'have you ever taken this test yourself?'

'Within five seconds,' said Sahra, 'Alex will be doing his Rutger Hauer. I guarantee it.'

'I've *seen* things you people wouldn't believe,' said Alex. 'Attack ships on fire off the shores of Orion . . .'

Luke joined in and they did the last lines together, perfectly synchronised: 'All of those moments will be lost . . . in time, like tears . . . in rain.'

Nicole and Sahra did a perfectly synchronised yawn.

After three hours they turned off the autoroute and stopped for petrol and lunch in a smallish town. Sahra was not a great parker. As she reversed into a space she thumped into the car behind. Luke got out and looked at the damage.

'It's pretty bad,' he said.

'Oh no!'

'I'm afraid so. I thought it was going to be bad, from the

noise,' said Luke. 'It was an amazing thump.'

'Like this,' said Alex, hitting the inside of the rear door with his fist, exactly as he had done a few seconds earlier.

'Idiot!'

'An English classic!' said Luke, pressing his hand against the rear side window. Alex pressed his to the same spot on the opposite side of the glass: the prison visit handshake.

'I'm paralysed from the neck downwards,' said Alex as they prised him out of the back seat.

'From the neck upwards you mean,' said Sahra.

It was nice sitting cramped round a table, facing each other after sitting cramped in the car, in two rows of two. The menu had been translated into English of a sort. Luke ordered oeuf brillées or 'Scream bled Eggs'. The waitress was friendly and gave them several refills of American-style coffee. They also had a conversation about coffee which they all knew they'd had before, word for word, but this added to the pleasure of this particular rendition. They took it in turns to use the bathroom. Eager to get under way again, they paid for the meal out of the kitty (which made it seem as if no one was paying), pushed back their chairs and got up to leave. It was raining hard outside.

Nothing in the past has any value. You cannot store up happiness. The past is useless. You can dwell on it but not in it. What good does it do anyone, knowing that they once sat with friends in a car and called out the names of cinemas and films, that they ate lunch in a town whose name they have forgotten?

Alex drove the second half of the journey. Luke again insisted that his long legs meant he had to sit in the front and so the two women arranged themselves in the back.

'This is more like it,' said Luke. 'Men in the front, women in the back.'

'So has it always been,' said Alex.

'So will it always be.'

'Can we have the heater on?' said Sahra.

'It is on.'

'But is it full on?'

'Affirmative,' said Alex.

'How about another round of *Pariscope?*' said Luke.

After only half an hour's driving the four of them fell silent. Luke glanced round and saw that Sahra and Nicole were asleep. He nudged Alex's arm. Alex looked at the sleeping women in the mirror and smiled.

'Sitting in the front seat of a car in winter, looking at our women sleeping in the back. That's what we're doing now,' said Luke.

He was supposed to be navigating but soon he fell asleep too. Alex didn't mind. He enjoyed being the only one awake in the car. It had stopped raining. The sky was clearing. On either side of the road were fields of ploughed corduroy. The landscape became steeper, emptier, colder-seeming. Trees adjusted themselves to the gradient. There was less and less traffic.

Nicole and Sahra woke, then Luke who consulted the map.

'Are we there yet, Dad?' said Sahra.

'Negative,' said Luke. 'About ten miles from now we get off the main road.' The sun was disappearing. The tops of the hills showed grey-white, whiter than the grey of the sky which began glowing pink.

'I think we've come the wrong way,' said Luke, soon after they had left the main road.

Alex manoeuvred the car around. Luke suggested another turning which also proved to be a mistake.

'Your navigating has left something to be desired,' said Alex.

'I've done . . . questionable things,' said Luke, back in Rutger Hauer mode.

The light was fading quickly. Alex switched on the side-lights. They turned on to a minor road which climbed and curved back on itself. Trees appeared black and stark against the sky which was infused with a deeper flush of pink. Everyone in the car was looking out for signs now: it was important, Sahra said, to get to the house before dark. There was a narrow turning to the right and she shouted to turn down it: a single-lane track lined by trees, gloomy. Alex turned on the headlights. A rabbit scampered across the road.

At the end of the track they came to a house. It looked dark and unwelcoming. The sky was burning red through the trees.

Alex turned off the engine. They sat there, a little disappointed after the long drive. Luke cracked open the door and got out. The call of birds emphasised the silence. He tipped his seat forward so that Sahra and Nicole could get out.

'So this is Colditz,' said Alex.

The walls of the house were tinged green with moss. Drain pipes. Windows the colour of slate. A bird cawed across the sky. It was cold but this cold was less a reflection of the temperature as it existed than a premonition of the cold which would come at night. Puddles were tense, preparing to freeze.

They walked round to the back of the house. Following her uncle's instructions Sahra took ten paces to the left, walked towards a tree and then looked for a large rock, beneath which the key was hidden. Allegedly. There were several rocks, none of them particularly big – and no key under any of them. All the ground floor windows were shuttered so Luke and Alex searched for ways of climbing up to the first floor where there were a couple without shutters. The only possibility was to get on to the porch round the side of the house, go up one of the drain pipes – risky – and move along a ledge – even riskier – to a window that might or might not be locked. They decided to attempt it. Alex was standing on Luke's shoulders when Sahra came and asked what the fuck they were doing.

'Going up to that window there,' grunted Alex as he clambered on to the roof of the porch.

'Oh OK. But you could come in through the door if you like. It wasn't even locked.'

'See you inside, Alex,' said Luke, following Sahra.

It was dark and cold in the house, colder than outside. Sahra lit a couple of candles and got the paraffin lamps working. Luke began laying a fire in the huge grate in the living room. Fortunately there were some large logs and pieces of kindling by the fireside. The problem was that there were few small pieces of wood, nothing to bridge the gap between kindling and logs. Luke was secretly glad of the challenge. There were few tasks that he could perform well and he took great pride in his ability to lay fires. He placed sheets of newspaper in the grate and scattered kindling over the top. Then he rolled up pages of newspaper and tied them in knots, threw in more kindling and the few small pieces of wood that were around. Nicole began carrying things from the car while Alex, having scrambled down from the porch, went out to the woodshed in search of small logs. It was dark now.

Luke put a match to the fire. The paper blued into flame,

then the kindling crackled and blazed. The heat was sudden, tremendous. A few minutes later the smaller blocks smouldered into life. Alex brought in some medium-sized logs, 'almost dry'. Luke chucked them on and very soon the flames were replaced by smoke. Alex looked alarmed.

'It'll take,' said Luke, unsure if it would.

Sahra, meanwhile, had turned on the water and electricity. The wiring in the house, her uncle had said, was 'uncertain' and should only be used for lights (as far as she could make out there were no heaters anyway). This was not a problem, he claimed, because once the fire was going the back boiler would generate plenty of hot water ('enough at any rate'). In the kitchen there was a gas canister and a cooker with a kettle which she began to heat. Alex kept bringing in logs. Nicole had transferred everything from the car to the kitchen. By now the fire looked like it *was* going to stay lit though the living room was still chilly. The bedrooms were freezing, damp.

When the fire was blazing – 'as I never doubted it would,' said Alex – Luke took some logs from it and started fires in the kitchen and the two bedrooms. Soon these too were burning brightly and in each bedroom a mattress was propped against chairs to dry out near the fire, even though it was not clear whether the mattresses were damp or just cold. It seemed likely that in a few minutes the house would go up in flames but it seemed more important to generate as much heat as possible.

Luke began cooking while Nicole and Sahra sat drinking or dashed upstairs to check that the mattresses weren't on fire. The fire in the living room was roaring. The water began running hot. Alex rolled a joint and then he and Sahra took a bath.

After dinner they checked the mattresses, decided they were dry and made the beds. Sahra put hot-water bottles in both beds and then they sat in the living room not speaking: sleepy, enjoying being by the fire which Luke prodded and rearranged constantly even though the thick bed of red embers meant that it was self-generating. A new log – part of a fence post – gave off a tiny jet of deep green flame: 'because of the wire at the top there,' said Luke, tapping it with the poker.

Apart from the track leading up to it to they had no idea what lay beyond the house.

What lay beyond the house turned out to be fog. When Nicole got out of bed in the morning and pulled back the curtain she found that the window was blurred with condensation. The view did not improve when she wiped it. The condensation was outside as well: fog. Alex disputed this at breakfast. Fog, he claimed, was not condensation, but since he was unsure *what* fog was they settled for Nicole's definition.

Luke had become obsessed with the fire, with keeping it burning at all times. He spent the morning bringing in logs and piling them by the side of the fire so that they would dry out and catch as soon as they were thrown on.

'It's the caveman thing,' explained Alex. 'He's got back in touch with the prehistoric origins of his desire to regulate temperature. Vulcan, that's what we should call him.'

Sahra and Nicole decorated the house with streamers and silver and red tinsel. The living room looked so nice that Alex went out and chopped down a Christmas tree. They wedged it upright in a pot of earth, decorated it with the fairy lights and angel-hair.

It was not until midday that they were ready for a walk in the forest. Quite a production: sweaters, boots, scarves, hats . . . Alex had forgotten his gloves and had to unwrap one of his presents early. Then he rolled and lit a joint. At last they were ready to set out. The stillness was primeval, as if history had never happened. The fog was so thick that even nearby trees were indistinct. Nicole was wearing a red embroidered hat with ear flaps that made her look like a Mongol invader. Blurred and mossy against the grey, it was by far the brightest thing in the forest. No animals were straying. The calls of birds were eerie-sounding. Sahra shook the branch of a small tree. There was a long pause and then a few drips fell to the ground. Nicole could see Luke walking ahead. She turned to speak to Sahra and when she looked back he could no longer be seen. She called to him – 'Vulcan! Vulcan!' – and he walked back towards the others through the fog that had engulfed him.

'We should stick together,' Nicole said, surprised by how quickly she had lost sight of Luke. They walked on, had a sense, sometimes, of moving up or down a slope but apart from gradient nothing changed: just the greyness and the darker greyness of the trees. Luke had been hoping vaguely that they would become lost. Until they became lost, it seemed to him, they had not really given themselves to the fog; until it obliterated everything it was still only a species of mist. And then, gradually (even the speed of realization was in keeping with the blurred, indefiniteness of the fog) they did become lost.

'Does anyone know where we are?' said Nicole.

'No idea.'

'Nor me.'

'Nor me,' said Luke, understanding now that everyone had been slightly hoping that they would lose their bearings. Each of them had been content to give themselves to the directionlessness of the fog because they had all assumed that someone else in the group would not have done so and would be able to steer them back to safety. The idea of being lost was nice but now they were faced with the need to become unlost. Being so stoned did not help. Sahra was conscious of her damp feet. Soon it would grow dark.

'What shall we do?'

'I'm not sure. Panic?'

'My impulse, of course, is to start blaming someone,' said Luke. 'Nicole!'

'The problem,' she said, 'is that the fog is not thick enough.'

'Not thick *enough*?'

'In Siberia the fog is so solid that as you walk through it your body makes a tunnel. It remains intact for hours, long enough to trace your way back home.'

'If we had anything to tie we could tie it to trees to avoid going through the same place twice.'

'If we had a ball of string we could unravel it.'

'If we had a compass we could look at it and be none the wiser.'

'If we had a bar of chocolate we could divide it into four and eat it. For energy.'

'I have chocolate,' said Nicole. 'Who would like a square? Except for Luke, I mean.'

They decided to keep on walking even though they had no idea of where the house was or which way to go. After half an hour nothing had changed. It was growing dark. Usually when it gets dark the light changes, deepens, but here the descent into darkness was marked by a gradual dimming of the already dim light. It seemed possible that they would have to spend the night outside and wait for the fog to clear. They walked silently, anxiously. Earlier in the day they had wanted the fog to press in on them, to shroud their vision still further; now they were trying to peer through it, hoping it would suddenly disperse.

They continued walking – 'What else can we do?' said Luke – and then, when they had almost lost hope, Nicole saw a light in the distance. Hardly enough to be seen, just a faint square of yellow. And it was not even 'in the distance': it turned out to be less than fifty yards away. Within minutes they were home. The timing was perfect: they were getting near to temper loss, recrimination and tears but, like this, the afternoon took on the exhilarating cast of a catastrophe narrowly averted.

Luke threw more logs on the fire and started the fires in the bedrooms. He and Nicole took a bath and then, by a tacit understanding, both couples went off to their bedrooms and made love. The house was silent. Nicole and Luke lay under the heavy duvet, watching shadow-flames writhe around the room. Across the corridor Sahra lay in the crook of Alex's arms and then they fell asleep. When they woke Alex's arm was numb, dead. Luke got up and made tea and turned on the Christmas-tree lights. The angel-hair made the lights glow soft and wispy. Alex came down. They heard the bath running, footsteps, Sahra and Nicole's voices, splashing. Nicole lay in the bath, Sahra sat on the toilet, chatting, laughing. The two women thought nothing about being naked together but neither appeared naked in front of the other's boyfriend; the two men – who were sitting at the kitchen table, chatting, laughing – never appeared naked in front of each other.

It was Christmas Eve.

In his Christmas stocking the next day Luke found underpants, socks and a purple baseball cap.

'Do you like your presents?'

'Yes,' said Luke.

'They're intimate presents.'

'They're lovely.'

'The underpants are intimate because you'll wear them against your bottom. The socks are intimate because you'll wear them against your feet.'

'Right. And the hat is intimate because I'll wear it against my better judgement.'

'You don't like them do you?'

'I do. I promise. Here's your stocking,' he said, handing it to her. She unwrapped a pair of ear rings, a tube of the chocolates she loved, and the skimpiest pair of white knickers imaginable.

'You must be joking.'

'Are they too big?'

'If they were any smaller they wouldn't exist.'

'You'd be surprised how hard it is to get very skimpy knickers made of cotton. Once you get into that degree of minimalism you're into porno, a world where natural fibres cease to exist. Speaking of porno, there's one present you've still not unwrapped.'

Nicole unwrapped it gingerly: a vibrator: in special seasonal packaging.

'Oh how lovely. An electronic toothbrush. Thank you.'

'Merry Christmas.'

'Luke, you are too much.'

'You've no idea how embarrassed I was buying that. If it hadn't been for the holly on the box I don't think I could have gone through with it.'

'Have you bought me anything that isn't totally perverted?'

'That depends,' said Luke.

The rest of the morning was spent cooking and wrapping up the 'official' gifts. An atmosphere of benevolent conspiracy prevailed as the four friends arranged themselves in different rooms to wrap each other's presents. In order to increase the sense of overflow and abundance Nicole and Sahra began wrapping up bottles of wine from the communal hoard. Alex and Luke joined in by wrapping up a selection of other communal items.

They pulled the crackers (which were useless) and ate lunch wearing coloured paper hats, always on the look-out for the chance to say, 'Are you still with us, Trevor?' The presents were unwrapped after lunch, between the roast and the pudding no one felt like eating. Nicole had bought Luke a sweater that he had seen in a shop but which, at the time, he could not face trying on. She unwrapped the present Luke had bought her and found a Polaroid camera. From Alex, Sahra got exactly what she wanted: a leopardskin jacket that was not made out of leopardskin at all. Sahra gave Nicole a pair of socks with toes on. Sahra and Alex had bought Luke a Walkman. Surprised and somewhat disappointed that Luke and Nicole had bought them nothing, Alex and Sahra moved on to the small items that the men had wrapped up. Expecting to find another pair of ear rings, Sahra found a tiny sachet of cocaine; Nicole unwrapped a chunk of hash; then Alex himself tore open the stash of grass he had wrapped up a few hours previously.

'Look,' said Sahra suddenly. It had started to snow outside, swirling silently beyond the window. Luke arranged four lines on a mirror like thin streaks of snow and they took it in turns to sniff them up with a red Christmas straw.

By now Nicole had loaded the Polaroid. They started with straightforward group shots, crowding round to watch the first pale smears appear, smudges of pink that traced the ghostly blank of a face. Background blurs became walls and shelves. Hair and eyes emerged, colours. After taking a few of these Nicole began running a fork through the wet prints so that the images, when they emerged, were patterned with luminescent streaks. Alex could not wait to have a go himself and proceeded to score a picture of Luke in such a way that red and gold antlers emerged from his head, like an extreme form of tribal head-dress, some trace of the spirit world, of his animal soul which the Polaroid had picked up. Luke loved these Polaroids, loved the way the present became a memory as soon as it occurred: an instant memory. When they had finished the first film Luke, feeling jittery after a second line of coke, immediately loaded another. He had bought the camera for Nicole but now refused to relinquish it. He wanted, he said to push the form forward, towards more abstract, less representational work in which the image was more severely distressed ('i.e. ruined,' said Alex on seeing the results). Many mistakes were made, and not only by Luke. Nicole wrestled the camera away from him, taking an unintended shot of the ceiling as she did so.

They were all feeling jittery; Alex rolled a joint to take the edge off the coke. Nicole claimed that she knew how to do multiple exposures but nothing came of her portrait of Sahra except the vague trace of hair and the black dot of an eye, like a fresco worn away over hundreds of years to almost nothing.

It was totally dark outside. They were still high from the coke but now they were stoned as well which was much nicer. Nicole said,

'I think it's time Luke, don't you?'

'Time for what?' said Alex.

'For us to give you your present,' said Luke. 'You thought we'd forgotten didn't you?'

'Not for a second!'

Luke went out and came back with a bulky, badly wrapped something. Sahra tore off the paper and found a reel-to-reel tape recorder – secondhand, obviously – with only one large spool instead of two small ones. Attached to the rim of this spool was a little red light bulb and, nearer the centre, a yellow one.

'So, what do you think?' said Luke.

'Well it's great,' said Alex. 'But, with respect, what the fuck is it?'

'It's something Nicole made. One of her Put-Togethers. Watch – and prepare to be overwhelmed with gratitude.' He turned off the main light. Nicole switched on the tape recorder. It whirred into life and soon all that could be seen in the darkness were two circles of quivering neon: a red and yellow catherine wheel.

In their bedroom that night Nicole and Luke took a series of pornographic Polaroids. They made love with the images of their passion coming to life on the bed around them: Luke's prick, veined, swollen, in Nicole's mouth; Luke with his face between Nicole's legs, his nose jutting over her pubic hair; the brilliant white of the vibrator – overexposed by the flash – disappearing into a flesh-coloured smear.

After they had made love they lay in each other's arms while, propped on the bedside table, the pictures went on developing, the colours darkening, the angles becoming more sharply defined, as if they were breathing, living.

The snow that had fallen tentatively that afternoon fell heavily in the night. The friends slept especially deeply because of the silence laid over everything by the snow. Luke dreamed of being asleep, which seemed to prove that he had slept as deeply as it was ever possible to. When he woke in the morning he was aware, first, of the silence. Not the simple absence of noise but a crisp, ringing silence. He looked at the Polaroids which, in daylight, seemed stunningly obscene. Outside, the trees were thick with snow that was still drifting past the window.

In the living room the fire had burned down almost to nothing. He raked the embers and piled on some kindling. When that began blazing he added a few small logs. He could hear the others moving around upstairs. Still groggy with sleep, Alex opened the bathroom door and saw Nicole, naked, one foot on the edge of the bath, rubbing moisturiser into her leg.

'Whoops!' he said, closing the door quickly. 'Sorry!'

As soon as Alex came down Luke hustled him outside. They threw a couple of snowballs at each other and then called up to Sahra.

'Look at the snow!' called Luke. He was standing in front of Alex, shielding him. 'Open the window.' As soon as she did, Alex let fly with a snowball that fizzed past her head and disappeared behind her.

A few minutes later the door opened slightly. A snowball exploded against it immediately.

'We're not coming out unless you promise not to throw anything at us,' Sahra called. There was no answer. Again there was only the silence of the snow. 'Quick!' said Sahra to Nicole. They dashed out of the door and were caught in a crossfire of snowballs. They cowered and screamed and then, suddenly, alliances changed. While Luke was packing snowballs to throw at the women Alex tackled him from behind and pinned him to the ground while Sahra and Nicole, screaming, shoved handfuls of snow down his collar and trousers. Then they went inside for breakfast.

In the afternoon, when it had stopped snowing, they set out on another stoned walk. Two days earlier the forest had seemed uniformly dense; now they could see that there were large patches of open ground, swathes of untouched snow.

'Nothing but coke,' said Luke, 'as far as the eye can see.' They walked for an hour, skirting the edge of the forest, tramping through perfect snow. They had all been so terrified of getting cold that they now found themselves sweating under too many layers of clothes. At times they sank up to their knees in drifts. They all wore sunglasses. Nicole had lent Luke her Mongol hat. Hidden behind his shades, Alex remembered her as he had seen her that morning, in the bathroom, his chest as tight as the snow creaking underfoot. Apart from that there was no sound. Then

Nicole thought she heard something. Almost like a scream. They stood still, listened, and a moment later they all heard the noise.

'I think it was over that way,' said Sahra, pointing. They walked into the woods, stopped and listened again, hearing the sound more clearly this time. They saw tracks in the snow: the tracks of an animal that no one could identify.

'Fox.'

'Deer.'

'Bear.'

'Wolf.'

'Too big for a wolf,' said Sahra.

'Big wolf,' said Luke.

They followed the tracks, obliterating them with their own. A few minutes later they came upon the dying animal: a deer, caught in some kind of trap. The snow was spotted with blood. Hearing them approach, the deer thrashed around in terror, its eyes wild. The friends stopped dead. Nicole buried her head in Luke's shoulder. Sahra was speaking to the deer, urging it to calm down but by now it was in a paroxysm of pain and terror. More blood began spraying on to the snow. The trap was self-tightening. The wire had already cut through one of its legs. The hoof lay like a wretched slipper on the blood-drenched snow. The other foreleg was almost cut through. The four friends stood where they were, hardly able to look, not knowing what to do. The deer was still thrashing around wildly. They moved back.

It was impossible to get a vet: there was no phone, they did not know if anyone lived nearby and, besides, the car had no snow chains. Alex said he had heard of something similar happening. The deer had been destroyed, he said. The only thing to do was to put the creature out of its misery but they had no idea how to do so.

'What can we do?' said Luke. 'Club it to death with branches?' Suddenly they were all laughing, shocked into hysteria. Alex suggested they cut the deer's throat or stab it to death with Nicole's Swiss Army knife. Their deranged laughter made the deer panic and they fell immediately silent. Blood splashed from its leg again. What seemed terrible was not the creature's injuries – though they *were* terrible – but its tenacity, the way it was obliged to hang on to life by a thread as thin as the fur and bone that connected its hoof to its leg. Resilience, clinging to life: that was what was awful. It should have given in, should have lain down and died but instead it persisted, wounding itself more grievously with every attempt it made to release itself from the trap its life had become.

'We've got to do something,' said Alex, moving forward. At that point, as if sensing that Alex's attention was focused on ending its life, the deer made a final lunge and its hoof came off. Blood sprayed over the snow. Nicole screamed and averted her eyes. The maimed creature lunged off, its two damaged legs sinking into the snow, leaving ghastly pink holes where it went. It was in agony but fear over-rode pain and it careered off through the trees. And *that* was the most terrible thing of all: to have it demonstrated so plainly that mutilation and pain were not the worst things that could be suffered, that it would endure these in order to evade whatever was represented by the four humans who watched it disappear. They were relieved to have been spared the effort of trying to kill it, horrified by the thought of the deer skidding and lurching through the snow on its ruined legs, dying later of cold and hunger. They turned away, leaving the two hoofs lying in the snow.

They walked back to the house in silence. Their footprints from earlier in the day were like evidence leading to the scene of a crime. They felt implicated in the cruelty they had witnessed. The sunset, too, dyeing the snow a delicate rose-colour, was incriminated, culpable. They saw no other animals on the way home, no birds even.

That night the four friends were quiet with each other. The deer's agony – 'all that shit with the deer,' as Luke and Alex would later term it – had tainted their stay. They ate the leftovers of lunch (itself the leftovers of the previous day's meal). Alex opened a bottle of wine but no one felt like drinking. Nicole washed up in the kitchen and stayed there when she had finished. Alex, Luke and Sahra were in the living room, sitting, not reading, not speaking. They heard Nicole moving around, putting away plates, heard her turn off the light in the kitchen. They expected her to come into the living room but there was absolute silence, as if she were standing very still. Then, after more than a minute, she walked in, quietly.

'Come,' she said. 'Quickly but quietly.' They followed her out into the dark kitchen. Nicole opened the door and stepped outside. The others followed. It was very cold. The sky ached with stars. The snow was lit by the light of the porch – and standing there was a deer, smaller than the one they had seen earlier in the day. It was standing quite still, on four perfect feet, its skin a light fawn colour. Its eyes were shining with the light from the porch.

'I was sitting in the kitchen, eating an orange,' whispered Nicole. 'And I looked up and it was standing there, looking in.'

Sahra reached for Alex's hand. Luke put his arm around Nicole's shoulders. The deer stood in the snow, breathing, twitching.

Then, unhurriedly, it turned and swayed off, picking its way through the snow, disappearing into the trees.

I want to tell now, as quickly as possible, a little of what happened later, much later. It should come after everything else, but I find that I don't want things to end like that, as they did. Perhaps that is what led me to tell this story that is not a story: the chance to rearrange, alter, change; to make things end differently.

The four of us remained extremely close for another year but we did not go away together again as we did that Christmas or the following summer (I will come to that later). Sahra and I began to see less of Luke and Nicole. There had been a time when all four of us had wanted the same things, had wanted to do the same things. We rarely noticed who proposed something and who went along with it. Then an element of give and take entered into our dealings; we became conscious of saying 'no' to each other. Sahra and I, for example, stopped taking E – we felt it was fucking up our heads but the more we took the less easy it became to tell how – which meant that there was a peak of intimacy, of rapture, the four of us could never reach together again. Saying no to E – or anything else for that matter – was like saying no to Luke.

Especially as what had seemed so vital and affirming about him ('yes, always yes') became, exactly as Sahra, half-jokingly, had claimed, simply greedy ('more, always more'). He fell for the easy part of the Rimbaud myth, the prolonged and systematic derangement of the senses, but – like many before him – he had none of the discipline or drive of the genuine artist and ended up with nothing to show for it, except what he'd done to himself.

By then I was seeing very little of him. He was too out of it too often. We'd begun to want different things. It was inevitable, I suppose: we had wanted the same thing for too long. There had been a couple of quarrels between us, nothing serious, ostensibly repaired – 'Forget it,' he'd said, quoting Nicole, 'life is too long' – but by then it didn't really make much difference either way. We were growing apart. Whenever we were together we were aware of how many things we no longer shared. Instead of great nights out we settled for those non-evenings that pass without incident because they were better than evenings that ended in argument, animosity or embarrassment. Sahra saw Nicole more often than I saw Luke but, according to Sahra, their meetings began to have the feel of diplomatic initiatives. She was worried about Nicole and had begun, almost, to despise Luke for her sake.

Not that he would have cared. He had changed, hardened. His idea of happiness became petrified. He was grabbing happiness, snatching at it. The feelings of euphoria and empathy which had marked our relationship from the beginning – and which had then been chemically intensified – had begun to turn into their opposites. Luke's happiness had begun to have a desperate edge to it. He was still aching after a possible future, some yet-to-be-achieved ideal, some crowning moment of happiness; then he realized – and this, I think, is what was so hard for him – that, far from being an intimation of the future, such a moment, a moment that had lasted for more than a year, was actually a part of his past, was already a memory.

He left Paris. He wrote from time to time, usually a post-card: a few lines, just about legible. We heard from him when he was living in America, and, later, in Mexico. Eventually he ended up back in London, which is where he was living the one time we met after he left Paris.

I was in England for the funeral of a relative. I had an address for him but did not want to turn up without calling. Directory Enquiries had no record of a Luke Barnes at the address I gave them. Feeling sure that it was pointless, that he would no longer be living there, I decided to go to the address anyway. I took a cab but asked the driver to stop a few streets away, by an Allied Carpets warehouse. I walked past a row of shops: a newsagent, a takeaway kebab place, an off-licence, the Taj Mahal Curry House, a small supermarket, a betting shop, a minicab office that had the look of a place under siege. The sky was full of dead light.

The address I had was for a block of flats. I pressed 5 on the entryphone and recognized the voice as soon as he answered. Just one suspicious word: 'Yeah?'

'Luke, it's Alex. Alex Warren.' I could hear the clunk of the phone being moved and that weird electronic hum that makes it seem as if an intercom has some kind of intermittent existence of its own. The pause went on long enough for me to try another question: 'How are you?'

'I'm OK. It's a surprise.'

'For me too actually. It was a spur-of-the-moment thing.

I was in London. If I'd had a number I'd have called.'

'What do you want?'

'Nothing. I just thought I'd see if I could see you.'

'D'you want to come up?'

'Sure,' I said quickly, as if it had not been a question but an invitation. There was another pause.

'Third floor,' he said, and the door was buzzed open.

He was waiting in the doorway, not smiling. I was shocked by how he looked: not because he had changed dramatically or terribly – or no more dramatically than most people we haven't seen for close on eight years. 'You look great,' we say in such circumstances and we say it because it is almost never true. We say it to buy time, to try to adjust to the way they look so bad. In Luke's case it was the subtlety of the change that affected me. His hair had greyed, but he was still thin. He was wearing a cardigan and dull trousers. His skin was stretched tight, his face looked sore from shaving. What was shocking was the resignation in his face. Anyone who passed him in the street could see it immediately, in his eyes, his mouth. His face had that unsupple look of someone who gets few opportunities for talk and laughter.

We shook hands: his handshake had not changed but, since it had never developed into the handshake he hoped it would, it *had* changed, totally.

'It's been a long time.'

'Eight years,' he said, standing aside to let me in. The flat was at least as dismal as the apartment he had moved into – and out of – on rue de la Sourdière. As soon as I stepped inside I could feel the loneliness, could smell the life he led: how he wore the same clothes for many days, how his body never got a chance to breathe. There was no variety in his life. Every day was the same as every other. It was too warm in the flat. The TV was on. Rugby. I asked him the score.

'I don't know,' he said. 'I'm only watching it because it moves.' We sat and watched the rugby, a game neither of us was interested in. Eventually he offered me 'a drink, or tea if you prefer'.

'I'll have a beer,' I said. I would have preferred tea but the atmosphere in the apartment was so unyielding that it seemed essential to try to do something to change it, to soften it. He went to the kitchen. I looked around the walls which were bare except for the photograph of the demonstration in Bucharest. I heard the fridge door gasp open and slam shut.

'Nice place,' I said when he came back.

'Sure,' he said, sitting down. I poured my drink carelessly: it was all froth. We held our beers and looked at the game. After a while, without taking his eyes off the screen he said, 'Are you still with Sahra?'

'Yes.'

'How is she?'

'She's great.'

'Do you have children?'

'One.'

'Do you have a photo?'

'Of the kid?' I said, reaching for my wallet. 'If you want to see it, sure.'

'Actually I don't. I hate pictures of children.'

The froth of my beer had subsided enough to drink. I said, 'So what about you Luke?'

'What about me?'

'How do you pass your time?'

'It's like Sahra said that day, at the coast. There is no more time.'

'What do you do?'

'Nothing. Actually that's not true. I wait.'

'For what?'

'For it all to come round again,' he said. We watched the game in silence. A fight started between two players and in seconds half a dozen of their team-mates were piling into each other. That was when I asked if he remembered the time we had beaten the guy up, on our way home from football. It was the only thing I said that afternoon that made him smile. We fell silent again. Then he asked the question I knew he would be unable to stop himself asking.

'Have you heard from Nicole?'

'Yes.'

'Where is she – in Paris?'

'Yes.'

'And does she have a child also?'

'Yes.'

'Then she's no longer beautiful. No longer a woman in fact. Once women have children they stop being women. They become mothers.'

I could have said something. I didn't. I was too . . . what? Not angry, something milder, indifferent almost: to the bitterness, to the hate I felt in him. To the hate he felt for himself.

There is an extreme form of meditation – I forget the name – which requires that you concentrate on your dead body, in its grave, rotting, crawling with worms, turning to earth, becoming nothing. I had read also of an American writer who, while doing something as ordinary as drying the dishes, found himself thinking of his dead mother, lying in her grave. Death appeared to him 'a force of loneliness, only hinted at by the most ravening loneliness we know in life; the soul does not leave the body but lingers with it through every stage of decomposition and neglect, through heat and cold and the long nights'. Both ideas are shocking but are they any more disturbing, really, than one we take almost for granted: that the soul rots, or wears out, like cartilage, *before* the body dies?

'I was going to ask how she was,' said Luke. 'But I think I'll leave it at that.'

'What happened Luke?'

'When? What? To whom?'

'You know what I mean.'

'To Nicole and me?'

'To you.'

'Nothing.'

I knew, from Nicole, some of the nothing that had happened. I knew about their last moments at the Café Bastille, knew that Luke had said he was leaving Paris, leaving her; abandoning everything, even himself. I knew that she had placed her hand on his and looked at him, and I knew what he saw: all the love in the world a man can ever be given by a woman.

'You know, Nicole,' he said, 'you've never once tried to restrain me. Never held me back. Never tried to stop me doing what I wanted.'

'I've never had to.'

'Not till now.'

'Not even now.' They were holding hands. 'Whatever you want, Lukey.'

'What I want,' he said, 'is for you to get up and leave. To watch you walk away.'

'Why?'

'So I can see you. So I can see you until the last possible moment.'

She gripped his hand. He moved his face towards her. They kissed. Then she moved her face and he felt her lips moving by his ear. She looked at his eyes that gave nothing back. Right up until the moment that she turned and left everything was reversible, saveable. The whole course of their lives, of our lives, hung in that one ordinary moment, indistinguishable, to anyone looking on, from the hundreds of other times that he had sat and watched her walk away. Perhaps that was why it was so easy for her to comply. They had rehearsed this moment so often that it required no effort, no will. As if nothing was at stake. She put her spectacle-case into her bag. Stood up, pushed her chair back into place and he watched her walk away, banging one table with her hip as she did so. He watched until he lost sight of her. He sat for a few moments, paid the bill and then stood up. He left Paris the same evening and, until that afternoon when I visited him in London, none of us saw him again.

After Luke left, Nicole came and stayed with us for a few days. Then she returned to the apartment but we still saw her every day. I remember thinking that it was less fun like this than it had been when there were four of us, all together. I remember thinking, too, that she would never recover from what had happened. I held her in my arms while she sobbed, could feel myself, even then, desiring her, wanting her. Several months later she went back to Belgrade.

We wrote, exchanged Christmas cards, talked on the

phone sometimes. She wrote to say she was married, that she'd had a baby. Then we lost touch for several years until she phoned, out of the blue, and said she was back in Paris. She had split up with her husband – her choice – and had come to Paris because of an offer of a job.

'So you're back for good?'

'I hope so. What about you? How is Sahra?'

'She's great. She'll want to see you. She's not here at the moment. When can I see you?'

'Whenever you like.'

'What are you doing this afternoon?'

I drove over to the apartment where she was staying, in the Thirteenth. She looked older, tired. We hugged each other. It was almost a relief to find that I was no longer attracted to her. Her face looked brittle. Her skin had lost its promise. She was still thin – like Luke – but whatever it was that had made her beautiful had passed. Maybe it *was* Luke's loving her that made her beautiful. Beauty, I thought, is a moment. It passes.

Her little girl was sleeping in the bedroom. She was three, a year older than our own son. We left her sleeping and went back into the kitchen.

'How does it feel to be here again?'

'It feels fine Alex,' she said.

'I spoke to Sahra before coming out,' I said. 'She's dying to see you.'

'And me she,' she said.

'It's great to see you,' I said.

Sahra and I helped her find an apartment, to get settled. We saw a lot of her. The three of us became friends again, real friends. I saw her more often than Sahra did. She had a great need to talk about the past, to tell things to me. I came to see that I was wrong. Beauty is not a moment. Or if it is a moment, it is one that can last for ever.

I had finished my beer. I said to Luke, 'Do you have any idea of how much unhappiness you caused?'

'I've done . . . questionable things.' That was the only thing he said that afternoon that made *me* smile. Then, serious again, he said, 'Do you have any idea how much unhappiness I have experienced myself?'

'Your choice.'

He shrugged. 'There's a café near here – I use the word café in its broadest, very unParisian sense – and I always go in there for a tea on my way back from the supermarket. The owner has a dog, a Dalmatian, and I go in there because of that, because I like the dog. When I went in there last the dog was nowhere to be seen. The owner said he was dead, he'd been hit by a car. And I sat down there and sobbed like . . .'

'Like what?'

'Like someone still alive.' I looked at my glass. 'Anyway,' he said, 'I was just telling you what happened in the café.'

'Why Luke?'

'Why am I telling you what happened in the café?'

'No. The big "why?" '

'That's a question I don't understand. It makes no sense. I don't think about that any more. "Why?" Because that's what happened.'

The game had ended. The two teams tramped off the field, caked in mud. Luke flipped through the channels. There was nothing on but he did not turn the TV off. I stayed another ten minutes. Then we said goodbye and shook hands and I walked to the tube.

It was not yet four and already it was almost dark. A black cab went by, For Hire, but I walked. It was not raining. There was a fifteen-minute wait for a train. I looked at posters for the latest films. London, England. It seemed awful to me: the weight of the place, the hardness. I was glad to be leaving the next day. I took out my wallet and looked at the picture of my son. A picture of a little boy like hundreds of other little boys. Except this was my son, Luke. He looked like his mother, like Sahra.

The day after getting back from what Luke had taken to calling their 'skiing holiday' Nicole took the train to Belgrade, to visit her mother. Luke saw her off at the Gare de L'Est. She pushed down the window of the carriage door. They kissed.

'It's nicer to part at a railway station than an airport isn't it?' said Nicole.

'Much. More cinematic,' said Luke. 'You've got the Walkman, yes?' She pulled it out of her pocket and held it up. Luke had some reservations about lending her his new Walkman. In his experience it was a good idea, as soon as you lent something to Nicole, to prepare yourself for never seeing it again – at least not in good working order.

'You won't break it, will you?'

'Of course not.'

'Or lose it?'

'No.'

'Promise?'

'I promise.'

A guard said the train was about to leave. A whistle sounded and the train began inching its way out of the station.

Luke ran alongside for a few yards, as you are supposed to. They called to each other and then they waved and then the train was gone.

When Luke went to bed that night he found an envelope under the pillow. Inside were two triangular pieces of black card, L written on one, N on the other, joined by a length of her hair.

Within four days Luke was beside himself. He gazed at the photograph of Nicole in Belgrade and the Polaroids they had taken. He pulled her knickers out of the laundry basket and masturbated with them pressed to his face. His head ached. He was suffocating. All his longing was focused on Nicole but it was exacerbated by everything he saw, even the photograph in *Pariscope* – of a woman squatting, her back to the camera – advertising a sex show. He translated it into an image of Nicole squatting over him, her cunt in his face. He shoved the thought almost physically from his mind but then found himself dreaming of her smell, her neck, her breath, her hair. Unable to remain indoors he went for a walk in the frigid air, hurrying in the direction of his old apartment and the Tuileries.

Grey boulders of snow lay piled up outside the gates of the park. Inside, the statues were rigid with cold. Having endured the blaze of summer they now waited out the brittle agony of winter. The trees were dark as iron. The sky was grey, heavy. Apart from that, as far as the statues were concerned, nothing had changed. Not even the old woman who sat there with her sign: 'DITES MOI'. She was wearing a coat, wrapped up in a scarf, sitting in the same place she had occupied all summer, carved out of a silence as extreme as that of the statues around her. Luke ignored her and, repeating *his* habit of the previous summer, went to the cinema.

The film was an adaptation of *Homo Faber*, a book Luke had heard of but never read. It began in Athens airport, in 1957, and then flashed back a few months to another airport, in Central America. The plane crashes and Faber finds himself stranded in Mexico. He gets back to New York and then decides to take a boat to Europe.

During the ocean-crossing Faber finds himself falling for a young woman called Sabeth. He watches her play ping-pong, and then he joins in, not because he wants to play but because he wants to participate in the act of watching her. When he is not watching her he is filming her with a super-8 camera, as if he were already anticipating remembered happiness. Every moment is a promise – of how it will seem on film, in retrospect, when it has passed. She tells him that his name, Faber, means forger of his own fate. From Paris they drive down through France and Italy. They become lovers, they travel on to Greece. Faber films her with his little camera, too fascinated by watching her speak to listen to what she says.

Words have nothing to do with happiness, they can only frame it. Happiness is a question of colours: the blue of the sea, yellow fields of rape, her hair against the sky.

In Greece Sabeth suffers a terrible accident. 'What was the use of looking?' Faber asks himself when he hears that Sabeth has died as a result of this accident. 'There was nothing more to see.' He is back at Athens airport and the film is back where it began. 'I wished I'd never existed,' says Faber, pale, devastated.

On the day of Nicole's return, still haunted by the film, Luke woke early. How was he going to survive until she came? The minutes were sweating by. He could hardly breathe. He had cut his nails down to the quick and put clean sheets on the bed. It took the will-power of a saint not to masturbate. He turned up at the station early and found that the train would be an hour late. He drank a shitty café au lait at one of the station bars, enjoying the commotion of departure and arrival, the rapid flick-a-flick of the departure board, the potential for robbery and harm suggested by the hundreds of strangers milling around in a place designed with getaway in mind. There was a sense of the whole of Europe converging here, on this station, and Luke at this moment felt that he too was in the precarious centre of something: of his life, of the life he had dreamed of. No, not the life he had dreamed of: the life he had willed, the life he had achieved. An unshaven man next to him lit up a cigarette. Luke left his coffee and headed to the platform.

The train curved into view, ground to a halt. The doors opened. Passengers began spilling out of the carriages, lugging their bags, embracing relatives, hurrying for taxis. Then he saw her. She was wearing a new coat, black. Her hair was long, loose, her skin pale. She looked tired, drawn. She walked down the platform, unhurried as always. She saw him. They were smiling, waving, then kissing. He breathed in the smell of her skin, her hair. He took her bag and they walked to the Métro.

'How was Belgrade?'

'It was like Belgrade.'

'And your mother, how was she?'

'She is happy. I showed her a photograph of you. She thinks you are handsome but immature.'

'Which picture?'

'The one of you when you were a boy, in the cowboy hat.'

'It doesn't do me justice.'

Sitting next to Nicole on the Métro Luke saw his Walkman in one of the side pockets of her bag.

'Incredible,' he said. 'I'd resigned myself to never seeing this again.' To his surprise it showed no obvious sign of damage. He checked there was a cassette and pushed the headphones into his ears. 'How was it?'

'Fine.'

He pressed Play. Nothing happened. He tried again.

'The batteries must be flat,' said Nicole.

Luke spent the rest of the journey wondering what he most wanted to do when they got back to the apartment: make love immediately or check that his Walkman was working properly.

As soon as they arrived home Nicole ran a bath and undressed.

Luke knelt in front of her, his face in her pubic hair. 'Let me lick you before you get in the bath,' he said.

'I've been on a train for ages. I need to wash.'

'No, before you wash.'

'I'm embarrassed. Is not too much?'

'No, it's beautiful.' She raised one leg, put her foot on the edge of the bath. He squatted so that he was almost under her, pushed his tongue as far into her as he could. She reached down and held his head with both hands, pressing his face against her.

Nicole lay in the bath, reading her mail. Before Christmas she had applied for a job in an architect's office and in this batch of mail was a letter asking her to come for an interview on the twelfth—

'Tomorrow!' she exclaimed. 'Luke!'

'Yes!' He was in the other room, hunting for batteries.

'I've got an interview for that job at the architect's. Tomorrow.'

'Good timing!' He put new batteries in the Walkman and went into the bathroom. 'The moment of truth,' he said, sitting, cautiously, on the toilet seat (it had never been fixed). Even with new batteries the Walkman did not work. Nicole stood up in the bath, began drying herself with a white towel.

'I'll take it back to the shop,' said Luke. 'I hope Alex and Sahra have the receipt. It must have been faulty.'

'Yes,' said Nicole, walking, naked, into the other room. 'Though I did get honey in it.'

In the morning she got up, showered and dressed while Luke lay in bed, watching her and her reflection in the mirror. He was always hoping that the mirror would begin to ghost but for months now it had worked completely normally.

'You know, I could spend my life watching you get dressed and undressed. However many times I see you naked I can never get over the shock of actually seeing you with no clothes on. And then, when I see you getting dressed again, when I see your pubic hair disappear into your knickers, when I see your breasts covered by your bra and your back by a blouse. Or when I see your legs going into your jeans . . .'

'Yes?'

'I don't know. I don't know what I was going to say. It's a simple thing but complex. Without clothes you're naked. With them, you're not. On the floor your clothes are just clothes, then when you put them on they're part of you.'

'That's profound Luke.'

'Maybe all I mean is I love watching you get dressed.'

'I like you watching me.'

'But you don't watch me in the same way, do you?'

'I've never been fast enough. You're dressed in less than ten seconds. Also watching's not the same as noticing. You don't need to watch to notice. Men watch, women notice.'

'Good distinction. Did you notice that I jerked off into your knickers while you were away?'

'I hope you washed them afterwards. How do I look?' She was wearing her smartest suit, green, shoes with slight heels.

'You always look beautiful.'

'Thank you.'

'Though naturally I would prefer stockings to tights.'

'Nothing if not predictable. See you later.' She kissed him on the cheek and put on her new coat, the one she had bought in Belgrade.

She was early for her appointment. The interviewer, her prospective employer, was late. His secretary made Nicole a coffee and said she could go through and wait in his office. She picked up the photo on his desk: wife and child, smiling, happy. She was surprised by how intensely she disliked this picture. It wasn't the people in the photo she disliked: it was the executive convention of *having* such a picture on your desk. The daily presence of the photograph, its sheer obviousness, probably meant that the executive-husband became oblivious to it. Pictures like that didn't help you to remember people, they helped you to forget them, and having one on your desk like this was a conventionally coded declaration of status: I am in a position to have framed snaps of my wife and children on my desk. And this advertisement, she suspected, was also a come-on. I have a wife and kids, the picture declared, therefore I do not try to sleep with my secretary or colleagues. But that statement somehow enhanced the chances of his being able to contradict it, to prove it wrong. By comparison the torn centrefolds, the oil-smeared nudes that mechanics stuck up on their workshop walls were images of felicity and integrity, faithfulness. She thought of the Polaroids she and Luke had taken: his face in her pubic hair, his swollen penis in her mouth, disappearing between the blur of her buttocks . . . If she became head of a company, she decided, these were the pictures she would have on her desk. Either that or the one of Luke when he was a little boy, in his cowboy hat. She was chuckling to herself when her prospective boss came in.

'Bonjour,' he said. 'Vous avez l'air tout guilleret.'

'C'est à dire, oui, je suis en train de penser à un truc tellement drôle.' She stood up, held out her hand. He was forty, handsome, smartly dressed, had kept himself in shape. She saw his eyes take stock of her, could almost see the thought bubble coming out of his head like in an American comic: 'Well, get a load of *this* . . .'

From that moment on it was obvious she was going to get the job.

She started the following Monday, the day the coldest weather for fifty years swept into the city like an invading army. It was so cold that Nicole was on the brink of abandoning her bike – unheard of – and travelling to work on the Métro. The cold was unbelievable, exciting. Things stopped working. Trains became glued to the tracks. Streets were stained with the frozen piss of dogs. Soil froze hard as iron,

iron became brittle. Fountains froze into meringues. News bulletins were given over almost entirely to discussing the weather (effectively, the news had been replaced by the weather). It was too cold to snow. Old people were urged to stay at home. The freezing winters of Chicago and Stalingrad were invoked constantly. Luke looked, aghast, at the electricity meter in the apartment, spinning round at the speed of a compact disc. He was better off at the warehouse, at Ice Station Zebra, as Alex had taken to calling it.

Then the warm weather – the weather that was simply cold as opposed to glacial – returned and life settled into its drab winter norm. It drizzled the whole time, as if the sky were a pipe that had frozen, burst, thawed, and was now leaking over the city.

At the beginning of March Sahra and Alex moved into a new apartment together. Alex's sub-let had come to an end and Sahra's place was barely large enough for her, let alone for both of them. They were getting desperate when they found the perfect apartment – at a far lower rent than they had expected. Since they were both foreigners and neither of them had salaried jobs, however, the landlord was reluctant to let it to them. Another couple were also interested and it was only by offering to pay six months' rent, in advance, in cash, by the next morning, that Alex and Sahra were able to swing it. Luke and Nicole – who had to ask her new boss, Pierre, for an advance on her wages – lent them half the money and the rest they cobbled together with credit and bank cards.

The apartment was over a watchmaker's. Right outside their window was a large clock which kept perfect time. Across the road was a cinema, so near, Alex insisted, that it was possible to check the time on the clock, see that the film was about to start and still get to your seat without missing anything. It was a good cinema but, over the years, many of the letters used to display the films that were showing had been lost. Substitutes were used – W (upsidedown) for M, N (sideways) for Z – but Alex and Sahra suspected that the programme was determined, principally, by the availability of letters. It seemed a good omen: the contingent letters of the cinema echoed the message Alex had constructed on the door of the fridge.

Nicole and Luke helped them move in and arrange the apartment (pride of place was given to Nicole's catherine wheel light) but, for them, the big event in March was the arrival of Spunk. Nicole liked her new job and had settled quickly into the routine of going to an office. It brought an element of stability and purpose into her life with Luke, creating the conditions in which they could think about acting on one of their longest-held wishes: to get a dog. They both wanted a dog but neither could face the responsibilities of looking after it. They wanted a dog that didn't smell, moult, eat or – heaven forbid – shit. No such breed existed. Then, in the aftermath of their worst quarrel, Luke found the perfect specimen.

It was a Sunday. They had been cooking lunch together: curry. Nicole was wearing the sweater she had bought for him at Christmas. Luke loved seeing her in it. He picked up a jar of pickle by the lid. The jar crashed to the floor and smashed.

'You know, one day I'm going to draw up a list of all the things you haven't put the tops back on,' Luke said as he began clearing up the mess. 'Maybe even sub-divide it, for ease of classification, into jars – glass tins, I mean – pots, bottles and tubes. Under bottles, for example, we would have:

olive oil, mineral water, shampoo et cetera. Under tubes, toothpaste . . .'

'You can't think of anything else that comes in a tube can you?' said Nicole. She was leaning against the cooker.

'Actually I can't, but the general point still applies. Put a lid on it.'

'Why don't you pick things up properly? That only smashed because you picked it up by the lid.'

'I'll tell you what Nicole. Put a fucking lid on it.'

'You put a fucking lid on it.' She had still not got the hang of swearing convincingly in English.

Luke kissed her. 'You know, the things I love about you are absolutely the things that drive me out of my mind with irritation too. I don't want you to put lids on things because I love the way you don't put lids on things.'

'But you wish I did put lids on things?'

'Exactly.'

'And it never occurs to you that I might be irritated by things you do?'

'Actually, now you come to mention it, no. Are there?'

'Yes, of course.'

'Like what?'

'The way you always splash in the bathroom, for example.'

'When I'm pissing?'

'No, when you're *wash*ing. You splash everywhere. You don't wash, you splash.'

'To wash is to splash. To wash brackets verb: to splash water on one's face. What's that smell? Is something burning?'

'I think so.' She turned away from the cooker to check what was burning and Luke saw immediately that it was his sweater. In flames. He grabbed the washing bowl out of the sink and emptied the soapy water over her. Water and cutlery sloshed and clattered to the floor. They stared at each other. She was soaking. The kitchen floor was drenched. The curry they had been cooking was awash with grey suds.

'You did that deliberately,' she said.

'You were on fire.' It was true but he had thrown the water over her out of anger as well as alarm.

'You didn't need to do that.' She was on the brink of tears.

'You ruined my fucking sweater,' Luke yelled, suddenly livid. 'You ruin everything you touch.'

'No. You do.' She pushed him away. He gripped her arms.

'You're hurting me. Let go of me.' He tightened his grip, dug his fingers into her arms as hard as he could.

'You fucking bastard!' She spat in his face, kicked at his shin. He let go of her arms and she grabbed a handful of his hair with one hand and clawed at his face with the other. It was agony. He felt like his scalp would come off in her hand. He yanked her hand free, shoved her away. She banged into the cooker and up-ended the frying pan of curry which slopped on to the already soaking floor. She grabbed the pan, threateningly, ludicrously, but by now the scene was too diluted by curry and washing-up water to sustain anger.

'Now look what you've done,' she said.

'What *I've* done?' said Luke. His face was burning where she had scratched him. His shin felt like it was broken. 'Christ, what a mess.' He moved towards her, hands raised as if in surrender, careful not to slip on the bilge-water floor.

When they had cleaned up the kitchen Luke limped out

for a walk. Nicole stayed at home. They were both stunned, exhausted by the sudden fury of the scene. They had quarrelled before but never as violently. It was like they had skipped three or four intervening stages – raised voices, heated arguments, recriminations, rows – and moved straight on to the fully fledged, all-out domestic riot. There was an element of novelty, of absurdity, to what had happened but they were both fearful that they had crashed through to that other dimension of domestic relationships where arguing and making up, yelling and apologising become the norm. Then the making up and apologising fall by the wayside. From there it is a small step to plate-smashing, hatred and attritional dependence.

At the Bastille Luke saw a weary Indian selling balloons. In addition to silver, helium-filled hearts he had a lovely Dalmatian: knee high, smiling, with a tightly inflated tail. He even had a little bell tied round his neck with a pink ribbon.

Nicole was sleeping when Luke got home. He lay on the floor and, using a broom, pushed the dog towards the bed. Nicole was awakened by the noise of the bell. She loved him immediately.

'He's the same one that followed us that night. The first time we went out.'

'Exactly,' said Luke, sitting on the bed.

'I knew he would turn up again.' She touched his face. 'Your face is all scratched. Does it hurt?'

'It stings a bit.'

'Is your leg OK?'

'It's broken but it doesn't matter. What about your arms?'

'They're OK.'

'You really do have a temper.'

'I'm sorry.'

'I'm the one that should be sorry Nic. I'm sorry. God, I feel like I've been dragged backwards through a Greek tragedy.'

'Me too.'

'That was some serious splashing back there in the kitchen wasn't it?' said Luke. Then he pointed at their new dog. 'What shall we call him?'

'Let's call him Spunk,' said Nicole who had developed a fondness for the crude English words she had learned from Luke.

He was perfect. He stood by the bed waiting for them to wake up in the mornings. When they came home at night he was waiting by the door, always smiling, tail wagging. They would have taken him for walks but that would have seemed like an affectation and so he remained a house dog. Nicole bought a bowl for him. He was no trouble. In no time at all he acquired a personality of his own. They loved him.

Alex was more sceptical. 'That dog of yours,' he said, 'has got an inflated sense of his own importance.'

'Very funny,' said Luke. They were due to play football. Alex had turned up for breakfast, as arranged, but Luke and Nicole were still in bed, drinking coffee. Spunk was by the side of the bed, eager, smiling. Alex was holding a bag of warm croissants.

'The clocks went back today,' said Nicole.

'Forwards,' said Luke.

'So either I'm an hour early or an hour late,' said Alex.

'Early,' said Nicole. 'Which is nice. The coffee's only just made. Have a cup.' Alex fetched a plate for the croissants. He poured himself a coffee, sat at the end of the bed. Sun was streaming through the window. Their clothes were piled on the floor. A large mirror was propped against a wall. Nicole was wearing a white T-shirt, spooning jam on to a croissant. There were bruises on her arms.

'Hmm. Fine jam,' she said in an improbable English accent. She looked sleepy. Alex pictured her sitting dreamily at her desk in school, rubbing her eyes. Luke kissed the side of her head.

'How many croissants did you bring, Alex?' he said, finishing his first.

'Six.'

'Great,' he said, plucking a second from the bag.

'D'you often have breakfast in bed?' said Alex.

'Oh yes. You see, we do so like fine jam,' said Nicole, spreading more on her croissant. A blob fell on the sheets and she began scraping it off.

'Actually we never have breakfast in bed because I hate spillage. Today was an exception,' said Luke, holding up both hands. 'Look at this. I don't know what to do with my hands. They're greasy from the croissants so I don't know where to put them. I can't get out of bed and wash them because I haven't got any clothes on and I can't put my clothes on because I haven't washed my hands and I don't want to get greasy stickiness over my clothes.'

'What are you going to do?' Nicole said.

'Make a run a for it,' said Luke, climbing out of the bed and dashing, thin, naked, out of the room. Nicole was laughing. Alex was aware of a dryness in his throat. He was surprised that the mere fact of Nicole's being in bed, a few feet from him, naked beneath her T-shirt, could generate such a tension.

'What's Sahra doing today?' she said.

'Nothing really. She's going to call you, I think.' He took a big gulp of coffee and looked at the window, the tray, the clothes in piles on the floor – everywhere but where he most wanted to. He glanced at the wall and saw her reflection in the mirror. She was looking away and he let his eyes rest on her image. He could see himself too, and then he saw Luke's reflection coming into the edge of the frame, his hair wet. Alex looked over his shoulder, surprised to find that Luke was already by his side. In the mirror Luke saw Alex as he had been a few moments earlier, his eyes fixed on Nicole's reflection.

Alex stood up and took the tray over to the sink where he washed the cups and plates more thoroughly than was necessary. Luke sat on the edge of the bed, one hand on Spunk's head, the other on Nicole's shoulder.

'What are you doing this morning?'

'I'm sleepy. Maybe I'll see Sahra.'

'I'll see you later.' He kissed her on the mouth, her lips buttery.

'Bye Alex,' she said. 'Have a good game.'

'See you Nicole.'

Luke and Alex walked to the station. Nothing they saw on the way there seemed worth mentioning. Alex said he was looking forward to the game. Luke too. A train pulled in as soon as they got to the platform. The carriage was empty and clean, new.

'We're going to be early,' said Alex.

'Yes.'

They sat in clanging silence for a couple of stops. Then Alex said, 'You know when you first came here, you were planning to write a book?'

'Indeed I was.'

'What was it going to be? A novel?'

'I suppose.'

'And what was it going to be about?'

'Ah, I never gave that much thought.'

'You had no idea what it was going to be about?'

'It was going to be about . . . Well, that's the funny thing. I suppose it would have been about the life we lead now. About you and Sahra and Nicole. About that house we stayed in over Christmas. It would have been about you and me and Nicole eating breakfast in our apartment. About our dog, Spunk. About you and I sitting on the Métro on our way to football . . .'

'Having this conversation?'

'Yes. Reflecting on things. So to speak.'

'And why didn't you write it?'

'I didn't have the faintest idea how to. It was just an adolescent idea.'

'There's still time.'

'But there's no need,' said Luke. 'What's the point? Why write something if you can live it?'

'Because you can't live it for ever, I suppose,' said Alex, getting up. 'This is our stop.'

It was only a five-minute walk from the Métro to the football pitch. They passed a homeless guy with a dog, hustling for change.

'That'll be you in a few years' time,' said Alex. 'Sitting there with your bowl and your plastic dog.'

'His name's Spunk,' Luke insisted.

They had been playing for less than ten minutes when Luke

stretched to block a shot on goal. He felt his foot twist horribly, forced round by the impact of his opponent's kick. His team-mates applauded the tackle but Luke could not play on, could not put any weight on his left leg. In minutes his ankle swelled up like an orange, then a grapefruit. He felt as if his foot had been torn off. His ankle was broken, he was sure. He sat behind the goal, on the brink of tears. Then, not even waiting for the game to end, he pulled on his tracksuit and told Alex he was taking a taxi home. Alex offered to come with him (Luke was emphatically not a taxi-taker, he had obviously hurt himself badly) but Luke urged him to stay and play on. He held his leg very still in the taxi, paid and hobbled up the stairs to the apartment. Nicole was still in bed. When she opened her eyes he began crying. Swollen beyond the realm of fruit, his ankle had assumed the colour of a bad banana, the kind of banana Sahra liked. He lay on the bed. Nicole put his foot on a cushion, wrapped a pack of frozen peas in a towel and wrapped the towel round his ankle.

'You should have done this straight away,' she said. 'And we should go to the hospital.' Luke lay on the bed, lost in pain, on the brink of throwing up.

At the hospital they waited for two hours to see a doctor and then waited another hour for an X-ray. The ankle was not broken but the ligaments were torn so badly that it would be best to have it put in plaster. The doctor said this as though there was a choice. When Luke asked if there *were* a choice the doctor said no, not really.

It was five in the afternoon by the time they left hospital with crutches and a bottle of pain-killers. Back home they found three messages from Alex on the answering machine.

Nicole was tender, loving. Luke had never loved her more: a predictable enough reaction, partly comprising self-pity, shock, helplessness; but Nicole, too, felt as if her love for him were being raised . . . no, not raised, the opposite: deepened. They had tapped into some elemental current that has always existed between men and women, that causes nurses to fall in love with the crippled men they are caring for. And this did not extinguish or run counter to the sexual energy between them. Having arranged Luke comfortably on the bed she undressed and knelt over his face. She closed her eyes and began stroking her breasts, reached down and separated her lips with her fingers. She stopped after a while and walked over to the filing cabinets. When she returned she knelt over him again, facing away from him, rubbing the vibro along her cunt.

After Nicole had come she said, 'Can you move over on to your side?' He did so slowly, careful not to jolt his ankle. He felt the slick touch of saliva and her finger slipping inside him. Then the harder buzz and pressure of the vibrator. He had never wanted anything more. He pressed back. At first there was a sensation of extreme tightness and then he felt himself open up. She had often pushed her finger inside him but he had never felt anything like this. It was as if he were dissolving. He moved his right knee up towards his stomach and felt her move more deeply into him. She touched his prick and in seconds he was coming.

'Now we're quids,' said Nicole.

'Quits,' he said, correcting her English for once.

For three days Luke didn't leave the apartment. Then he began hobbling around, going to the shops for milk, to the

Petit Centre for breakfast. The world had changed utterly in
the interim. Now, he realized, it was peopled overwhelmingly
by the halt and the lame. Everywhere he went he saw fellow
limpers, hobbling and shuffling their way through the world.
Infirmity was the norm. The highly mobile minority were
missing out on a fundamental fact of life: getting around was
difficult. It was like a premonition of being old, when even the
smallest task would require planning, concentration and
determination. Everything changed. Those men who levered
themselves along the street in gallant, hour-long expeditions
to the tabac for a Lotto card seemed less like unfortunates,
more like the elders of the city, gurus in possession of the final
secret of debility.

Lazare transferred Luke to what Alex termed a 'desk job'
at the warehouse: filling in orders and manifests, checking
deliveries. The lunch-time kick-arounds were starting again
and Luke went along too, on his crutches, feeling sorry for
himself, to watch. He was glad when the lunch break was
over and they went back to work.

An outsider might have thought it strange that we stayed
so long at the warehouse, working at what must have seemed
a dead-end job. It *was* a dead-end job but everyone was happy
to stay there. Several people – Matthias, Daniel – had vague
plans to paint, to write, to make films (Luke's *Route 29* was a
case in point), but no one showed any sign of putting these
plans into practice, possibly because working at the warehouse, surrounded by other people who had no immediate
plans to get on, made it easy to forget that in the world
beyond the warehouse people *were* making plans and films,
holding exhibitions and forging careers. And at the same
time, because the guys at the warehouse were working – as

opposed to being miserably unemployed – and because most of them were foreigners, working abroad (gastarbeiters, according to Alex), this easy-going purposelessness had an automatic element of achievement built into it. Besides, Luke insisted, it didn't matter if they weren't achieving anything.

'Life is *there* to be wasted,' he joked.

At her job, meanwhile, Nicole was becoming increasingly aware of the attentions of her boss, Pierre. He was approachable, polite, friendly, interested. He complimented her on her work, listened attentively to any suggestions she had about the projects that were coming through the office. He sought out her opinions and then, when they had finished discussing work-related matters, he asked her about films, books. They had lunch together (he paid). He found himself wanting to stand closer to her when they were talking in the office, drinking mugs of coffee. Pierre loved his work, was ambitious, had always looked forward to going into the office, but now what he most looked forward to was seeing what Nicole would wear to work, how she would wear her hair. He came to recognize her perfume. Sometimes she was sure she could feel his eyes on her back, the touch of his gaze. When she turned round he would be looking the other way, doing something else, but he was there, always. Nicole was efficient, reliable, friendly. She never flirted. Describing her to a friend at lunch one day Pierre said that what fascinated him about her most was her absolute chastity. What he didn't say was that he felt – as surely as Nicole could feel his eyes on her back – her to be a woman who would give herself utterly to a man. Her chasteness was somehow the outward proof, the external manifestation, of a potential for sexual abandon all the more alluring for being hidden, invisible. This certainty –

a conviction whose strength derived, paradoxically, from an apparent lack of evidence – drove him to distraction. He came to love and, almost, to hate her. He bought her a present – an expensive fountain pen – and then made light of it. On several occasions Nicole made a point of using the word 'boyfriend' but to Pierre this nameless boyfriend seemed just that, a boy who was not to be taken seriously, an impediment. When he heard that the boyfriend had injured his ankle this seemed less an accident than a manifestation of his physical inadequacy. The knowledge, the certainty, that Nicole's erotic 'potential' – and he found himself using that word frequently when telling her about future business ventures – was still to be unleashed, caused his attitude towards her gradually to coarsen. Pierre was urbane, charming, but Nicole was becoming increasingly aware of a leer in the things he said. As she came to know him better his charm began to falter. His habitual poise only just managed to prevent his flirting and innuendoes appearing crude rather than suave, suggestive. Nicole came to dread days that ended with just the two of them alone at the office: not because she feared him but – as she told Luke – because it was becoming tiresome dealing with him.

One evening Pierre pushed back his chair, took off his glasses, stretched his arms upwards and outwards to relieve – and signal the end of – the accumulated stress of eight hours of hard work, and suggested a drink.

'I'm sorry. I have to go home.'

'To your boyfriend? What's his name?'

'Luke.'

'Luke, yes. How is his ankle?'

'He moans and groans but he is getting better, I think . . .'

'It must be frustrating, physically,' said Pierre. 'For him, I mean.'

'He wishes he could play football.'

'I'm sure. Oh well, another time maybe.'

'Yes, for sure.' Nicole gathered up her things and put her jacket on. 'Au revoir Pierre.'

'Au revoir Nicole.' He watched her leave, noticing about her the same things that Luke had noticed.

The weather became warmer, the days longer. One particular Sunday, Sahra declared, was The Day That Was The First Sunday of Spring, the first day when it was warm enough to sit comfortably in the sun on a café terrace. The four friends met at the Café Bastille but the terrace was jam-packed so they went to the Kanterbrau which was also packed. All cafés with terraces were packed so they went back to the Bastille and waited for fifteen minutes before a table became available. It would have been an even longer wait if Luke had not had his crutches.

People were crowded together as tightly and neatly as an audience at a cinema but here they were both audience and subject; in watching everyone else they were watching themselves. Everyone had a part to play and everyone played the same part. In these circumstances, sunglasses – looked at, looked through – came into their own. Implicit in the idea of sitting on the café terrace was both question ('It's nice sitting here isn't it?') and response ('Yes, lovely') and all conversations were more or less elaborate versions of this basic call-and-response of reflexive affirmation: 'What better place to be in the world than here at this café?' 'Nowhere, this is perfect.' The friends sat together, playing their part, letting the sun warm them. It grew hot. Nicole took off her cardigan. Her arms were thin, pale.

'I've developed a liking for olives,' said Alex.

'I hate them,' said Luke.

'I've always liked them,' said Sahra who wanted to write down the recipe of a meal that Luke had cooked for everyone a few nights previously. Nicole thought she had a pen and began looking in her bag.

'Oh no,' said Luke. 'Every time I see Nicole looking in her bag like that I get tense. Implicit in the idea of rummaging is not finding, and implicit in not finding is losing: usually something of great importance, i.e. belonging to me. Oh how I used to love my property.'

'Used to?'

'I've had to renounce it as a condition of being with Nicole. Now all the things I most love are Nicole's. That is to say they *were* mine once and either she's broken or lost them, or has come to have absolute ownership of them.'

It was true. The surprising thing was that he had come to love Nicole's infuriating disregard for her – and his – things. Every time he saw her wearing a favourite dress – the blue one, for example, with the knotted halter neck that he had bought in a sale at the shop next to a place where they had eaten minestrone soup one lunch-time in November – was, potentially, the last. There was no telling how or when she was going to ruin or lose it.

After dredging the depths of her bag Nicole triumphantly held a pencil aloft. It was broken, unfortunately, prompting another bout of rummaging. This time she came up with a pencil sharpener, shaped like a jet whose cockpit gradually filled up with shavings from the pencil. Sahra wrote down the recipe. They ordered another round of coffees. Alex took off his sweater and said how greatly the discovery of fabric conditioner had improved his life. Luke also took off his sweater, revealing a T-shirt of which he was immensely proud. Across the front, in red letters, was written: TRY BURNING THIS FLAG, ASSHOLE. Sahra loved it too. Nicole was unsure. Alex asked him to put his sweater back on. Miles walked by, laden down with shopping from the market. Luke called out, waved. Miles called back that he couldn't stop: 'omelettes to make, wine to drink'. A young woman distributed green pieces of paper which demonstrated the deaf and dumb alphabet. She returned a few minutes later, smiling, silent, and picked them up again. A waiter, carrying a full tray of drinks, tripped over Luke's crutches. He looked like he was about to go flying but managed, somehow, to stay on his feet *and* keep the tray level. It was an heroic, awe-inspiring performance, applauded warmly by all who witnessed it, especially Luke. The phone box opposite was out of order. One person after another went in, tried to call, and came out looking disappointed and, surrounded as they were by the many people using mobile phones, anachronistic. Trees were coming into leaf. The traffic lights went about their business.

'What shall we do next?' said Alex.

'Sit here some more,' said Sahra.

'We could ride the 29,' said Luke. 'That is, we *could* ride the 29 if it wasn't a Sunday.'

'When are we going to start shooting the movie Luke?'

'*Route 29*? Today would have been perfect but the frigging 29 doesn't run on a Sunday.'

'Plus there is the small obstacle of not having a camera,' said Sahra.

'A mere detail,' said Luke. They sat just looking for a while. At each other and the people going by, looking at the people who were sitting down, looking.

'What about *seeing* a film?' said Luke. 'As opposed to making one.'

'In this weather? Crazy.'

'A searing indictment of racism, that's what I'm in the mood for. Or maybe a film noir where people are always turning up their collars against the rain and throwing cigarettes into gutters.'

'Or throwing away the murder weapon.'

'A great trope, that.'

'They're all lovely tropes.'

'Some are horrible,' said Sahra. 'I hate the laugh that turns into a deranged cackle.'

'I hate that too,' said Nicole.

'Me too.'

'And me.'

'I like the Styrofoam cups that the cops drink coffee out of on a stake-out. Sitting in a car, eating burgers and drinking out of Styrofoam cups.'

'Tossing the Styrofoam cups out of the window and squealing the car round when the dealer – "It's him!" – finally shows.'

'Or drinking out of them in the overworked precinct. A place where the phones are always ringing.'

'Hookers being brought in.'

'Handcuffed Chicanos.'

'The phones always ringing.'

'Desks crowded with papers and Styrofoam cups.'

'The Styrofoam cup is crucial. It's easier to knock over

when you're rummaging through your papers on your over-worked desk. The spilled coffee adds to the chaos.'

'Also to throw it in the bin in the corridor as a way of emphasising a point. Walking along a corridor, tie askew, on your way to interview—'

'Q and A.'

'Right. The shooter—'

'The perp.'

'Right again. Shoulder holster revealed. Tie askew, drinking coffee from a Styrofoam cup, draining the last drops and throwing it in the bin.'

'Maybe we *should* go to a film,' said Alex. 'Could you pass me *Pariscope*, please Sahra?'

An hour later they were in the cinema, watching a film from the pre-Styrofoam era: *The Man With the X-ray Eyes*.

'A parable,' claimed Alex afterwards, 'if ever there was one.'

A month after trashing his ankle – a month of shoving knitting needles down the cast to ease the itching which doing so exacerbated – Luke had the plaster removed. He was shocked when he saw his leg, amazed at how withered, white and useless it had become. The physio instructed him in exercises to build up the muscles in his legs and to restore movement in his ankle.

'Comme exercice y'a pas mieux que la natation,' said the physio. 'Faut nager!'

'Je déteste nager,' said Luke.

But he *did* like the swimming costume that Nicole bought herself the day after his plaster came off. It was yellow, a one-piece, but so much of that piece had been left out that it looked, if such a thing were possible, like an all-in-one bikini. Nicole swam twice a week at the pool on Alphonse Baudin but this costume, she said, was only for best. Luke took a Polaroid of her wearing it, smiling, patting Spunk on the head, framed by a sky so blue it was impossible to tell that it was taken indoors, by the window in their apartment. This, Luke discovered, was one of the great features of Nicole's apartment: the distinction between outdoors and indoors was not absolute – which is why, by the time he took that picture, Nicole was already slightly tanned. When the sky was clear it was possible to lie stretched out on the floor for an hour in the afternoon, bathed from head to foot in sun. As the summer approached so the length of time that the sun perched in the right place extended itself. Luke loved to watch her lying there, naked, her breasts rising and falling slightly, her hair streaming over the red cushion. Looking at her, it seemed to Luke, was a form of thinking.

On one occasion, as she dozed, he took down from the shelves the anatomy textbook that had belonged to her father. Photos showed the body stripped of successive layers: clothes, skin, fat, muscle. There was not a drop of blood to be seen, hardly even a hint of red or pink. Cuts and injuries revealed a pulsing arterial richness; these photos showed a world of uncured, brownish leather. Luke kept looking from the pages of the book to the naked woman lying asleep on the floor, then back to the book again. The photos became more explicit by the page. Every nook and cranny of the body was held up to impartial scrutiny. A foot, ankle ligaments (he winced), a shoulder, a shrivelled brown cock. It was like pornography taken to some numbing stage of total disclosure. By comparison pornographic or bodybuilding magazines seemed gentle and elusive as fairy tales. Everything was displayed, nothing was revealed. By the closing pages he was half expecting to see the soul itself revealed as a dark tumour-shaped lump or a resilient piece of gristle which, like the appendix, served no real medical function and could be disposed of as superfluous.

It was depressing, looking at this book, to think that this is what we all were and would become: a mass of dry, spongy material, nine tenths of which seemed dedicated to waste disposal. He looked at Nicole: her stomach growled. She was the only woman he had ever seen shit. Not *seen* her shit exactly, but at least been in the bathroom *while* she sat on the toilet, shitting . . . Inside, as this book made plain, every man and woman was exactly the same as every other. There was nothing to choose between anyone. But there was Nicole, the woman he loved, lying on the floor.

He thought of *The Man with the X-ray Eyes*, with Ray Milland as the doctor trying to find a way of seeing through the skin of his patients to offer immediate and accurate diagnoses of their illnesses. He applied drops of chemical solution to his eyes and, at first, was able to see through a few sheets of paper. Then – the fun part – he was able to see through nurses' dresses and underwear. The experiment got quickly out of control because he couldn't control the duration or depth of penetration of his vision. After a while repeated, unregulated exposure to the X-ray solution caused Milland's vision to be filled entirely by the ghastly viscera and skeletons he'd hoped only to glimpse in the course of his medical research. All the time his eyes were getting more and more bloodshot, like someone who'd been sleeping in gritty contact lenses for a month. God, his eyes looked sore. People and walls began to fade altogether. To control this creeping omniscience he wore sunglasses which had to get thicker and thicker and darker and darker. Eventually only dense lead sunglasses could prevent his peering through buildings. By the climax of the film the world was melting away and he was staring into a psychedelic infinity of colour.

Luke closed the book and looked again at Nicole, bathed in light, her flesh stretched perfectly over her hip bones. Her eyes flickered open, taking in the room, squinting in the light, seeing him.

'What have you been doing?' she said

'Bending and straightening my leg eighty times.'

'I had such deep sleep. Am I really awake? I can't tell.'

'You're asleep.'

Nicole stretched and then lay with her eyes shut. They were still shut when she said, 'How are you my Lukey? Happy?'

'Oh yes.'

'Say why.'

'Why I'm happy?'

'Yes.'

'I could list things, things that make me happy. You. Looking at you. Looking at you naked. Talking to you while looking at you naked.'

'And what about other women?'

'What about them?'

'Do you ever look at other women?'

'No.'

'Do you ever want to?'

'If I wanted to I would.'

'So you never want to?'

'Do you want me to answer absolutely truthfully?'

'You're an only child, remember? You don't know how to lie.'

'Never.'

Nicole stood up and walked to the fridge. 'Would you like some water?'

'No thank you.' She took a bottle of faucet-filled Evian out of the fridge, opened it and took a sip.

'What else makes you happy?' She was standing with her back to the open fridge, naked, one arm propped on the door. Steam coiled round her.

'Wearing my new T-shirt.'

'That horrible one?'

'Yes. What about you?'

'What makes me happy?'

'Yes.' She put the bottle back and shut the fridge. Luke watched her cross the room and lie down again in the hot puddle of sun.

'Knowing you. Knowing, not looking. You see the distinction?'

'It is, so to speak, staring me in the face.'

'I know you so well, Luke. I like that. That makes me happy. Suppose they cloned you, made another one of you, absolutely identical. I could draw up a list of a hundred or a thousand things that distinguished you from it.'

Is this what it means to love someone? To take pleasure in itemising the smallest things about them? Except the list is never definitive, never complete. Things have to be added to it constantly: things that have never been noticed before, new things that turn out to be essential things.

'Let me qualify what I said about looking at you making me happy,' said Luke. 'I have X-ray eyes. It's not just your outside that I had in mind. It's your kidneys and liver and all those hidden bits of offal that make you work the way you do, that make you smell the way you do, that make you what you are.'

'Is that why you're always trying to get your fingers up my arse?'

'Yes, that makes me happy too.'

'It's easy isn't it, happiness?'

'It's all in the lubrication.'

'Happiness is just the harmony between a person and the life they lead.'

'That's lovely. Is it you or someone else?'

'Someone else.'

'Who?'

'I forget. Are you still bending and stretching your leg?'

'No. Now I'm just chatting.'

'I love chatting with you.'

'Me too.'

'Is it still all withered and feeble?'

'My leg? Yes.'

'Like your prick then.'

'Yes, exactly.'

'I'd like to make love.'

'Me too.'

'Tie me to the bed,' she said.

Nicole had to work late the following evening. She and Pierre had just put the finishing touches to a proposal for a competition for an extension to a museum in Provence. Everyone else had left. It was hot. Pierre had taken off his tie, his shirt was unbuttoned at the neck. He went to the fridge and came back with a bottle of champagne. He opened it and poured two glasses.

'A toast!' he said. Nicole held her glass, waited. 'To you . . . For all your hard work.' She smiled, held up her glass, sipped from it and then looked down into it. Pierre was sitting on the desk, one foot on the bottom drawer. He poured himself a second glass, angled the bottle towards her.

'No thank you.'

'Come on. We're celebrating.' She smiled. Took another sip. Looking behind her, through the blinds, she saw a light go off in the office opposite. She heard Pierre moving from the desk. He was standing up. He put the glass down on the desk, quietly, and reached his hand towards her, touched her shoulder.

'Nicole,' he said. He moved his hand to her hair, pushed it behind her ear. She looked at him. He angled his face towards her. She felt his breath and then his lips on her. She averted her face, took a step back. Pierre remained where he was, his hand in the air.

'Nicole,' he said. 'The truth is, Nicole . . .' He took a breath, looked at the floor and then at her face again. 'I am in love with you.' His words were tender but there was a threat contained in this tenderness. He reached towards her, fingered her hair behind her ear again.

'Please. Don't do that.' It had been so slight a gesture, and her reaction to it so excessive – to refuse him even this! – that Pierre felt as if he had been hit. He was embarrassed and his embarrassment made him angry. He left his hand where it was. With the other he touched her shoulder. He leaned towards her. She turned her face away. On the filing cabinet nearby was a pile of paper and the pen he had bought her.

'I want to kiss you.'

'No.'

'Not even that?'

'Let go of me.'

'What do you think I'm going to do? Rape you?'

'You couldn't.'

He gripped her shoulder. She craned her head back, pushed him away. He pushed harder. She stepped back and rattled into the blinds. She reached for the pen and held it in her fist, as if she were about to plunge it into his face. His hand was still on her shoulder. For several moments they stood there like that, their faces inches from each other. Then Nicole reached up, moved his hand from her shoulder and manoeuvred past him. She put the pen on the desk and picked up her bag. Pierre had pulled out the chair from the desk and slumped into it. Ignoring him, Nicole left the room and closed the door, exactly as if she had just finished a normal day's work.

Luke was sitting on the floor when she got home. He was wearing his ridiculous T-shirt, checking film times in *Pariscope*, munching his way through a bowl of cherries. Spunk was next to him, tail wagging, eyes fixed on the door, awaiting her return. She told Luke what had happened while he held her, his vision focused, for no reason, on a little area of the wall opposite where the paint had been applied too thinly. Women withheld themselves from men and then, for a while at least, they gave themselves to a man, to one man. And what a stroke of fortune it was, what a miracle, if you turned out to be that man! I am her man, Luke thought to himself. But how arbitrary it was, this privilege, and how precarious. There could come a time when he would find himself excluded as totally as Pierre from the invisible field of her consent, her desire, her trust. He held her tighter, as if this extra exertion of pressure could indefinitely forestall such an eventuality. Everything he could think of saying was inadequate. He was her man. Nothing he could do or say could do justice to this fact. He kissed her.

'You taste of cherries,' she said.

Nicole was out of a job and, at the warehouse a few days later, Luke and Alex became convinced that they were heading the same way. Unusually Lazare said that he wanted to see them at three o'clock: normally he simply put his head out of his office and shouted to whoever he wanted to speak with – i.e. yell at – to get in there immediately. The uncharacteristic formality seemed ominous and, sure enough, when they turned up promptly at his office everything about his manner suggested imminent redundancy. He was sitting in his chair, smoking one of his non-Cuban cigars.

'Sit down,' he said. Luke and Alex looked round. There was only one chair. Perhaps this was how it would be settled: whoever sat down would get the bullet: a comfortable version of Russian roulette. They remained standing.

'How's that ankle Luke?'

'Great. Almost back to normal.'

'Good. Listen, we're coming up to a very quiet period. There won't be enough work to go round.' The phone rang. He picked up the receiver, hung up, and then left it sprawled on the desk: his own no-frills version of 'No calls, please. I'm in a meeting.' The dull dial tone could just be heard. 'I can't keep everybody on here. You two were the last to arrive. So it's you who have to go.' The dial tone turned to the higher pitch intended to alert the caller that he had taken too long to dial. 'Which is a shame because I like you both. And the other guys like you.' He shifted in his chair, a little embarrassed by this admission of affection. His cigar was not drawing well. He stubbed it out and picked up a pen instead. 'But there's something I could suggest to you that you might like anyway. I bought this house in the country. A small place, very run down. It's very pretty. It's been done up but there are a few things still need doing. A lot of things actually, but nothing too major. Plastering, painting, cleaning, tidying. So if you want to you can do that for me: do the place up. In return you get a nice – well, a place that will be nice when you finish working on it – home for the summer. Plus I'll pay you something. Not much, but something. Take those sweet girlfriends of yours. By the end of the summer things will have picked up here. You can come back. So what do you say?'

They said they would let him know tomorrow, when they had talked to their sweet girlfriends.

Since she had lost her job and had no chance of finding work before September, Nicole said yes immediately. Sahra, too, could think of nothing she would rather do: there was never much work in the summer.

'It's a unanimous yes,' Luke told Lazare the next day. 'We'll do it.'

'That's good. When d'you want to leave?'

'The week after next?'

'That's good too because I was going to have to get rid of you then anyway.'

Both couples advertised their apartments in FUSAC and were immediately inundated with calls from eager sub-letters. They boxed up their belongings and arranged to set off the following Monday: a year to the day, Luke realized, since he had first arrived in the city – just as everyone else was leaving for the summer. Now, by leaving, by joining the exodus that had rendered his first weeks so desolate, he felt he was demonstrating how completely he had come to belong in the city, to feel at home in it.

In the biography of Luke's time in Paris, the area around his old apartment, the Tuileries especially, constituted his childhood. A few days before leaving he took Nicole there on a valedictory tour. They rode the 29 to the Opéra (the nearest Luke had ever come to taking it with a purpose, in order to *get* somewhere). Nicole's hair blew across her face as they leaned on the balcony rail, looking back, watching life recede. A roller-blader clung dangerously to the back of the bus as it snaked along the narrow streets by the Musée Picasso. Waiting on lights, a couple squabbled furiously in the front of their car. An old woman's shopping bag split, spilling oranges on to the pavement and into the road. Nicole spotted Alex and Sahra, arm in arm, walking along rue des Archives, laughing. She called out, too late. A wild-looking African berated a traffic warden for the ticket she had just written. The balcony filled up and thinned out. Louis XIV and his horse were framed, briefly, against a whirl of blue as the bus nipped around the Place Des Victoires. Something had set off a car alarm; a thin man conducted the noise serenely. When the bus was held up in traffic two workmen crossed the road carrying a large mirror which flashed back the image of Luke and Nicole in the balcony of the 29.

'You see what an inconsequential film it will be?' said Luke when they got out at Opéra. Nicole laughed. She was wearing a white dress, plimsolls, Luke's sunglasses (the ones she had mislaid), a single bracelet. It was hot. There were a few scars of cloud; otherwise the sky was empty blue. On rue de la Paix Luke went into an alimentation and came out with two plastic bottles of fresh orange, one of which he threw to Nicole. She caught it, just. Luke was wearing a linen shirt, jeans. She watched him unscrew the bottle of orange and gulp it down as if he were pouring sun down his throat.

The park was packed with tourists. Litter bins were overflowing with Coke cans, buzzing with wasps. The grass had not yet been scorched by the summer heat, there were not too many cigarette butts in evidence. A group of boys were playing football. The ball bounced over to Nicole and she toe-poked it back. Sun dazzled the statues. To Luke's surprise and disappointment the centaur was no longer there. It too had left the city for the summer: for restoration, a plaque explained.

Since seeing Luke that afternoon in London, and while writing this account of the period when our lives overlapped, I have thought constantly about what happened to him, have come up against that 'big why' again and again.

I think now that certain destinies are the opposite of manifest: ingrown, let's say. Hidden, rarely revealing themselves, probably not even felt as a force, they work like the process or instinct that urges a seed in the soil in the direction of the light: as strong, silent and invisible – as imperceptible – as that. In Luke's case, something took him away from the light, from what he most wanted and loved. As if the seed's impulse towards the light becomes warped or damaged so that it takes itself deeper and deeper into the soil. As it buries itself deeper so it redoubles its efforts to attain the light. But in doing so, like the deer we saw exhausting itself by struggling in a trap, it succeeds only in burying itself still further. Eventually the urge towards the light withers because, as if through the workings of some last-ditch, built-in fail-safe, only by ceasing to struggle can it hope to survive. At some very late stage it senses that it is its *longings* which have condemned it. And so it remains where it is, a faint pulse of life in the darkness, directionless, not moving.

I think Luke could feel something tugging him, exerting not an attraction but a pull that was very faint and yet so insistent that he began to wonder if, by giving in to it, he might have found a way of being faithful to his destiny. Maybe some truth would be revealed to him that was denied to happier, more contented people. Even as he thought this he must have suspected that such a truth would be distorted, rendered false, because it would, inevitably, be encrusted by bitterness. We all want to believe that truth is incompatible with bitterness but this is wishful thinking. Perhaps truth *is* bitter, mean, miserly. The hankering to make of truth something ennobling and pure is itself a falsification. Perhaps it is actually the truth itself that twists you, that is twisted.

Obviously things could have turned out differently for Luke, could have worked out better. But by letting things occur as they did he believed he was penetrating more deeply into himself, getting closer to his core. Luke fell short of what he was capable of. He could have been many things, could have achieved more than he did. To all outward appearances he failed: he failed to keep the woman he loved, to pursue a career, to raise a family, to be happy. All of the things he associated with happiness came to be lodged absolutely in his past. But there was a sense, I think, in which he did fulfil his destiny. There are people who are destined to have lives like this and, in some way, his falling short was a kind of triumph; he was being faithful to some part of himself, to his destiny.

There are all sorts of propensities in people; we tend to look only at the positive side – their potential for success, for happiness – but there are other kinds of negative potential:

the potential for wasting the talents we are given, for blighting our prospects of happiness.

So, as he sits there, staring at the TV that has been on all day, waiting for time to pass, as he looks at the bed where he has slept every night, or at the crumbs of bread scattered over the kitchen table, as he postpones for a little while longer the first drink of the day, or decides that he has waited long enough and opens the first bottle – perhaps he feels that at some level he has achieved his destiny, that he has been true to some part of himself, has touched some possibility which had been latent in him from his earliest beginnings. Perhaps he feels at home in himself.

I can imagine him sitting there, his mouth numbed by beer, knowing that he has ruined his whole life, that nothing will remain of him when he dies – no book, no children – and wanting nothing to be any different, accepting it. I can even imagine him almost happy.

Alex and Luke had a meeting with Lazare who gave them a list of things he wanted done to the house, how he wanted them done. There was no phone, he said, but they should call whenever they got a chance, to let him know they weren't ruining the place.

'And don't be surprised if I turn up one day to check on you.' These were his final words on the subject.

As at Christmas they loaded up Sahra's car and found that they were once again pressed for space. They bought a roof rack but even with that piled dangerously high there was not enough room for everything they needed. The bikes were the real problem. Not taking them was unthinkable so they arranged to send them on ahead by train. They threw out other things that weren't strictly necessary, decided they *were* essential after all and crammed half of them back on to the roof rack.

'What are we going to do about Spunky?' said Nicole. 'We can't leave him.'

'You're right. We'll have to take him.'

He was waiting for them in the apartment. Luke kicked him in the face and sent him floating across the room.

'Luke!'

'It's for his own good. To stun him.' Luke picked up their dog and put his arm around his neck.

'I can't look,' said Nicole. Luke reached under him and pulled the stopper from his stomach. Spunk sagged and shrivelled. Nicole listened to the long hiss of air as Luke squeezed the life from him.

'He feels I'm letting him down,' said Luke.

When Nicole turned round he was holding a lumpy square of black and white plastic, tied with pink ribbon.

They had hoped to leave in the afternoon but by the time they had taken the bicycles to the station and finished loading, unloading and re-loading it was growing dark. This was probably for the best, Alex thought. The already defective car looked so unroadworthy it would be more prudent to drive at night when there was less chance of getting pulled over. They were further delayed by Daniel who – though the women knew nothing of this arrangement – was supposed to be getting some acid for them but, two hours later than promised, he called to say that it was impossible. He'd have to post it on to them.

It was almost eleven when they finally set out. Even at that late hour there was still a bluish tinge to the sky: the sharp indigo that is unimaginable except as a backdrop for petrol stations, signs, neon. The moon was in orbit. Sahra was driving. Since their top speed was only 75 k.p.h. and they wanted, in any case, to avoid being towed off the autoroute in the event of a breakdown, they stayed on B roads, passing through villages whose backs seemed resolutely turned away from the road, wanting nothing to do with it. Houses did not seem asleep so much as barricaded in. They drove through the night, stopping for fuel whenever they found a petrol station that was open. Sahra had made a flask of tea which they passed round, sipping in the faint light of what Alex liked to call the instrument panel.

The miles slipped by. They fell silent. To no one in particular Alex, who had taken over the driving, said,

'Has anyone ever said to you: "cat's eyes – what a great invention!"?' There was no answer. He glanced over at Luke who was sleeping in the seat next to him. In the back seat the women were also asleep, exactly as they had been during the winter trip. Smiling, Alex concentrated on the road ahead.

It got light so early it seemed the darkness had not really slept, only taken a nap. The light was bleary-eyed, uncertain, then it began to brighten. The sun stumbled over the hills in the distance. Already, when they passed through villages, people were up and working. At the first patisserie they saw Luke got out and bought coffee and disappointing croissants. They ate in the car, as if they were on a stake-out, 'even though it's really only a take-out'.

'Very funny Luke,' said Alex, his eyes sore with tiredness. They wanted to toss their Styrofoam cups out of the window but were worried about littering. Luke took them over to the bin and Sahra took over the driving.

A road drifted up to the house, winding not so much to negotiate the slight gradient as for the visual pleasure afforded by doing so. The house itself was perched on the edge of a field of wheat. It was a low, sprawling place with a roof that sloped almost to the ground. The walls were thick, made of clumps of what was, presumably, some native stone, sand-coloured. This was the architecture of bitter winters and blazing summers. The front door scraped over the tiled floor as they pushed it open. They opened the shutters. White light rushed in, filling every angle of the interior.

Most of the structural work had been completed. The floors required varnishing, the bathroom had to be tiled, everything needed painting. The whole place needed cleaning. There was dust everywhere, it was a mess, but, essentially, Alex declared, the problems were cosmetic. There was gas but no cooker as yet (though they had instructions from Lazare about which model he wanted, and money to pay for it) and there was almost no furniture: a few fold-up chairs, a table, two thin mattresses, some loungers for outside.

Nicole heard Luke calling her. She went out and saw him standing by the car. Spunk was perched on its warm bonnet, full of life again, tail wagging.

The village was three kilometres away but apart from a bar and butcher there was almost nothing there. The town was another twenty-five kilometres beyond that. On their first trip there they bought the cooker Lazare had requested and ate lunch at Chez Marianne, a restaurant run by an old couple who took a liking to them. On a napkin they sketched a time-table: Monday to Friday, in the mornings (start-time optional), they would work without fail (at what was not made clear). Afternoons and weekends were optional.

After agreeing these terms they took a stroll round the town. It was a nice place with a river and church and a market on Wednesdays. They drove there every Wednesday and sometimes on Saturdays, to stock up on supplies, to phone Lazare to let him know how things were progressing , and to

eat lunch at the restaurant. Strictly speaking these
Wednesday-morning outings contravened the time-table but
the purpose of scheduling their time like this – Luke argued –
was not so much to ensure that the work was done as to make
the pleasure of not working as intense as possible.
Uninterrupted idleness would have turned quickly to boredom. As it was, the obligation to work each day for four hours
or so meant that their free time maintained its idyllic, valued
quality.

The problem with the work was that Alex was the only
one who knew how to do most of it. Luke, Sahra and Nicole
could paint and tidy up but only Alex was capable of performing more advanced functions. Luke liked the idea of
putting up shelves but Alex had to do the sawing himself if
any vestige of accuracy was to be maintained. While capable
of planning lavish and complex changes to the basic layout of
the house Nicole had relatively little experience of actually
putting these plans into practice. She was adaptable, versatile,
learned quickly and in the chain of command she became
Alex's second-in-command. (Alex had appointed himself
'supreme commander' without opposition but Luke advised
him not to get too excited about being Nicole's boss: the last
one, he pointed out, had almost been stabbed in the face for
his pains.) Sahra had the invaluable skill of being a meticulous
finisher. Luke, it became apparent, was hopeless even at mea-
suring and his task, consequently, was to sort out and clean
the barn which was crammed to the rafters with useful and
useless stuff accumulated over a period of more than five years.
It was an immense, filthy job and he complained about it on
a daily basis.

'That's the price you pay for being totally unskilled,' said

Alex. 'Sweat is cheap. Were you capable of performing a more complex, rewarding task, we would consider assigning it to you. As it is, you're not. Hence . . .'

'THE BARN!' shouted Sahra and Nicole together.

While working on the house the other three became used to hearing cursing and swearing as Luke dragged another load of dusty rubble or rust-encrusted implements into the yard. Often these yells were violent enough to make them think that he had injured himself. One day, though, a wild shriek emerged from the barn, followed by the call to 'come quickly'. They dashed out, expecting to find him pinned beneath a ton of farm equipment, only to find him struggling with—

'A ping-pong table!' Alex was as excited as Luke and together they dragged it out into the sunlight. It was warped slightly on one side, a chunk appeared to have been bitten out of a corner, a leg was missing: these things aside, it was easily 'of championship standard'. The net, when they found it, was ragged but Nicole managed to tie string across the rips. They set up the table in a sheltered spot by the side of the house, using bricks to prop up the sagging, legless corner.

'There *is* one small problem,' said Alex. 'We haven't got bats or balls.'

'Shit!'

They bought them the next time they went into town and began playing as soon as they got back. It was years since anyone had played and at first they tapped the ball back and forth mechanically, rarely deviating from the safety of the backhand. Spin was introduced gradually. Then, occasionally, one of them would finish the rally with an aggressive fore-hand, either winning the point (very rarely) or (more usually) whacking the ball into the net. After a few days the success rate for forehands went up – but so too did the frequency with which these shots were returned. From there it was a small step to returning an attacking forehand *with* an attacking forehand of still greater ferocity. Instead of simply taking it in turns to play, Luke and Alex forced through the principle of Winner Stays On. Nicole dropped quickly out of the rankings and tended not to play. Sahra, who claimed to have played for her school team, won some games but the table came to be dominated, predictably, by Luke and Alex. Alex attacked relentlessly but Luke, relying on twisting combinations of spin – the ping-pong equivalent of judo – began to use his opponent's strength against him. Standing way back from the table he kept looping the ball back until Alex finally over-hit or slammed it into the net and lost the point.

For a while ping-pong dominated their lives. Then it was sidelined by a more important discovery. On most days one or all of the party went out 'on reconnaissance' (as Luke and Alex termed it), 'for a bike ride' (as Nicole and Sahra termed it). They were all out together, about two miles from home, when they came across an old clay tennis court. It was at the edge of a field and seemed to belong to no one. Luke and Alex tore home, snatched up their rackets, cycled back and launched immediately into what turned out to be a gruelling four-setter (won by Alex) in ninety-degree heat. The women returned from their ride to find both men cowering in the shade, dehydrated, on the brink of heat-stroke.

Sahra and Nicole liked to play too, in the early evenings. The men played singles and then, when it was cooler, the women turned up for mixed doubles. The games between Luke and Alex were always fiercely competitive but if the match was still under way when Sahra and Nicole arrived the sight of their girlfriends cycling up spurred them on to new heights of aggressiveness. Alex was the stronger and more skilful of the two but Luke ran down every ball, stretching out his thin arms and somehow getting it back. This was both the strength of his game and its fundamental flaw: he loved soaking up punishment but in tennis this proved a less successful strategy than in ping-pong. He stood too far back, behind the baseline, putting himself under immediate pressure. What he most enjoyed was chasing lost causes and refusing to accept defeat – but he could never convert this determination not to lose into an ability to win. On the contrary, he had such a dread of losing that it became inevitable that he would. He believed that he was the kind of person who could pull himself back to equal terms from a two-set deficit – and he was, he did. But then, having drawn level at two sets all and gone four games ahead in the fifth, he contrived, somehow, to blow it. He tensed, choked, lost.

After these encounters Luke and Alex came off court and rested while Nicole and Sahra knocked up. They sat on the clay, drenched in sweat, drinking bottles of water, occasionally rolling back a ball that had bounced towards them.

'I had my chances,' said Luke.

'You did.'

'I didn't take them.'

'You didn't. And do you know why you didn't take them?'

'Why?'

'Because I didn't let you.'

'That's not true. If I hadn't hit those volleys into the net,

I'd have been flying. As it was I was crashing. But if I *had* made those volleys . . .'

'Do you know what I'd have done then?'

'What?'

'Raised my game.' They laughed and settled back to watch Sahra and Nicole play. Both women had been coached when young, they had the strokes, but both suffered from incredible lapses of concentration that sometimes lasted for the best part of the game. Nicole also got into weird tangles when the ball came straight at her, trying desperately to play a backhand and forehand simultaneously. She had no anticipation, waited for the ball to come at her, made no allowance for spin. After twenty minutes Luke and Alex joined the women on court and they played a set or two of mixed doubles together.

The favourite game of the whole summer, though, was Bombing the Television. Cycling back from tennis they always crossed a small river. From the bridge one evening they saw a television, screen-up, floating downstream.

'Great,' said Luke. 'Let's smash it up.' Alex needed no encouragement and immediately they were scurrying around looking for suitable rocks. The TV was ten metres away and was proving difficult to hit. The women joined in and soon were hysterical with delight, desperate to sink it. As the TV drifted nearer it was hit, twice, on the walnut surround but no one could get the screen itself. It floated closer to them but they were running out of decent ammo. Alex was about to propose a cease-fire which would give the TV a sporting chance of survival – no throwing until it had passed a certain distance beyond the far side of the bridge – when Sahra caught it with a direct hit. The screen did not just crack: it exploded, and the TV immediately sank without trace. Nicole and Sahra high-fived each other, weak with the excitement of destruction.

'It just goes to show,' said Luke as they clambered back on their bikes like a gang of delinquents, 'there is nothing in life more pleasurable than destroying things.'

They decided to take a different route home and soon became lost. The sun was slipping behind the remains of a cloud. Trees grew black. Birds were heading home (they could have been heading out but that seemed unlikely). Everything, it seemed, was packing up and heading home, even the clouds: only a few were left. They came to a railway crossing.

'Let's walk along the tracks,' said Sahra.

'Where do you think they're going?'

'In this world there is one path that only you can walk,' said Luke, echoing Miles. 'Where does it lead? Don't ask: take it.'

They locked their bikes together and walked along the railway line, into the embers of the sun. Sahra kept looking behind in case there was a train coming. Alex said there was no chance.

'How do you know?'

'Because the rails are rusty, one. And, two, there's no shit on the tracks.' He was right but the other three still felt a little uneasy as they stepped across the sleepers. After a point it did not get any darker. Instead, the twilight became more intense. The light faded but the darkness glowed. They followed the rails which kept everything in perspective, lent an automatic purpose to their steps. It seemed possible to walk like this for ever. Then Nicole said she was hungry. The others agreed that they were hungry too, starving in fact.

And thirsty. They turned back and walked in two pairs, holding hands.

The rails held what was left of the light. Black against the deepening blue, the last birds dipped by, also in pairs.

If initially it had seemed that there would be nothing to do but relax and read and cook, soon there was too much to do. The days were long but they were not long enough to contain all the happiness we needed to cram into them. How different from now when we have learned to measure out our happiness, distributing it evenly through the week so that there is enough to go round even though happiness is, precisely, an abundance, an overflowing, and even to think about rationing it is to settle for contentment – which anyone who has known real happiness rejects instinctively as the form despair takes in order to render itself bearable.

A few days before Luke's birthday Nicole came up with another of her Put-Togethers. She retrieved the sunken TV from the river, removed the whole of the back and brought the rest home. For three days she let it dry in the sun and then installed it in the living room which – in order to keep the heat at bay – was kept dark. By placing the screenless walnut surround in front of a window, and blacking out the rest of the window, the TV broadcast a perfect image of the fields and sky outside. It was not just local TV, it was site-specific. The reception was perfect and for Luke's birthday a customised version of *Brief Encounter* was being screened.

Luke sat in the darkened living room and watched Nicole and Alex playing Celia Johnson and Trevor Howard; Sahra took all the other roles. Alex was the only one who had seen the film and since he had only a vague recollection of all but a few lines, most of the script was improvised. In some ways Luke thought it an improvement on the original: it was in colour for a start, and the scenery was stunning.

'It all began quite simply,' said Nicole in her best English accent, 'in the refreshment room at Milfordhampton Junction. I was trying to get to Altonhampton but the train had split and I was terribly, terribly lost. I walked out of the refreshment room along the platform when suddenly—'

At that moment Alex kicked a ball at her. 'Oi,' he called out. 'Any chance of a shag, love! You look like you're dying for it!'

That pretty much set the tone for the whole piece. When Celia said she was upset and confused Trevor passed her a strong joint and suggested she 'have a toke on that'.

'Might I?' said Celia.

'I'm a bit of an idealist really,' said Trevor. 'You see I have this idea that I would like to manufacture enough acid to keep everyone in the world tripped out of their minds for the rest of eternity.'

'It sounds frightfully complicated,' said Celia. When they began meeting for their afternoon matinées they consulted *Pariscope* to decide which film took their fancy.

'What are you in the mood for darling?' said Celia.

'What about *Sous Les Jupes Pas Des Culottes*? Or *Les Suceuses*?' said Trevor.

'Oh I don't like those highbrow art films. Isn't there something lighter?' said Celia.

'What about *Pénétrez-Moi Par Le Petit Trou*?' said Trevor.

'That sounds interesting, let's try that,' said Celia, her eyes brightening.

It went on in this vein right up until Trevor's final, heart-broken goodbye: 'Fuck off then you prick-teasing slag!'

In response to this fond farewell Nicole walked towards the house until her face filled the screen in tight close-up. Luke got up and advanced towards the TV, assuming the role of Fred, the almost-cuckolded hubby.

'Whatever your dream was, it wasn't a very happy one was it? You've been a long way away. Thank you for coming back to me,' he said, reaching through the screen and taking her in his arms.

At breakfast the next morning the postman delivered a birth-day postcard from Daniel.

'How sweet of him to remember your birthday,' said Sahra, going inside to make more coffee.

'Let's hope that's not the only thing he remembered,' said Luke. 'Oh, could you bring some scissors when you come back Sahra?' He handed Alex the postcard: a Bonnard show-ing his wife Marthe, standing in the bath, blazing with naked light. Alex passed the card to Nicole who gave it back to Luke. When Sahra came back he began cutting into it with the scissors.

'You're spoiling it!'

'Only the top corner,' said Alex, watching attentively as Luke cut into one of the two stamps. It was not stuck in the middle, only around the edges. Luke eased the scissors under the stamp and slit it down the centre. Underneath were two squares of grey blotting paper.

'Is that what I think it is?' said Sahra, reaching out her hand.

'I rather think it is,' said Luke.

'*What* are they?' said Nicole.

'Well, whatever they are,' said Luke, fiddling with the scissors again, 'there are two more under the other stamp.'

'Good old Daniel,' said Alex.

That afternoon Nicole and Sahra made the most important discovery of all: the lake. One side of it was popular with tourists – at the weekend it was jam-packed – but they had found a track to the far side that was inaccessible by car and therefore almost deserted. The edge of the lake was dark, muddy. Your toes sank in as you entered the cold water and spooky-looking reeds waved around your ankles and shins as you got deeper. The women loved spending whole afternoons there, swimming, sun-bathing. Luke and Alex preferred to play tennis and come along later, sneaking up quietly, like schoolboys, hoping to discover their girlfriends naked. If they came for the entire afternoon they brought a football and played head tennis on the shore. Sometimes they stayed at the lake until late in the evening and then cycled home in the twilight, slowly, in a group, until Luke or Alex suddenly staged an impromptu speed trial as far as 'that gate', 'that tree', even the house itself. In the course of their time in the country Luke and Alex had worked themselves up into a frenzy of competitiveness. As well as killing themselves on the tennis court and, on windless days, monopolising the ping-pong table, they took any opportunity to throw down a challenge: running races (sprints and middle distance), stone-throwing (who could throw furthest, who could hit a Coke tin balanced on a stick pushed into the silt at the lake's edge), skimming pebbles. The world had become an arena in which to test themselves against each other.

'If we had boxing gloves we'd build a ring and I'd knock his fucking teeth out,' said Luke as the four of them sat by the lake's edge.

'Luke!' said Nicole.

'How would you do that when you'd be in a coma with a broken jaw and brain damage?' said Alex.

'It must be an English thing,' said Sahra, shaking her head.

'Actually, I tell you what I wish was here,' said Luke. 'A place where you could jump from cliffs into deep water from incredibly high up.'

'I *love* doing that,' said Sahra.

'Me too,' said Alex. 'Though I'd dive rather than jump.'

Back at the house Luke and Alex leaned a ladder against one of the walls and took it in turns to see who could climb highest using only their arms. This was a potentially dangerous game – for Luke. Alex was able to get to the top and down again but Luke could only get two thirds of the way up. By that stage he was too high to drop safely to the ground but his arms were so numb that it was only by wrapping his legs around the ladder and waiting for the fire in his shoulders to diminish that he found the strength to descend.

'Luke, you're so stupid,' said Nicole when he was back on terra firma. 'If you fall from there you'll be back in plaster again.'

'That's exactly what kept me hanging on,' laughed Luke, shaking the blood back into his hands. Undeterred, he continued practising, adding a few rungs every couple of days. While ostensibly taking a dim view of their boyfriends' antics on the ladder, the women actually enjoyed this particular event.

'It's so horny isn't it, watching men hanging by their arms like that?' said Sahra.

'It *is* isn't it!' said Nicole. 'I was just thinking that.'

'I always used to get turned on watching trapeze artists at the circus when I was young.'

'Me *too*!' giggled Nicole. 'Don't tell them that though. They'd probably rig up some kind of trapeze.'

Not to be outdone, the women organized a swimming race – the only event in which Luke and Alex did not compete against each other. A hopeless swimmer, Luke was reduced to refereeing. Alex, being strong, could swim well but could not keep up with the women who pulled ahead of him and then, having left him in their wake, achieved their own kind of victory, undermining Luke's motto of 'Victory at all costs' ('an inappropriate motto for a compulsive loser,' according to Alex) by finishing neck and neck.

Although he did not enjoy swimming Luke did like going out with Nicole on the blue lilo she had bought in town. They lay across it, using it to keep them afloat, kicking with their legs for propulsion. When they had gone a good distance from the shore they clambered aboard and sat on it together, their combined weight pushing it a foot beneath the surface. Using it like this was well outside the lilo's performance envelope, but each time they went out they strayed a little further from the shore, passing through sudden bands of cold and warmer water until Luke judged, one day, that they were in the dead centre of the lake. As he lay on the lilo with Nicole in his arms, her tanned body pressed against him, the sun drying them, Luke wondered what would happen if the lilo exploded, burst, sank. Would he be able to make it back to the shore? It was a freshwater lake. There was no salt to keep him afloat. The water was dark. Reflected in it he could see the single cloud that skirted the sun. Nicole's wet hair was streaked across his arm. He glanced across at her. She was wearing her yellow swimming costume. Her eyes were open, smiling oddly, watching him.

'You're thinking about drowning aren't you?'

'I was actually, yes. Or at least wondering if I would drown.'

'If what?'

'If the lilo burst.'

'We can see if you like.'

'What do you mean?'

Without replying Nicole reached down and pulled the stopper. Air whooshed and bubbled out of the lilo. It began deflating immediately.

'Nicole!'

In his panic Luke capsized the lilo and they both rolled under the water. When he bobbed up again, spluttering, he saw Nicole clinging to the lilo, reinserting the stopper. He stroked towards her. The lilo sagged but was still floating.

'Fuck Nic.' He rested his arms on the lilo, his face close to hers. 'You're crazy. What if you hadn't been able to get the thing back in?'

'Then you would have seen how stupid you are, thinking about drowning like that, little boy Shelley.'

His anger vanished immediately. 'You're right, I would have done,' he said, leaning across the lilo and kissing her.

'I wouldn't have let you drown,' she said.

'I love you,' he said, aloud, for the first time.

'I've heard you before,' said Nicole.

'When?'

'In the mosque was the first time. But I heard all the others too, my love.' She put her arms round his neck, kissed him.

'You're so beautiful,' he said.

'It's your loving me that makes me beautiful,' she said.

Cycling home they stopped by an oak tree. Luke lacked a vocabulary of landscape. He didn't know the names of trees or birds, could identify only the most rudimentary crops: wheat, rape, vines. As a result he saw the landscape only in the vaguest terms: trees, fields and colours. Yellow, shades of green, slopes and gradients, the shadow-drift of clouds. Even as he noticed the landscape he was, simultaneously, oblivious to it. He looked but could not listen. It appealed only to his eye. There was nothing for him to learn from it, it had nothing to tell. Perhaps the fact that he knew the name of this tree is why the scene struck him so forcibly.

They propped their bikes against the oak. The wheat had been taken in on either side of the road. The grass was scorched yellow: it had been months since there had been any rain but that did not matter. Life here had adjusted long ago to the huge thirst of summer. There were a few scars of cloud; otherwise the sky was empty blue. The light struck Luke almost as a moral force. Nicole was sitting on the grass at the edge of the road. Her hair was still wet. She took an orange from her bag and offered it to him. He nodded and she tossed it to him. Luke retreated a few paces and then threw it back. Nicole caught it easily and threw it to him again. Luke walked further back. Nicole stood up and clapped her hands. Luke threw her the orange which she caught, just. Then she stepped back and threw it to Luke who had to stretch to catch it, head tilted up to the sun. They continued throwing the orange back and forth like this, the distance between them increasing all the time. The orange looked like a planet as it hung in the blue sky. Neither of them dropped it but, as the distance between them increased, so the accumulated impact of catches made it leak. Snags and rips appeared in the peel. It became mushy and then Nicole's fingers grasped the sky instead of the orange and it splatted on the road. She raised her hands, shrugged, smiled, wiped her hands on her dress. Began walking towards him. The road wound out of sight behind her. On either side of the road were fields of wheat. The oak cast a shadow across the road. She was wearing plimsolls, her white sleeveless dress, a single bracelet. Her hair was long, still wet, black. She walked towards him but, even as she moved, there was a stillness about the scene, something Luke recognized, something it shared with other moments from his life that he could neither recall nor anticipate. A windlessness, a silence. The landscape breathing and rippling. Time going nowhere else, staying.

Sahra and Alex had prepared dinner. As usual the table had been set in front of the house. Nicole sat down with them and Luke brought out two beers from the fridge. He tried to open one of the bottles Zimbabwe-style and, as always, failed. He passed them to Alex who flipped off the top and handed back the open bottle.

'You're going to break your thumb if you keep trying to do that,' he said smugly. Luke rolled a joint and he and Sahra played a couple of games of ping-pong. Then they opened a bottle of wine and ate dinner. For dessert they each ate a grin of melon. Alex rolled another joint which only he and Luke smoked. The sun had sloped off somewhere else and they were waiting for the moon to show. Nicole was sitting on the floor between Luke's legs, her eyes closed. Stoned, Alex watched Luke combing her hair with his fingers.

If you watch someone's hands closely enough, can you feel what they have felt, touch what they have touched?

Alex became aware of a tightening in the atmosphere: an alertness. Feeling Sahra watching him, he shut his eyes, blanked off his thoughts.

The long curve of the days was marked by the movement of the sun, by the changing light. Every day was like every other: they worked on the house, ate lunch, played tennis, swam, went for cycle rides and walks, got stoned, cooked dinners. The passage of the weeks was marked by their deepening tans and the gradual improvement of the house. Luke finished cleaning out the barn. The house had been painted. Only odd jobs remained to be done. The house was still sparsely furnished but in every other respect it looked like a home.

Alex was cleaning paint drips from the floor in the living room. The window was open. Straight ahead was a view of the blue unclouded weather but the window itself reflected an angle of the exterior that he could not see directly. The reflection in the window was darker than reality, imparting a tint to the sky like a premonition of thunder. He went over to the window and opened it inward. As he did so the view in the glass panned round to reveal the gravel path leading to the barn. It was like a form of elementary surveillance and Alex felt as if he were spying. He opened the window wider, until he could see the barn itself. At the extreme edge of the window frame, he saw Nicole walking into view. With the window open as wide as possible he watched her lay a towel on the parched grass and take off her shorts and T-shirt.

Underneath she was wearing her yellow swimming costume. She sat down and rubbed sun lotion on to her arms and legs and shoulders. She picked up a book but put it down again almost immediately and lay back in the sun. Alex heard the door open behind him. He glanced round as Sahra stepped into the room. She saw him silhouetted against the shock of light.

'Hi!' he said, moving the window slightly.

'Alex?'

'Yes.' He stood up, giddy with the blood draining from his head.

'Are you busy?'

'Not at all.' Sahra walked towards him, put her arms around him, kissed him. 'What is it?' He held her.

'We're still looking in the same direction aren't we?'

'At this moment, no. We're looking at each other.'

'You know what I mean.'

'Yes, of course. I mean, we are still looking in the same direction.'

'Promise?'

'I promise. Look,' he said, moving so that they were both facing the open window, looking out at the blaze of wheat and sky.

One night, when Alex and Sahra had gone to bed, Nicole and Luke carried their mattress and bedding out into the yard. They made love, Luke manoeuvring, selfishly, so that he was underneath and could see the sky. Nicole moved slowly, pulling away from him until he almost came out of her, then sliding back over him, taking him inside her again.

'Shoulders,' she said. He moved his hands up to her shoulders, stroked them.

'Shoulders,' he said.

'Back,' she said.

'Lovely back,' he said, moving his hands down the steps of her spine and then back up again.

Next she said, 'Waist.' He repeated the word and moved his hands down to her waist.

'Hips,' she said.

'I love your hips,' he said, moving his hand over the angle of bone.

'Breasts,' she said.

'Breasts.' He touched her breasts and kissed her on the mouth.

'Lips,' she said.

'Lips,' he said.

'Tongue.'

'Tongue.'

'Ear.' He kissed her ear, whispering the word in her ear.

'Neck,' she said, and he touched her neck as softly as he could.

'Hair,' she said. Her hair was falling over his face. He gathered it loosely in his hand and let it run through his fingers.

'Hair,' he said, gathering it in his fist.

'Hair.'

He pulled her hair, gently, then harder until her head was pulled backwards.

'Hair.'

'Hair,' he said, threading it with starlight.

Afterwards they lay side by side, staring up at the star-drenched night. Neither of them was able to recognize the constellations. To attempt to arrange the swathe of stars into patterns, designs, shapes or outlines of objects was to diminish them, to scale down the immensity of what was seen and render it manageable. Even to look at them through your own eyes, to seek to hold the view in your head seemed compromising, belittling.

If only we could see without *being* – then we could *be* what we see.

'How many stars do you think there are up there?' said Nicole.

'An astronomical number.'

They watched for shooting stars, taking it in turns to call out: 'There's one!' 'Look, there!'

'I've never been happier in my life,' said Luke.

'Nor have I.'

'And I never will be happier.'

'How do you know?'

'There's a ceiling. A limit.'

'Funny to say that now, now that there is no ceiling to be seen.'

'You don't think those stars are a ceiling?'

They lay still. A satellite skimmed the earth. Passing, passing.

'What are you thinking now?' said Nicole.

'I'm wondering if it's possible that happiness could become unbearable,' he said. 'I think I can imagine it, not being able to bear happiness any more.'

Nicole said nothing. He moved to kiss her. Her face was wet against his lips.

To see without being, to be what is seen . . .

A few days before they were due to return to the city the

four friends drove to the coast. It was an hour's drive, and when they were almost there they took Daniel's acid. Alex had done a trip once before, years ago, and so had Sahra. After much negotiation Alex took a whole blotter while the women – Nicole having once again been persuaded and reassured by Sahra – took a half each. Luke swallowed the rest.

They parked the car and began walking. The wall beside the road was tumbled down and broken. It didn't matter: its dereliction was part of a cycle that led ultimately to its being repaired. Everything had its season here. The road was dusty, dry. At the side of the road were stones, left over from whatever process had been used to make the road. All along the roadside was the sizzle of cicadas. They turned on to a smaller road. To the left were trees, bare and thorny as barbed wire. Leaves had been dispensed with as an unnecessary luxury. It was perfectly still but, after years in this normally windswept spot, the trees looked, even in repose, as if a gale were screaming through their spindly branches. Leaves had been sacrificed for roots, display for the more desperate task of clinging to thin soil. All energy passed down rather than out. All visual clues suggested the buffeting and howling of wind – even the grass was combed flat – but the only sound was of insects, twitching.

They found themselves walking across the very different grass of a golf course. A group of men in pastel sweaters took it in turns to tee off. Because Sahra was the only one with a watch they called her Chronos, a name she was more than happy with. Here and there they tried to give names to various land formations. Although, between them, they had many names at their disposal, no one was sure if the words corresponded to the features intended. Luke thought of rock types and forgotten processes of erosion taking millions and millions of years, proceeding, so to speak, at a glacial pace.

Unsure of the direction they were taking, they passed a car park where an old man and a woman stoically contemplated the view while drinking from a tartan-patterned flask. Odd things caught Luke's attention: a red phone box, English-style, with blue tiles of sky showing through the square frames of windows (two broken). What was *that* doing there?

'Hey Chronos!' called Alex. 'What's the time?'

'It's stopped,' said Sahra.

'Time has run out,' said Nicole.

'There is no more time,' said Sahra.

The road gave way to a path that followed the bend of the coast. Their feet moved over crumbled yellow stones. A single dark puddle – where had the water come from? – fixed Luke's face against a glinting bowl of sky. To the left was a low wall; to the right, a taut wire fence, tufts of grey fleece hanging from the barbs. A hundred metres further on this gave way to an electrified fence that hummed quietly to itself. They began to feel hemmed in by this corridor of fences and walls which was just one strand of an elaborate web, stretched over the landscape as far as the eye could see.

Luke vaulted over a gate, closely followed by Alex, as if they were the last survivors of a gruelling cross-country run. Fields rose and fell: a patchwork of yellow, khaki and green, cradling the sky. The sun became stronger, turning the sky from grey-blue to blue-grey. The sky circled the earth like a satellite. The horizon was a blue extinction of cloud. Without realizing it they had lost track of the sea: the path they were following had led imperceptibly inland and no one had taken any notice of where they were headed. They were stranded in the swelling landscape of camouflage-patterned fields. A middle-aged man and a woman in a headscarf appeared. They had the look of people who regularly reported anything suspicious to the police.

'Excusez-moi,' said Luke, surprised by how fluent he sounded. 'C'est où, la mer?'

'La mer?'

'Oui.'

'Vous cherchez une mer spéciale?'

'Non,' said Alex, glad to be wearing sunglasses. 'La mer d'une façon générale. Vous pourriez me l'indiquer?'

The couple did as they were asked. The four friends all called out 'merci' and walked on. Alex pulled a banana out of his jacket pocket and chewed on it. He threw the peel over a wall, flapping like a bird as it went. The air was even stiller. Is there a negative as well as positive wind-scale? A gauge of stillness? Today was stiller than a day when smoke rises vertically into the air or a shuttlecock, dropped from a plane, falls as straight as a builder's plumb-line. No molecule of air moved. The friends, by contrast, made their way to the cliff uncertainly like a river meandering to the sea. Not only had they drifted from their destination but they had drifted apart from each other. Luke let the landscape ripple through his head. When he looked around he saw Nicole and Sahra – was she still Chronos, now that her watch had stopped? – in a field near a patch of woodland. Still further away, Alex was lying on his back, feeling the land breathe beneath him. Fence posts cast shadows across the grey ribbon of the lane as Luke made his way towards him.

Together again, they walked past giant Swiss-rolls of hay and a farmhouse where a dog barked viciously. In a shed they glimpsed farm machinery that could mangle your arm terribly. Also a tractor with no cushion on the seat.

'How cold that must be in winter,' said Nicole.

'When the skies are like ice.'

'When the ground is like ice.'

'When the sea itself is ice.'

'When there is nothing but ice.'

'Where are the cliffs?' said Alex.

'The sea.'

'The coast.'

'The edge.'

They walked on, coming eventually to a steeply rising bank which, they were sure, was all that separated them from the cliffs. For ten minutes they scrambled up the grass of the bank. Cresting it they saw a huge expanse of sky and, off to the right, a lighthouse perched on the edge of the coast. They continued across the grass that covered the last fifty metres of land. Sun poured into their faces. Luke looked at Nicole and Sahra. They had their arms round each other and were laughing hysterically at Alex who had taken off his jacket and was carrying it over one arm, walking briskly as if late for an important meeting. Sahra trotted over to him and they walked on, holding hands. Nicole ran over to Luke and kissed him, her eyes shiny with laughter.

She was speaking. Her voice took a long time to reach him. 'Are you still with us, Trevor?'

A voice – his own, he assumed – said possibly not.

With every step they took towards the coast the light became stronger. The sky overhead burned a deep blue. The lighthouse gleamed whitely.

And then they were there. There was no more land. It

stopped. They had come to the edge, could go no further. Sea and sky were lost in a luminous haze. There was no distance or direction, only the weightless flow of light. All sense of substance – of earth, weight, mass – was lost, as if they were suddenly back at the first moment of creation when this was all there was, a mingling of light and air: blue draining through gold, light dissolving into itself.

As Luke became used to the glare he could see boats floating in the blue sky. The laws of perspective melted in the intensity of the light. There was no sound of surf, no noise of wind. Overhead the shimmer of gold gave way to a deep, clear blue. He looked back at the green grass rolling away from the cliffs, cropped short by absent sheep. He lay on his back and looked up.

A military jet pulled through the sky, very high. Beyond that was the uncertain region where sky turned into space, where everything began to peter out, where distance ceased to be measured as space, only as light. The plane itself was no more than a dot, would probably have been invisible but for the vapour trail easing out behind it. He watched it race around the sky, following the curve of the earth in a long silent arc. The sound lagged behind, a rumble that was only now making itself heard in a part of the country the jet had passed over seconds before, miles inland, in one town or another.

Acknowledgements

The text contains the following samples from *Fiesta (The Sun Also Rises)* by Ernest Hemingway:

p. 14:   'There were lighted bars and late open shops on each side of the street.'

p. 25:   'a way of getting an intensity of feeling into shaking hands'

p. 34:   Alex's 'glass was empty.'

p. 51:   'A man and a [woman] passed. They were walking with their arms around each other.'

p. 51:   'Across the river were the broken walls of old houses that were being torn down.'

p. 104: 'the music hit you as you went in'

p. 105: 'Lavigne's was closed tight, and they were stacking the tables outside [. . .] Lilas.'

p. 120: 'It was amazing champagne.'

p. 173: 'It was raining hard outside.'

p. 218: 'He took a big gulp of coffee'

These lines were quoted from the following sources:

p. 7:   'O light . . . their fate.': Albert Camus, *Selected Essays and Notebooks*, Penguin, Harmondsworth, 1970, p. 152.

p. 198: 'a force of . . . long nights.': John Cheever, *The Journals*, Cape, London, 1991, p. 119.

p. 234: 'Happiness . . . they lead.': slightly misquoted from Camus, *op cit.*, p. 98.

Although this book is dedicated to two friends, I would also like to share it with Tim, Hania, Charlie, Rupert, and Ollie Gross. And Valeria, of course.

I would also like to thank Alexandra Pringle and Richard Beswick for their persistence, Antonia Hodgson for overseeing the manuscript's progress, patiently and scrupulously, and Ethan Nosowsky for much-valued trans-Atlantic advice and friendship.

THE COLOUR OF MEMORY

Geoff Dyer

'In the race to be first in describing the lost generation of the Eighties, Geoff Dyer in *The Colour of Memory* leads past the winning post. "We're not lost," one of his hero's friends says, "we're virtually extinct." It is a small world in Brixton that Dyer commemorates, of council flat and instant wasteland, of living on the dole and the scrounge, of mugging, which is merely begging by force, and of listening to Callas and Coltrane. It is the nostalgia of the DHSS Bohemians, the children of unsocial security, in an urban landscape of debris and wreckage – "the one thing we really know how to manufacture". Not since Colin MacInnes's *City of Spades* and *Absolute Beginners* thirty years ago has a novel stuck a flick-knife so accurately into the young and marginal city. A low-keyed style and laconic wit touch up *The Colour of Money*'
The Times

'Of all the hyped novels about 1980s London it remains one of the most genuine'
Peter Jukes, *New Statesman*

'Captures the vigour and life of Brixton . . . There are vivid tableaux of street life, shot through a compassionate lens . . . sustained and powerful'
Sunday Times

'Dyer writes crisp Martin Amis-inflected prose, full of acute perceptions and neat phrases'
TLS

'Vivid and generous'
Independent

Abacus
0 349 10919 2

OUT OF SHEER RAGE

Geoff Dyer

'If there was a prize for the year's funniest book then *Out of Sheer Rage* would win hands down'
Independent on Sunday

Sitting down to write a book on his hero D. H. Lawrence, Geoff Dyer finds a way instead to write about almost anything else. In Sicily he is more absorbed by his hatred of seafood than by the Lawrentian vibes; on the way to the D. H. Lawrence Birthplace Experience, he is side-tracked by the Ikea Experience; in Mexico to steep himself in the white-hot beauty of the landscape he cannot get beyond a drug-induced erotic fantasy on a nudist beach. *Out of Sheer Rage* is a richly comic study of the combination of bad temper, prevarication and base appetite that go into a book: if you have ever wanted to write, then reading *Out of Sheer Rage* may cure you!

'*Fever Pitch* meets *Flaubert's Parrot*, by way of Blake Morrison'
Daily Telegraph

'Marvellous . . . a glorious truant from study . . . gives a better picture of [Lawrence] than any biography I know'
James Wood, *Guardian*

'An intriguing, magnetic, genre-rattling book'
Sunday Times

Abacus
0 349 10858 7

Now you can order superb titles directly from Abacus

☐	But Beautiful	Geoff Dyer	£7.99
☐	The Colour of Memory	Geoff Dyer	£7.99
☐	Out of Sheer Rage	Geoff Dyer	£7.99
☐	Anglo-English Attitudes	Geoff Dyer	£12.99
☐	Paris Trance	Geoff Dyer	£7.99
☐	Yoga for People Who Can't Be Bothered to Do It	Geoff Dyer	£10.99

──────────── ⬭ ABACUS ⬭ ────────────

Please allow for postage and packing: **Free UK delivery.**
Europe; add 25% of retail price; Rest of World; 45% of retail price.

To order any of the above or any other Abacus titles, please call our
credit card orderline or fill in this coupon and send/fax it to:

Abacus, P.O. Box 121, Kettering, Northants NN14 4ZQ
Tel: 01832 737527   Fax: 01832 733076
Email: aspenhouse@FSBDial.co.uk

☐ I enclose a UK bank cheque made payable to Abacus for £ ....
☐ Please charge £............. to my Access, Visa, Delta, Switch Card No.

☐☐☐☐☐☐☐☐☐☐☐☐☐☐☐☐☐☐☐

Expiry Date ☐☐☐☐   Switch Issue No. ☐☐

NAME (Block letters please) ....

ADDRESS ....

....

....

Postcode ....Telephone ....

Signature ....

Please allow 28 days for delivery within the UK. Offer subject to price and availability.

Please do not send any further mailings from companies carefully selected by Abacus ☐